DRIVING SHARON CRAZY

S H O R T   S T O R I E S

SUE PACE

'Driving Sharon Crazy : Short Stories'
Sue Pace

Published in 2017 by
Sue Pace
Seattle, WA U.S.A.

*To the mental health non-profits around the world
and also to the Wounded Warriors
and the Families of Wounded Warriors.*

Contents

Ralph's World   7

Wrestling with Demons   27

My Life as a Sane Person   40

Candymaking   63

Garret's Lament   70

Driving Sharon Crazy   75

Sibling Rivalry   85

Sex and Maple Bars   108

The Yard Sale   127

Seven Stages of Sin   143

Chant of Survival   169

This is What She Knew   179

Passing the Torch   192

Drinking Poems   214

Obituary for an Asshole   222

Acknowledgements   *236*

RALPH'S WORLD

AT HOME

The bad thing about going through Detox is that you make a lot of friends who turn out to be assholes. They mooch cigarettes and whine about how tough life is and then they try to borrow money. I've been in Detox three times and it's always the same. The guys try to out-tell any story I've got plus most are too shaky to hit the toilet when they piss. If staring at hosed down porcelain isn't bad enough, my uncle calls to tell me what a loser I am and threatens to cut me out of his Will. For a guy like me, getting cut out of a ten million dollar Will carries real weight. As far as I know, though, Uncle's more into growling than cutting so I'm still happily reading the obituaries with the rest of the cousins.

There's always a flip side and the good thing about Detox is that almost any of the women there will let you have sex with them for the price of a cigarette. Usually it's not very good sex because all the time you're trying to get it done they're thinking, "Jesus, hurry up before the orderly comes around" or sometimes they're just thinking, "God, I need a drink."

Sharon wasn't like that. She not only didn't smoke or have sex but she also still had good skin, good teeth, and good hair because she wasn't your run-of-the-mill drunk but, instead, a really smart chick who had blacked out at a girlfriend's wedding reception and got scared she was going to end up like her wacko mother, so she put herself in Detox for thirty days.

That's where I met her and that's one of many reasons why she hates me. Her husband hates me, too, but Stephen hates me because I know how many chicks he's banged on the mattress in the Graduate Student TA's office. Not just ordinary undergraduate chicks but also his advisor's sixteen year old daughter, which all adds up to playing with fire: student-teacher sexual harassment fire. Advisor's stepdaughter fire. Betrayal of a wife fire.

Stephen thinks he can get away with that kind of shit because he's smarter than everyone. Only he isn't smarter. I'm not smarter, either, but the janitor is and he's not above blackmail. I know this having learned it the hard way.

You probably already guessed that I'm in love with Sharon. It's an unrequited love. You probably already guessed that, too.

I'm a graduate student myself – I've been studying sponges. Not the descriptive nor the metaphorical kind but specifically the *sheepswool* and *grass sponges* (phylum Porifera) some of which are found off the coast of Florida and particularly in the warm currents of Key West. These are not plants (like most folks think) but are colonies of animals with amazing powers of regeneration. That's what my experiment was supposed to be about. I was going to chop up a living sponge and sift it through extremely fine cloth – a la the experiments of Brody & Cox – only I was going to use the electron microscope at the school to *really* look at things.

I wanted to discover something special about the mitochondria of these *Hexactinellida* sponges; something that could win me recognition as a real scientific genius plus make me some big bucks because of its commercial application.

I had to quit with my experiment because I started drinking (for the third time) during the chopping up process. That was Stephen's fault. He kept joking about the silent cries of all those tiny mouthless creatures.

"If you really want a grant-winning experiment, Ralph, you should try to figure out just how fucking much pain they are in when you run them through the blender..."

I wanted to run *him* through the blender. "They can't feel pain, asshole," I said to him, "they don't have nerve endings!"

But he wouldn't shut up. "Theoretically, neither do plants but the studies are there to show the shock they feel when a chainsaw bites into them or a lawnmower starts up. Don't you read, Ralph? I would have thought you'd at least have skimmed Lebber and Warshowski or Antias, Grummel and Bates. Hook your little spongelings up to a couple electrodes and start up the blender. Then maybe you'd have something worth studying."

He didn't really give a damn (he was torturing snakes for his own doctoral dissertation) but he wouldn't let it go. Not even when Sharon begged him to stop. It was the second year of grad school when we were all done competing for TA slots and alpha position. By then everyone knew Sharon was Alpha and Stephen would never forgive her for that. Me? I'm just the class fuckup.

Which is the second of many reasons that Sharon hates me. So why on earth she let me put my arms around her that bright May morning was a puzzle. Crying was part of it, I guess.

"I can't take it anymore," she whispered.

"Stephen?"

She snorted which I guess was supposed to mean she could take Stephen for decades. "I'm talking about my brother, Danny."

"Is he the crazy brother or the other one?" (Group therapy is part of any decent Detox and Rehab program, thus I knew more about Sharon than probably anyone on campus including her husband. I knew, for example, that most days she loves her pets – two dogs and two cats and a rabbit – better than she loves any member of the family she grew up in.)

"Danny's the one who's nutty as a fruitcake." She sort of laughed when she said it. As if calling your own brother nutty meant he was vaguely embarrassing, like being in junior high and having the class dork for a brother.

"What's Danny done now?"

"I have to help him but you have to promise to not tell anyone where I've gone. Not Stephen. Not my advisor. And especially not the FBI."

A promise like that would be hard to keep, but Sharon's vanilla-scented hair was in my mouth and her arms were tight around my waist. Not to mention the feel of her thighs against mine and her soft breasts against my chest. Of course I said 'yes'. Sure. Whatever you want. I would have promised her anything.

"What's Danny done now?" I repeated.

"He and my mother are on a road trip – in a used Good Humor truck – and I need to catch up with them."

I was harboring a hard-on the size of a banana and her half-filled suitcase was on the bed. I knew that because she had taken my hand and led me from the porch into the house. We walked down the hallway, past the kitchen, to her bedroom. I was so caught up in the moment I could hardly breathe.

It never occurred to me to pull back, to be afraid, or to question her motives. Maybe she didn't have any motives. Maybe she was just hurting so much she grabbed the first person who came by the house, which was me delivering a note from her advisor. A note that said she'd damn well better have some answers as to why she left in the middle of one lab and didn't show up for the other.

We didn't have sex. She simply collapsed into tears and I held her tight and stroked her hair and murmured something like, "there, there, sweet baby it will be alright."

ON THE ROAD

Sharon wasn't into physical fitness and environmental responsibility, but she'd been riding her mountain bike to and from class which was no mean feat given that they lived along Green Lake and the University District is half a hillside away. But she wasn't planning on chasing Danny and her mother on a bicycle. Stephen had taken ownership of their Volvo when they split. So all her sobbing in my arms really boiled down to wanting my Jeep. Not me. Just the Jeep.

"Hell no," I said, "you can't take my wheels without me coming along, too." So I drove and she did the navigation thing with a map as big as a pup tent.

We headed south on Interstate 5 and I drove all the way to Sacramento, CA, the first day which was a total of 754 miles. It was a start. The second day she drove from Sacramento to Flagstaff, AZ, which was another 768 miles. We spent the night in the Motel 6 that was three feet from the railroad tracks. It brought out an uncharacteristic tenderness in Sharon. Not passion. Make no mistake on that point. She said she'd stayed there ten years before with her baby brother (the schizophrenic) and her wacko mother.

The room had two queen-sized beds and we talked between, over, and through the lonely sound of train whistles and the clackety-clack of wheels on rails.

"Do you have any idea where the fuck we're going?" That was me, burn scars and all, flat on my back in my underwear and facing the inert ceiling fan. It was late May and the air conditioner was broken. Flagstaff at night wasn't hot but it certainly wasn't cold, either.

"Yes. I do."

She'd been saying those three words for a total of fifteen hundred miles but wouldn't give me the grand scheme, the overall plan, the end goal of our travels. She wore gray athletic shorts and a sleeveless tee shirt with a faded butterfly on the front. She also wore anti-zit cream on her nose and callous-go-away cream on her feet. I thought she looked terrific.

"What's so special about Flagstaff?"

"I need to talk to someone."

I scratched my belly. "There are inventions called telephones, you know. Sometimes people call long distance and they don't have to spend all that money on gas."

"Go to sleep, Ralph." She got up off her bed (the one next to the window) and walked to the bathroom. There was the sound of water running in the sink and the toilet flushing and then the shower pattering. She wasn't getting clean. I knew that and she knew I knew it. After awhile she started shouting and screaming and crying and then she came out of the bathroom and threw the soft-sided cosmetic bag at me. It was big and heavy because of the portable hair dryer and all the bottles of hand lotion and shampoo and hair conditioner.

"You goddam fucker! Where are they?"

I turned over and pretended to be asleep but she bashed me again and again with the bag and then she started hitting me with her fists so I had to duck my way out of bed, wrap my arms around her, and hold her tight until she finally stopped.

"I threw them away," I said. This time her hair smelled like key lime pie. "You don't need them."

"I do," she said. "I need them a lot. I saved three little airline Baileys for tonight. Please, I need them."

"No, you don't," I said, "it's all in your mind. You're not addicted to anything."

"What the... fuck do you... know! Stephen lets me drink," she was hiccupping into my chest.

Stephen doesn't love you the way I do. That's what I wanted to say but I didn't. I just said, "I'm not Stephen."

"You pop pills," she muttered.

"Minerals and vitamins and shit. You can pop some, too, if you want. They'd be good for you."

She went back to her bed and neither of us slept for the rest of the night.

Morning in Flagstaff in late May is worth the trip – even with eyes that feel like a used cat box and crappy Motel 6 coffee burning a hole in my stomach. Brown and Green mountains loomed up behind us and the air felt cool even while the sun was beating down out of a sky the color of a 1957 Chevy. I could stay here, get a job teaching biology to high school snots, and just never leave. We could both stay here and forget uncles and brothers and the whole sorry mess. We ate at some dumpy but crowded hippy place where I had two hard boiled eggs and orange juice and she had french toast with half a gallon of syrup and extra-spicy tofu sausage. She kept looking at her watch and finally said, "Okay, let's go. I need to talk to Georgie."

I drove north through town to the old Safeway and she went inside. When she came out she had a bottle of wine, a carton of cigarettes and a local newspaper. The paper was for her, but the wine and cigarettes were for the wizened, toothless guy who lived in a box on the hillside behind the store. (She didn't get anything for me, but I had my bottled water, Vitamin E, and Calcium tabs so what did I care.)

I sat in the car, behind the steering wheel, and watched her climb a hill covered with piles of garbage and hundreds of bleach bottles. She snagged a guy out from under a lean-to of a crap brown tarp attached to a rusted-out pickup camper. The windshield was a spider's web of cracked glass and the whole place smelled like cat spray. Meth lab, I thought. She's going to get us both killed. Sharon bent forward, talking earnestly. I saw this vagrant piece of shit give a toothless smile before he figured out what she wanted. He frowned and took a step back. For her part, she kept right on talking, holding the paper sack low enough for him to see inside but just out of reach. He kept on frowning and shook his dirty head. I tried not to think of lice and fleas and god knows what-the-fuck-else flying through the air. Finally, he started talking and she handed him some folded money. He took the bribe (along with the cigarettes and wine) with greedy fingers. The transaction lasted three minutes – maybe four.

Sharon walked slowly back to the car, with the newspaper tucked under her arm. The sun lightened her hair and turned her skin golden but her eyes were dead tired. Any fool, even one who loved her blindly, could see that.

Georgie's pals were already pushing him around, demanding the money. Sometimes I wished I was the kind of guy who'd step in and stop a fight but I'm not. Not when it's five against one or two if I joined the dance. It didn't last long, anyway, and at the end Georgie only had the wine & cigarettes which he'd kept by sticking down his nasty-looking pants. What the fuck, if there's one thing I know it's this: except for the world of sponges, the animal kingdom can't survive without a pecking order.

Sharon got in the car. "Mother and Danny were here last week," she said. "They looped back and are headed east again."

"So is Danny a meth-head?"

"Not when he's with my mother."

"So that's good."

"Yeah, Ralph," her voice was sarcastic, "that's good."

"Where to?"

"Interstate 40. Mother thinks Oklahoma City is a good place to begin clearing the planet for the first shift of aliens." After Sharon climbed in the car she started to read the newspaper – the classified section. "No messages," she finally said and I knew the FBI or the CIA or somebody smarter and more powerful than me needed to be let in on the secret.

"How, exactly, are they planning on clearing things out?"

"Georgie didn't know that part." She snapped on her seat belt and we headed into the sun.

"Okay," I said, "is this Georgie reliable about information like the looping back part and the Oklahoma City part? You know, does he actually know anything or is he just blowing smoke up your ass?"

"Oh yeah, he's reliable."

"Convince me..."

"Georgie and Danny lived under the same overpass in Portland."

"Oh, well, there's a great reference for knowing anything."

"They were also in a halfway house for schizophrenics for almost a whole year."

"How old is this Georgie?

"How old do you think he is?"

"Questions like that are always a trick."

"Guess."

"I don't know, maybe forty."

"He's my age, twenty-seven."

Which goes to show that meth-heads fall apart a lot quicker than alkies. After we got past the mountains of Flagstaff and into the high plains, I put the Jeep on Cruise Control. "Do you have even the faintest idea of what the hell you're doing?"

"Yes, I do."

The same three words; why was I not surprised?

ALBUQUERQUE, NM

We went to the Museum of Space & Flight first. With a slow finger, Sharon went down the list of names in the visitor's book and, sure enough, there they were: Daniel and Mother from Portland, Oregon. "Why did they do that?" I asked.

"Do what?"

"Why didn't they put down their real address?"

"They're paranoid schizophrenics, Ralph. It would never occur to them to tell the truth."

"But they put down who they were."

"Actually, Danny did that. He knew I'd try to find him."

"How old is Danny?"

"Twenty-three."

"So why doesn't he just walk away from your mom?"

"When she's not around, he gets meth cravings and doesn't eat good. He doesn't sleep."

"Sort of like us only we want alcohol."

"He starts thinking he's a space age machine. He tries to fly."

"You never mentioned that in any of the AA groups. Don't lie to me, Sharon. I've come on this goddam road trip, you can at least tell me the truth."

"Deception is part of the animal kingdom, Ralph, and I wish I really was lying to you but I'm not. They don't do so well without each other. They can take care of each other and leave the rest of us alone." She was ashamed of that last part but I understood it completely. Anyone with half a brain would understand it.

"Okay. Logic tells us they're together, so what's the hurry to find them? What's the fucking big deal!" I yelled the last part but Sharon didn't flinch. That's one of the qualities that kept her in Alpha position among all the Biology Teaching Assistants. Nothing intimidated her.

"The big deal is this: they have to take their medication! Otherwise Danny starts talking like a robot and god knows where he'll end up, probably in some crappy nuthouse or at the foot of a cliff and none of us will know where. Mom will take off all her clothes and be put in jail again in Roswell. Or Chicago. Or Memphis. Half my family will disappear and I might never find them again."

By that time, we were in front of the exhibit on the first spaceship to the Moon. I pulled her into my arms and she got my shirt all wet with her crying. Tourists avoided us, but nobody told us to leave. This is what sponges were for, I thought. They soaked up whatever came along and didn't expect anything more.

"I got to tell you Sharon, your family is about as fucked-up as any I've ever heard of."

"Well, now you know why I won't have sex with Stephen."

That little nugget of information kept me quiet all the way to Amarillo, TX. We spent the night in a motel room that had western décor and enough silverfish to give the carpet a moving, three-dimensional pattern. The air-conditioning worked, though, and Sharon turned it up to High. The arctic cold made me wish for a down jacket and mittens. While Sharon did crossword puzzles, I pulled the bedspread up to my chin and watched MTV.

"Do you like sex?" I asked.

"Of course, I just don't want to have children."

I pounded my two flat pillows and repositioned them against the headboard. "A few years back they invented a thing called birth control."

"Birth control is a lottery."

"So you don't believe in playing the odds. I can appreciate that."

"Pregnancy is hard on a woman. I could get sick." The sound of her voice – low, with a tremor –made me want to cry. "I could have a psychotic break," she said.

I tried to sound reasonable yet sensitive. You know, like they teach you in therapy. "I read all the stuff you passed out in group, Sharon. It's not statistically likely and shit, if you're worried about pregnancy, you could always have an abor –"

"Don't say it!" she said.

Fuck *sensitive* and double fuck *reasonable*. I got up and turned off the air-conditioner. I also put on my socks and sweatpants and switched TV to one of the late night rerun channels. The Red Planet was on – one of the episodes I'd seen half a dozen times – so I turned the set off and went back to my double bed. The motel's Vacant sign flashed on and off outside out window.

Sharon turned out her light. "You don't know anything," she said. I figured she was right about that.

It was another night of tossing and turning, but by the time the sun came up I'd thought of the question I should have been asking from the moment Sharon held out her hand, palm up, for the keys to my Jeep. It was the question my analyst would want an answer for and if I lived to make another appointment I should be able to do something besides stare at his Rolex watch and how he made his fingers into the intellectual I'm-really-thinking-about-what-you-just-said shape of a steeple. I waited until we were packed up, through New Mexico and all the way out of Texas before I asked it.

"Why?"

The Jeep windows were open and the shifting air currents lifted and released Sharon's hair until it moved like something possessed. "You're supposed to be a scientist. Be precise."

If she wanted precision, I'd give her my version of it. "Why are you chasing after Danny and your mother?"

"Because."

"Not good enough, Sharon, plus it's sure the hell *not* precise and since that's what you claim to want right now don't you think you should practise it?"

"I owe him," she whispered – which was also three words but at least not the same fucking ones she'd been using for an answer since we'd gone on this godforsaken road trip. The subject was obviously closed because she turned on the radio and we listened to country music and the farm report until I thought I'd lose my mind.

THE OKLAHOMA CITY ZOO

I am doing research and writing a dissertation on sponges. I like sponges because there are no surprises with them. Sharon doesn't like sponges because they keep the same shape from infancy to old age – in other words, all they do is grow. She wants something that changes completely and dramatically thus she is doing her research on butterflies.

(At least that's why I think she is...)

Stephen is doing research on poisonous snakes because he likes to toy with danger. And they are easy – just throw them a gerbil or a handful of crickets and you don't have to go back for days. I don't understand how someone as smart as Sharon can be so stupid when it comes to her husband. I mean, the guy is a whore and she's still mooning around after him. Sure, she threw him out but that won't last. It never does. The janitor has set up a pool on how long it will be before Sharon takes him back. Even the head of the biology department put in $5.

The Oklahoma City Zoo has a 20,000 square foot butterfly garden. I didn't know that when I parked the Jeep and we headed for the entrance kiosks. Sharon paid. Where the hell she got the money for this trip I'll never know – maybe her dad, who's a big name plastic surgeon, sent it to her. Anyway, the butterfly garden has (according to the sign above the door) 15,000 plants to sustain the complete life cycle of over a hundred species. Even I (who liked sponges) was impressed. Inside, the warm air was moist, aromatic blossoms were deep-throated, and hundreds of butterflies flitted, rested, and sipped from shallow dishes where fruit sat gently rotting.

The Monarch was the Oklahoma State butterfly. I didn't know states had butterflies, but there were plenty of them in the compound. Also exotics and commons. Sharon liked the Western Pygmy Blue – which was small, but not really blue which seems like a bad trick but, fuck, we all knew she was into things not being what they seemed.

Sharon had worn a turquoise-colored tee shirt and the butterflies couldn't get enough of her. That's because they didn't know that for her research she Super-glued their tiny feet to a glass slide and watched when they tried to fly away. She took digital pictures of the air foils that made their wings work. The Defense Department was very interested in her research. They could give a crap about mine but Proctor & Gamble had given me a small grant plus there was always my uncle in times of emergencies. Stephen was getting a grant from a cosmetic conglomerate and also a pharmaceutical company. This is graduate level education in the land of the free and the home of the brave.

Sharon and I went to the zoo three days in a row. She sat, rapt, in the butterfly house the whole time, letting them climb on her arms and shoulders and get tangled in her hair. I went other places: to the aquarium, the cat forest, and also the bird sanctuary. I loved the zoo but, for me, three days in a row was two days too much.

On Friday, around lunch, Sharon jostled her way through the crowd to the center plaza hotdog stand. I was having a Western special with barbeque sauce & curly fries.

"I thought you didn't believe in fast food," she said.

"Everything in moderation," I said.

A tall, skinny kid was with her. He had short, clipped hair, wire-rimmed glasses, and a funny look around his green eyes – like a rabbit about to be taken down by a red tailed hawk. It didn't take a brain surgeon to figure out who the hell he was.

"Hi, Danny," I said, "want some fries?"

"Yes."

"No," Sharon said. "We don't have time for that."

"I want fries!" In that short sentence his voice went from typical male to something out of a freak show. I saw the family resemblance in the stubborn set to his chin.

"No!" Sharon shouted.

"Mar-jorie-has-star-ted-coun-ting," he whispered, using his robot voice.

"Who the hell is Marjorie?" I asked.

"Mother." Sharon's face was almost as pale as his was. "Where is she?"

"Back at the motel." He gestured vaguely. "A few blocks over...."

I'm an only child and an orphan to boot. I just have cousins to rely on for genetic synchronicity. Most of the time we don't even come close to knowing what the other person is thinking, but with people in the same family you get this *look* and it's as if they're doing mental telepathy. Sharon didn't say a word but she gave Danny this goddam *look* and he dug around in his shorts pocket and handed her a motel key. He also took out a pill and popped it in his mouth. He used my Pepsi to wash it down.

"You stay here," Sharon told me. "Keep him out of the sun." Then she took off running. It's 80 fucking degrees and she's running sprints. In no time at all she'd disappeared into the crowd.

"Take the Jeep," I yelled, but Danny shook his head.

"Mar-jorie-listens-for-cars," he said in the grating robot voice. "It's-bet-ter-if-she-just-walks-in."

I looked at him for long minute.

"I should go inside," he creaked. "I get burned real easy."

We walked through the crowd, dodging babies in strollers and grubby-faced kids with balloons. "So, Danny, what's it mean when your mother starts counting?"

"She always counts. Sometimes ascending and sometimes descending." He leaned close and something about his face and the set of his body made me want to step back – about a mile back – but Sharon had left him in my care so I stayed there and looked him right in the eye.

"This time, Mother started at a smaller than usual pre-designated point. She'll keep counting in descending order in units of varying digital size until she runs out of positive numbers. When she reaches zero and moves into negative numbers the bomb goes off."

"Holy Shit."

Danny nodded and his metallic voice creaked. "Yes, ho-ly-shit."

"What was the, uh, pre-designated number?"

"Half a million."

"Okay. And when did she start the, uh, countdown?"

"Seven weeks ago."

I felt myself break out in a sweat and not because of the springtime weather. "So how close to the negative numbers are we getting?"

"She doesn't count every second."

"That's good."

"And sometimes she has to add numbers because of things that happen."

"That's even better."

"But she's down to ten thousand."

"Should we be, like, calling the FBI?"

"Sharon will."

He began making popping and whirring sounds with his mouth. Like a little kid playing with a microphone. It was annoying as hell and I began to understand Sharon's fear of sex and pregnancy. I even understood her fear of losing her own sanity, though it would seem that might be something worth striving for. I mean, fuck, wouldn't you rather be wacko than responsible?

While Sharon was out trying to save the world, or at least Oklahoma City, or maybe just her family, I took Danny on a tour of the zoo. He listened carefully while I told him all about the sponges at the aquarium. Sponges live a long time, I said. Sponges stick together when they can. Sponges aren't as beautiful as butterflies but they are useful and you can count on them to stay the same their whole goddam lives.

"I can see why you like sponges," Danny said. "I like them, too." We looked at the fish and shrimp and all the other water-dependent creatures. He read every placard and brochure and, except for his hand tremor and jerky gait, almost seemed normal. We went from the indoor aquarium exhibit to the indoor gift shop where he bought a whole packet of postcards. From there we went to the indoor butterfly garden.

That's where Sharon found us. Her face was blotchy and I could see her pulse hammering away in her throat. Even when she's a mess, she's beautiful.

"She wasn't there," Sharon said. She sank down beside us on the bench. "They're living in Earl's Good Humor truck behind the motel. The key is for the laundry room. I don't know how the hell Danny got it."

"Maybe you should call the police," I said. "Or the FBI."

Sharon wore a rose-colored sleeveless tee and butterflies were setting and rising from her chest like student pilots practising touch & goes. "Why?"

"Because of the bomb thing."

"There is no bomb thing, Ralph. It's all in Danny's and Mother's mind. They've done this for years. She counts down and she counts up. Sometimes she counts sideways. I was hoping I could at least get her started on her medication, but it looks like she's flown the coop."

"But the bomb?"

"She's been on the FBI watch list for years and there's never *been* a bomb. She's crazy, Ralph. They're both crazy. The main thing is to keep them on their medication."

"I'm not crazy," Danny said, "I'm eccentric."

"Yes, but even eccentrics have to take their medication. Every single day." Sharon stood and waved. "There she is. Thank God."

Marjorie was driving an electric wheelchair – the kind that can pull the load of someone who weighs four hundred pounds.

The butterflies liked her even more than they liked Sharon. They were tangled in her chopped-off hair, they covered her massive chest and arms, and they gathered upon her knees, each one the size of a Volkswagen Beetle. It must have been the perfume she was wearing or maybe it was the striped muumuu. Her face was distorted by the pounds of fat, but the family resemblance was there. It was in the clear skin and gold tints in the hair. Also the green eyes and, fuck, I don't know, it was spooky. Like looking at Sharon in a funhouse mirror.

When Danny saw his mother, his grin was like blazing sunshine pushing through the clouds of a cold, rainy day. You couldn't help but smile right along with him. Sharon was right, they needed to be together.

"I'll have to stay for a while," Sharon said.

"Stay? Here?"

"Until I'm sure they've been taking their meds every single day. Then I'll take the bus back to Seattle. Or I could fly."

"You'd leave them here alone?"

"They're adults."

"*Wacko* adults."

Marjorie had started counting under her breath. I couldn't tell if she was ascending or descending. Danny had started with the grinding and whirring sounds.

"They won't be wacko in a couple of days. They'll be fine."

"Until the next time."

Sharon nodded. Her face was frozen in a mask of pain – mouth open, eyes wide – like a guy I knew who'd blown out his knee during basic training. Even if I didn't love her – even if I *hated* her – I don't think I could have looked at that soundless despair without offering up something.

"What about school?"

"My advisor understands. It was part of my acceptance into the program."

"How many times has this happened?"

"This is the first time during the school year – the rest of the times have been during intercession or vacation."

"So this is where theory meets reality."

She nodded.

"Speaking of reality, why isn't Stephen here, helping out?"

She looked at me for a long time, tears still streaming. Finally, she hiccoughed and said, "Don't you ever get tired of being an asshole?"

"Apparently not."

SANITY AS AN ALTERNATIVE LIFESTYLE

Sharon, the butterfly researcher, wanted her life to metamorphose into something more wonderful than babysitting her mother and brother. Stephen, who works with poisonous snakes, married Sharon because she was dangerous, and danger is what he craves. Too many academics don't understand the importance of the sponge and I am hoping to not get thrown out of the graduate program because I don't know what there will be left to fail at and I'm afraid I'll return to drinking.

For the present, I telephoned my therapist and left a message saying I'd be missing a session or two because I was doing a good deed down in the Southwest and, no, I wasn't binging. Sharon rented a room (two double beds) in the Motel 6 across from Tinker Air

Force Base. Between the landing of planes and the whirr of cars and trucks on Interstate 40, I expected that fucker Insomnia to be my constant nocturnal companion. I was not disappointed.

Except for occasional forays into our bathroom, Marjorie and Danny lived in the Good Humor truck which was parked at the end of the building. A routine of sorts was quickly established. I ran in the morning, after the sky had lightened but before the Sun actually rose. Sharon ran at night, when the air was cool and the Sun a red ball in the Western horizon. In between, we all went to the zoo. The animals seemed very happy to see us. So were the hotdog vendors. Marjorie sat quietly, like an enormous mountain, on her motorized wheelchair in the center of the Butterfly House. Sharon sat beside her, taking notes on the behavior of the Western Pygmy Blues. I bought Danny some SPF 45 sunblock and we strolled among the other exhibits like goddam kings.

On the way home, we rented videos and the four of us spent our nights crammed in one room, watching an alternating kaleidoscope of chick flicks, Disney animation, and war movies. The crunch of buttered popcorn was deafening.

After the eighth day, it was as if someone had flipped a toggle switch and Danny quit sounding like something from Star Wars. The day after that, Marjorie stopped counting. When I woke up on the tenth day, they were gone and Sharon was on the telephone, talking to Stephen.

"No, I didn't sleep with him," she said. "Okay, we slept in the same room but we didn't have sex."

"He's an asshole," I said. "Tell him to go fuck himself." Then I went outside and tried to remember how many days it had been since I'd had a drink. That's how happy I was being with Sharon and her crazy family. There was no longing; all I could remember was laughter. When I went back inside, Sharon was in the shower. I packed all my stuff into the car (the postcards and tee shirts and all the other shit) and waited for the woman of my dreams to come out of the bathroom and break my heart.

Sharon didn't say a word at all while dressing and packing her own stuff and gelling her hair and smearing on lotion and all the other things a woman does to arm herself for the world. In the motel's cramped office, she whipped out her trusty charge card and paid for the room. The total was enough to buy one anatomy text and two biology seminar texts – which shows just what a rip-off college books are.

When she climbed into the Jeep, she said, "You're right. He *is* an asshole."

"So don't go back."

"I'm not leaving the dogs and cats. After I called him, he put them in a kennel."

"That's like putting them in jail," I said. "I would never do that."

"I know you wouldn't." Then she leaned over and kissed me on the lips.

"Does this mean you like me?"

"It means I don't hate you."

"That's a start."

I put the Jeep in gear and headed north, to Seattle, and away from the best family vacation I'd ever had. "Can I adopt your family?" I asked.

Sharon didn't answer, but she laughed for miles and miles.

WRESTLING WITH DEMONS

July 30 –

My Father (the Mayor) is furious because the outside of the house looks like shit. (His words, not mine.) He put a half inch ad in the college paper (*wanted – house painters*) because of the cheaper rate and also because he thinks that will show any voting age students he didn't really mean it when he called them a *bunch of raving communists*. Father wants white with green shutters but his trophy wife (Teresa, the Bitch Queen of Darkness) wants summer sunshine with autumn goldenrod. She's a thirty-five year old real estate agent who understands the value of color in the housing market and Viagra in a bedroom. It doesn't really matter what they want. Painting will have to wait until the trial is over because of the evidence factor.

I've started this journal against my will, but Dr. Jung (my court-appointed psychologist) said it would show I was invested in my rehabilitation. Addie says it might relieve stress – she walks three miles a day and lifts weights at the downtown YMCA. Since I'm not allowed to leave the house, I suppose writing is worth a try.

Note: Addie was our family chef de cuisine for twenty-nine years, but the Bitch Queen of Darkness (who cooks with boxes and cans) fired her to save money. My Father, being a thorough politician, settled Addie into the lap of luxury at a high priced retirement home. I'm sure you can see the underlying formula of need-more-money-must-spend-more-money. It's the American way.

August 1 –

Dr. Jung's secretary is in love with him. I, who have given up on love, can notice the cow eyes she makes whenever he passes her desk on the way to the Men's Room.

Dr. Jung's real name is Wiczencinski, which begs to be mispronounced so I'm sticking with Jung. At the end of our first meeting, he spilled coffee on my file. I helped blot the mess in order to get a quick peek. There wasn't much in there except scribbled notes about fingernails bitten to the quick and the sour smell of my unwashed hair. As if his breath didn't stink like cigars. Plus his cardigan was covered with dandruff.

Note: court psychologists tend to be a scruffy lot. My court-appointed attorney is brand new and hasn't, thus, achieved scruffiness.

August 8 –

Addie believes if you build, it they will come. Today she was going to begin another wedding cake – seven tiers with a faux basket weave design, chocolate cream cheese rosebuds, and yards and yards of trailing mint ivy – but decided instead to get a rinse and set. (The beauty school beautician claims fluorescent pink hair will make her look younger and more vibrant.)

Addie dropped off a magazine in apology. GUNS & AMMO. There was a handwritten note inside that looked like blackberry brambles in winter – thick curlicues and jagged lines. "I'd suggest a shotgun, up close and personal, but if you don't want to see blood, get something with a night scope."

I left the magazine out, note and all. It was an act of defiance. Let Father read it when he climbed the stairs to my garret to pick at my resolve. Probably Addie-of-the–night-scope wasn't thinking about my father. She was remembering Geoff, the fiancé who forgot to show up at our wedding. (Then again, she might have been thinking about Jillian who, if she really were my best friend, would have made it over to see me at least once during this house arrest, wouldn't she?)

August 15 –

Today Dr. Jung had to be in court, so our appointment was rescheduled. He left an email message of two words: "Write more."

"Why?" I emailed back.

"Because then it looks like you give a shit." That was in my cell phone voice mail. I could hear "all rise" in the background and someone else muttering, "put that goddamn thing away or Judge Curtis will (static, static) hates those fucking (static, static) in court."

I don't see the point of all this journaling. Emotions are emotions and words are words and seldom do they truly match up. I have taken to copying sections of Webster's Dictionary so when my time in court comes I can lift the journal and flip through the pages. "See all the words," I will say, "lots and lots of words."

August 30 –

My Court Date is marked on the calendar in red. Father did that. He figures I'll crack under the pressure and confess. He's desperate to get the trial over and the house painted.

Addie came over to raise my spirits. She beat me out of three dollars at gin rummy and also brought some gossip. She said my mother is on the Oregon coast at a combination artist's retreat and psychiatric sanitarium getting in touch with her personal Demons. I'm not making this up. That's the name of the sanitarium – GETTING IN TOUCH WITH YOUR PERSONAL DEMONS.

She also said after the trial Judge Curtis was having his wattle lifted. Dr. Jung's secretary quit. And Geoff, my ex-fiancé, eloped with Jillian, my ex-maid of honor. Where is GUNS & AMMO now that I need it?

September 2 –

Today is my mother's 50th birthday.

Note: According to my lawyer, I am not supposed to write anything prejudicial against my mother but as a subject, she can't be avoided entirely. After all, she was born on this day fifty years ago. It's a matter of public record. Just like it's a matter of public record that the love of my life married my once-upon-a-time best friend last week. Or that I'm on house arrest for refusing to testify against my mother and for calling the judge a blithering asshole in front of five lawyers and twenty or so criminals. It's ALL a matter of public record, dammit.

My lawyer feels there is a case to be made for diminished capacity dating from my first (and only) semi-suicide attempt with a bottle of Tums. I was fourteen and knew enough, even at that tender age, to not grab my mother's lithium or my father's migraine medication. My non-prescriptive choice did have advantages – it was palatable and I suffered no serious side effects except for a brief bout of constipation. Plus, I received a whole bunch of much-needed parental attention which was sadly lacking in my life. This is not to diminish real suicidal gestures which my older sister Kate almost died of in her first year of college.

As for my lawyer's hopeful case-making, my twenty-four year old mind actually does feel diminished, but not because of behavior a decade ago. It's because I'm stuck in my room. I'm masturbating twice a night and getting nowhere. With each failed orgasm I can feel my brain settling into a soupy kind of gray aspic. This is what happens when you resign your job as kindergarten teacher in order to put together the wedding of the year but your fiancé dumps you at the altar and a judge thinks putting you on house arrest will make you lie about your own mother.

Try living in your own bedroom (no matter how opulent) for seventy-five days in a row with the only distractions being random visits from an eighty-four year old pre-Alzheimer cook and nightly thumps and moans from your father's bedroom. Of course, capacities become diminished.

September 5 –

Dr. Jung had to be at court. I tried to use the time constructively by doing a web search (*www.restraints.com*) hoping I could connect with others who are living with electronic gizmos on their ankles. I found, instead, a homepage for girdles as a fetish – the kind with hanging metal fasteners. There were also a number of S & M sites filled with more dog collars, leather chastity belts, chains, whips and, yes, restraints, than the human mind could imagine. Well, obviously not more than the human mind, etc., but certainly more than MY mind wanted to. I do not have the gift of sexual exuberance.

Addie says it's because I'm depressed. I hope so. I would hate to think my days of passion were finished at the age of twenty-four. She said passion can be regained and used her marriage as an example of the ability of persistence to overcome cold hands.

Note: Lack of passion is one of the main reasons why Geoff and I are not married. Second on the list is he was overly concerned with appearances and I wasn't.

September 10 –

My sister left a two sentence message on the voice mail: "Jail will kill Mother. Do you want her death on your conscience?" Kate is in the Peace Corps and I assume she walked a day and a half over dusty roads to reach a payphone but West Africa has made a leap into the modern world. Perhaps there is one in the heart of her village.

Note: Sisterly love is only as thick as one-upmanship will allow.

Dr. Jung said my court date is very soon and we'd better get down to business. I said I'd showed up more than he had. He said that hostility was healthy up to a point but that my future was in his hands and unless I wanted to spend the rest of my life contemplating my bedroom curtains or the cold bars of a cell, I'd better shape up. I said he was as big a bully as my father. He smiled and wrote that part down in his little notebook.

This is, by the way, the longest conversation I've had with Dr. Jung.

September 15 –

The Powers That Be decided a color digital video and professional slides would be sufficient evidence for the trial. The house painter came – a grad student with a wolfish grin. He started at the top of the fireplace chimney. It is a matter of public record that our fireplace is painted exactly like a man's genitals.

I estimate it will be days before he reaches the testicles – which are nestled and splayed among ornamental shrubs and include not only the base of the chimney but the wood box and patio grill. The penis is pink and the testicles are blue with maroon veins and black snarls of hair. Did I mention that my mother is a well-known artist? She specializes in watercolor landscapes. The chimney was done in enamel – which is the main reason it will take the house painter so long to complete the job. All that chipping and scraping.

I do not see, at all, how there is a connection between my mother's art and the chimney's metamorphosis. I absolutely deny any aiding and abetting.

Note: It was a colder than usual spring and while my father was on his extended honeymoon, the fireplace sent forth smoke almost daily. That billowing whitish emission from the tip of the two story circumcised penis brought traffic to a complete stop along our street and, I've been told, also on the main arterial leading to the heart of the city.

I was not aware of changes to the once red brick chimney. They apparently happened while I was busy planning my wedding. I could only see Geoff (with me on his arm) walking down the aisle into a rosy-hued future.

Judge Curtis does not care that the chimney is at the far end of the house – away from the front door, the garage, and driveway. He refuses to understand the single-focused nearsightedness of a young woman planning a wedding *all by herself* because her mother had moved to an artistic retreat for a quiet nervous breakdown after being dumped by her husband of almost thirty years.

September 19 –

In ten days, Dr. Jung's report has to be in the hands of my lawyer and my mother's lawyer, not to mention the hands of the Prosecuting Attorney. Dr. Jung fires questions at me right and left.

"Do you hate your father?"

"Of course."

"Did you ever want to have sex with him?"

"I can hardly stand to have dinner with him. Why would I want to experience anything more intimate than unfrozen spaghetti and meatballs with garlic bread?"

"Did you help with the chimney's paint job?"

"I didn't know about it! If the neighbors hated it so much why didn't they ring the doorbell and say something?"

Dr. Jung scribbles furiously in my file. As for me, I'm working on growing my nails and clearing my complexion. I've tried a shampoo which has lent highlights and fullness to my hair.

When the house painter shows up again I will offer him a cold beer or an iced tea. He is my age and speaks three languages: Japanese, English, and German. Unlike my ex-fiancé, he is not interested in making a million dollars before the age of thirty or becoming the youngest senator in the state. He plans to become a Social Worker and help the downtrodden. I believe I fall into that category.

September 29 (morning) –

Addie came by to cook my favorite comfort food (bread pudding with whip cream swirls), but the Bitch Queen of Darkness had Father escort her out of the kitchen. Again. No matter what he does I'm not going to turn state's evidence against my mother. Not because I am a good daughter but because I can't. I don't know anything, dammit.

Addie said my father was a two-timing shit, his new wife was the devil incarnate, and the judge was, indeed, a blithering asshole. Also, my ex-fiancé was a jerk and my best friend a bitch. She handed me a tissue. "Plus your mother hasn't been a very good parent to you. Think about it, Clarice..."

(As if I'd been doing anything BUT think about that single fact for the past twenty-four years.)

September 29 (afternoon) –

The house painter's name is Joseph Takemura. He was engaged, married, and divorced in the space of five months. If he had it to do over again he would. "I learned a lot," he said.

"Like what?"

"Like doing things in a hurry isn't always a good idea no matter how horny you are."

"A cheap lesson at any price," I said.

Joseph Takemura was compactly muscular and covered entirely with chips of penis-pink and ball-blue paint.

Even his straight black hair was highlighted with Technicolor dust.

"My sister thinks I should plead guilty because jail would kill my mother."

"Your lawyer should be making a deal," he said. "That's his fucking job."

"Will you come visit me in prison?"

"Not so fast," he said. "What's in it for me?"

"Extra credit," I said. "Sociology profs love jail visits."

"Not any more. Now they're interested in pedophiles and the culture of terrorism." I started to cry, but he took me in his arms and kissed me, slowly and thoroughly, then put his painter's mask back over his face and climbed out my bedroom window.

"It's a morals charge," I called after him. "My mother and I are charged with willfully exposing the neighborhood children to pornography in the form of a two storey high penis."

His voice came through air that smelled like fresh rain and cut grass and all things clean and wonderful. "If it was in a fucking museum, they'd call it Art."

September 29 (late) –

The Bitch Queen of Darkness tapped at my bedroom door. She was wearing a filmy negligee and a slime-green cucumber-avocado complexion mask. She smelled like salad.

"Your sister quit the Peace Corps."

Her lips were moving but I couldn't make sense of the words so she repeated it. Only this time she added the word "idiot." As in: "Your *idiot* sister quit the Peace Corps."

"Kate quit? Why?"

"I think she preferred that to being thrown out."

"Thrown out?" I squeaked. "Why?"

"She didn't do her job. Surprise, surprise."

My father's trophy wife wore a hairnet and chin strap. She had wrist length moisturizing gloves with pink hands silk-screened on the top. I'd never seen her without styling gel and nylons; now she was a caricature. "She quit when your father and I were on our honeymoon."

I did the day-to-week-to-month math. "Where has Kate been staying?"

"Not here."

"Yes, but where?"

"Your father has been a train wreck, an absolute train wreck, since the penis thing and you are an ostrich. This family is nuts."

That part I agreed with.

"Take your head out of the sand." Her voice was really quite lovely; contralto with a delicious warmth that belied the frosty eyes.

"You feel sorry for me."

"You wish. Your father has gotten enough negative publicity for one election year, don't you think? If this charade keeps up much longer he won't *have* a campaign. He'll have a joke book."

"I don't know who painted the chimney."

"You're supposed to be the smartest one in the whole family," she said. "Well, Miss Smarty-pants, who gains the most from ruining your father's life?" Then she melted into the shadows of the hallway and I heard the door to the master bedroom snic shut, muffling my father's snores.

"Everything isn't about my father," I said.

September 30 –

I waited until dawn, then hoofed it to the Retirement Home. Addie was having breakfast. French toast and sausage patties. Fresh squeezed orange juice. Her pink hair was vibrant among all the nodding blues, whites, and grays.

"I'm running from the law," I said. "I need the keys to your car."

Addie set her tea cup back in the delicate saucer, sloshing some of the golden liquid onto the pure white tablecloth, and smiled.

Five hours later, we stopped at a gas station to pee while Addie shoplifted Twix, Almond Joys, and a disposable camera. "The old lady gets a real kick out of the old slight-of-hand," the cashier said. "That'll be $57.49 for gas plus extras."

That afternoon, we pulled into the parking lot of a sprawling resort surrounded by a stucco and brick fence. My mother was in the art room, dipping a brush into paint the color of unripe apples.

Kate stood at her own easel. The paper in front of her was blank.

"You're supposed to be in Africa," I said.

"I came home."

"Why?"

"It was hot."

"You could have gone to Nepal," I said. "It isn't hot in Nepal."

Kate picked up a charcoal pencil and began drawing stick figures. "I hate you. You ate in air-conditioned restaurants and sat in air-conditioned theaters while I was stuck in a place that didn't have ice cubes."

"My fiancé married my best friend. Just how much fun was that?"

"Move away from the window, girls," Mother said. "You're blocking the light."

Note: Our mother raised us to not linger at windows. No wonder I didn't see the chimney's transformation.

A silver Lexus turned into the parking lot. I didn't expect to see it so soon, but Father probably hadn't stopped for gas (once) and to pee (twice) and still another time so Addie could pick some wonderful bluebells growing beside the road. Father parked next to the Pontiac where she dozed in the front seat, snoring softly, bluebells wilting in her lap.

He did not look happy to see any of us, the women of his first family.

"I didn't do it," I said. "Maybe it was Kate."

Kate threw an eraser at me. "I've been here for weeks. Ask anyone."

Mother laid a dripping brush against hungry paper. "Kate can't draw and she certainly can't paint."

"And your Mother hates enamel, plus she's been here for months, doing the Demons thing." Father smoothed his hair and then his tie. "It had to have been you, Clarice."

"Wrong."

"Then who ruined my house? Who's ruining my campaign? Who, for Chrissake, is ruining my brand-new marriage?"

"Everything isn't about you," I said. "Try to remember that."

I drove Addie's Pontiac back to my ruffled prison. My father called Dr. Jung to talk about any Demons I might have and the possibility of involuntary psychiatric admission. I could join my nutty sister and fragile mother. This is what happens when your life falls apart.

Three days later, Joseph Takemura scraped all the way to *terra firma* and found the section under the testicular brambles that said, in very small pink and blue script,

Revenge is a dish best served cold.

I knew, then, that I'd been wrong. Everything WAS about my father and I also knew which spry ex-cook hated him enough to want to ruin the rest of his life.

Thanksgiving –

The Bitch Queen of Darkness left my father right after he lost the election. Mother and Kate continue to wrestle with Demons. No-one has the heart to prosecute an eighty-four year old resident of the Happy Trails Retirement Home, no matter how outrageous her behavior. The house remains unpainted (chimney draped in condom-style tarps) while neighborhood children follow me making rude noises. After Christmas, I'm leaving for Alaska to teach in a progressive private school. Joseph Takemura has promised to bring Addie up for a supervised field trip. I told him to not stop for gas and to bring lots of slight-of-hand money.

In the meantime, I'm working (with real success) on regaining lost orgasms.

MY LIFE AS A SANE PERSON

THE LABORATORY

I was in the third year of my PhD, studying the migration patterns of Western Pigmy Blues and teaching veterinarian wannabes the delights of comparative anatomy through the process of dissecting sharks and cats. If it were my choice we'd have been gutting pedophiles, but the cats came cheap and already dead from the pound. The sharks came finless from a Japanese fish outlet. We also went through several dozen sheep eyes, which were plentiful due to the fondness of the general populace for lamb chops. I, myself, am a vegetarian. Bottom line: I knew nothing until the FBI showed up while I was gutting Marissa. She was a formaldehyde-scented tortoiseshell tabby that I named after the woman who seduced my husband and stole my future.

The FBI came in a set of three: two males (Hispanic and Caucasian) and a female (also Caucasian.) They all wore chinos and lightweight jackets and had cute little cell phones that rang intermittently. I thought they were MBA grad students so I got a bit snarky. "This isn't a goddam phone booth," I said, "this is my lab, so get the hell outside!" Two of them flashed their badges and one flashed the butt of his gun. That one, the one with the gun, said, "We'd like to ask you a few questions." This was done very discretely, but pre-vet students have fast eyes and, also, I might add, big mouths. My advisor would have a few questions of his own before the day was out.

THE HALLWAY

"What's this all about?" I asked. The smell of Marissa clung to me and bodily fluids dripped off my rubber apron and gloves. The three agents took a giant, united step backwards.

The Hispanic put out his strong, tan hand. "Why don't you give me your weapon?" he said. I couldn't understand what he was talking about for half a minute, but then I got it and handed him my dissecting scalpel. Everybody seemed more comfortable once that glinting bit of surgical steel was out of my hand and secured by the very tippy-tips of his fingers. Later I caught him scrubbing up to the elbows with a KFC antibacterial soap packet. You wouldn't think such a tough guy would get so squeamish about a few dripping intestines.

"You're Sharon Hansen?" The woman had short cropped hair and hands with calluses in interesting places.

I nodded

"Do you know where your brother is?"

"Which one?"

"The one that's nutty as a fruitcake."

"I didn't think FBI agents got to use terms like that when describing people."

"We're only human."

"The one that was locked up for a few years," blurted the Hispanic. "The young one."

"Then you would be asking about Danny. No, I don't where he is. Not recently anyway."

"Do you know Earl Lambini?" He gave a slight Spanish twist to the Italian surname.

"Yes, but I haven't seen him for months." I could have told them more – like what a worthless piece of crap Earl was or how, until recently, I'd named all my dissecting cadavers after him. I could have also told them that Earl was unemployed and had been shacking up with my mother for ten years but, hey, they didn't ask and I wanted to get back to class.

"Tell us about Danny..."

"Last I heard he was driving Earl's Good Humor truck from Humptulips, Washington to Portland, Oregon."

"Maybe we could go someplace private," the woman said. "Do you have an office?"

That's when I knew Danny had finally done something so outrageous, so awful, that even the FBI wasn't going to talk about it in public.

GENETICS

My older brother and I were normal. So was our father. We liked regular meals and caps on the toothpaste and even though we never made our beds we washed the sheets once a week. My older brother played second clarinet in the Seattle Symphony. Our father was a plastic surgeon specializing in burn repair. I expected to spend the rest of my life doing research on the airfoils of the smallest butterfly in North America, *Brephidium exilis,* also commonly called the Western Pygmy Blue. My father and brother and I were the part of the family that practised precision and appreciated beauty.

Mother and Danny were not like us. They understood, from personal experience, the fleeting delight of beauty but they never practised precision. They knew not restraint.

THE TEACHING ASSISTANTS' OFFICE SPACE

Three of us shared a cramped, windowless closet on the fifth floor of the WILLIAM P. HARTZEL HALL which was called Hell Hall by the freshmen because of its overactive heating system. In the TA office, there was a twin-size mattress propped against the near wall. Two desks overflowed with yet-to-be-graded term papers, books, gerbils in glass tanks and crickets in egg cartons, computers, file folders, cold moldy pizza, and a jug of cheap burgundy. The crickets and gerbils were for Steven's snakes. Steven was my estranged husband. The mattress and the wine were for Ralph – who was the sole reason Steven and I still had anything in common. (We both loathed him.)

On one side of the closet there was a third desk, facing a poster of myriad-colored butterflies lifting from a field of flowers. There was a computer in the exact center of that desk along with in-boxes, out-boxes, pop quiz and term paper boxes, and computer disks in orderly packets. There was a bookcase beside the desk with everything sorted by subject matter and date of publication. There was a neatly-lettered sign on the wall above the desk and bookcase. "I am handy with a scalpel and I will eviscerate anyone who leaves even one crumb of pizza or one drop of burgundy on or around this work area." My office mates did not find this funny. Neither did the FBI. However, my desk was pristine thus illustrating the power of truth in advertising.

It was the middle of the day and the TA office was empty except for the gerbils & crickets in Steven's snake food bank. There was also the quiet hum of the ceiling fan. Everyone settled into chairs except me. I stood by the door, arms folded. "Okay," I said, "what's this all about?"

"Tell us about Danny," the Hispanic said. "Tell us everything."

"I don't know everything," I said. "I probably don't know anything. I haven't seen Danny, face-to-face, since Christmas."

"Your stepfather phoned us. He seems to think you're the one Danny would contact in an emergency."

"I don't have a stepfather."

"Then who's this Earl guy?"

"Not my stepfather."

"We haven't been able to talk to your mother," the female agent said. "Do you have any ideas about that?"

"No. Should I?"

MORE GENETICS

Mother was a product model who wanted to be a starlet. Not a star. A starlet. She planned to live off her looks until she could find a really rich doctor and get married. She figured being a model would help with that and she was right. She started out demonstrating blenders and toaster ovens. She laughed a throaty laugh while running her hands over the backs of sofas and easy chairs. She sat on the hoods of brand new cars. She met my father at a boat show. After she got married and then pregnant, her life as a beautiful person went straight down the crapper. She blamed the additional three hundred fifty pounds on her children and maybe she was right. Or maybe she simply achieved her aspirations too soon and didn't know how to move on.

Danny inherited Mother's thick-lashed, astonishingly green eyes and also her creamy skin. His teeth were straight and his hair tawny with red and gold highlights. He moved fluidly, in the way of jungle cats or thoroughbred horses. He was not pregnant three times and so avoided the extra weight but, genetics being a crap shoot, he could not avoid her schizophrenia.

MY HOUSE

I invited the FBI home because I hoped it would annoy Steven who lived in the bedroom off the hall. That bedroom had cable and was close to the front door which he used, frequently, on his visits to Marissa the Slut. Steven was not home and not annoyed. I lived in the Master bedroom because it had its own bathroom and also telephone. Our pets (we are, after all biologists and we love animals) lived in the den, the back yard, and the front room. Sometimes they tried to live in the kitchen and in the bathroom but we discouraged it whenever we remembered.

Steven and I had five pets and were living together (instead of apart) because we were poor and also because neither of us could stand to leave Silky the large dog, Stinky the small dog, Prudence the rabbit, or Kit and Kat the blue-eyed, loud-mouthed, identical Siamese neutered tomcats from the same litter. Steven and I were unhappy in our two bedroom house but we were surrounded by love.

The FBI asked if Danny had contacted me. Then they asked about mail – email and snail mail, both. I showed them a letter from the stack on the kitchen table. The return address was in all caps.

YOUR BRO DANNY
TOAD SUCK PARK
CONWAY, AK

The Gunslinger (with his regulation crew cut and striped tie) donned latex gloves to handle the envelope. He unfolded the single piece of paper and a pair of white and black wings fluttered to the floor. His one raised eyebrow asked the question.

"It's a *Pieris rapae*," I said. "The Common Cabbage butterfly."

"He mailed you a blank piece of paper and a dead butterfly?" He turned to the others. "This is bullshit."

I picked up the lacy white wings with black markings that looked like little eyes. They stood for all the summers Danny and I had spent fishing in the creek and running across the meadow. I was about to explain those good times but I thought, Fuck it. Let them be idiots.

"What's this?" The Hispanic picked up another envelope. The return address was equally geographic.

BROTHER DAN, ESQ
SCREAMING WOMAN CREEK, WY.

"Screaming Woman Creek?" That was the female agent.

"You didn't call the cops after getting this?" asked the Hispanic.

"It's a real place."

"Anyone with half a brain would have called the cops."

"Anybody with half a brain knows you don't have a warrant," I said, "so stop insulting me."

The Hispanic dropped the Screaming Woman envelope like it was on fire and out fell the porcupine quills – not even a blank piece of paper – nothing but quills spilling onto the hardwood floor like scattered pine needles on the hill behind the house we grew up in.

"Where's your brother?" The men were impatient but something else skittered behind the woman's eyes. Not pity and not fear but something very close to both those emotions. Maybe she'd dealt with a schizophrenic before.

"Right now? I don't know."

Squinting, the woman held a third envelope to the light. The postmark was Amarillo, TX, home of the 72 oz. steak. This steak is free if you can eat the whole thing in an hour and very expensive if you can't. It's a trick like all the tricks played on us by our mother. Everything costs more than you first thought: love, hate, disgust, joy. The envelope smelled like old blood and there was a rusty stain in the corner but it was empty because I threw out the steak bone. If, indeed, it really was a steak bone.

The female agent's voice was soft. "What was in it?"

I shrugged.

"We can get that warrant and go through your whole house."

"Do what you have to do."

She dropped the stained envelope back onto the table. "What we'd really like," she said, "is Danny's itinerary."

I spread my hands, helpless. "I've told you everything I know."

I counted floor tiles while they bickered about what to do next. Before they finally gave up on me, the female tried to hand me her business card and when I wouldn't take it she placed it on the stove, equidistance between the four burners. For some reason it reminded me of the things on my desk back at the TA office and I had to smile.

As soon as the front door closed I headed for the back porch where we kept a battered but functional coffin style freezer. It's where I stored all my mail from Danny, to keep it safe from the pets. I can't imagine why his old letters were on the kitchen table but I'd been preoccupied lately. There were deadlines to meet and I couldn't get my data to prove or disprove anything. I was going to spend spring break running the numbers for the tenth time. I confess I was also hoping Steven would come home and give me some scientific research pointers. He's brilliant when he keeps his prick in his pants.

I unlocked the freezer and dug through three feet of unopened boxes and manila envelopes. There were also various items for an emergency including Popsicle gerbils for Steven's snakes. It was lunchtime and I was hungry. Beneath the frozen rubble was a Lean Cuisine with an expiration date that was only two months overdue.

FORMS OF COMMUNICATION

My mother prefers the telephone to all other forms of communication. That way she can hang up at any time leaving you, the caller, with a dial tone. My father prefers email or text mail. My older brother prefers in-your-face conversations at two in the morning between impromptu jazz sessions. This is, you understand, after he's stoked on uppers and played thousands of crescendo and decrescendo sixteenth notes while trying to keep up with the flashing baton tip of the Symphony Maestro.

Steven's cell phone was on the coffee table. I used it to text message my father – the man who was perpetually washing up for surgery.

Me – The FBI was here.

He replied before I had time to get lunch out of the microwave.

Dad – How's Steve? (Steven is the son that Dad always wanted.)

Me – Steven's a shit.

Me – I hate him.

Me – D.I.V.O.R.C.E.

Father had already signed off, which was just as well because I wasn't up to thumbing any more letters to form-tortured sentences. You'll notice he didn't ask about the FBI.

THE MYSTERY OF THE THREES

My life is determined by one triangulation after another. A trilogy arrives with the predictability of the tides: three FBI agents, three classes to teach, the birthdays of my father's three ex-wives to remember. Three times I've been crushed under Steven's dalliances. My mother's February stroll, stark naked, down the main street of Roswell, New Mexico, was her third psychotic break. It may have been a decade ago but it marked forever our relationship and thrust me into the role of emotional caretaker. A role, I might add, for which I am not naturally talented. Now I'm trying to accept three parcels a week in the mail from my nutty-as-a-fruitcake-youngest-brother, Danny.

POSTAL WARS

A battered Volvo station wagon screeched into the drive. There was the low whistle Steven used to call the dogs, then metal against metal as the key scraped across the lock. He could fiddle all afternoon, but he wasn't getting in so easily this time. The doorbell buzzed for half a minute before kicking began at the brass plate along the bottom of the door. Shouts came through the thin wood.

"Sharon! Open the door, goddamit, I fucking live here!"

"Not anymore!"

"I pay half the rent on this dump. That means you can't change the locks."

"Can't isn't a word in my vocabulary."

"So this means you'll take over the lease? Fine. I want Stinky, Silky, and Prudence. You can have the cats."

I opened the door. "Over my dead body."

"That can be arranged. The mail carrier would do it for free." Steven held out a seeping parcel in a plain brown wrapper. The postal date was eight days earlier and the return address was Las Vegas. "He handed this to me when I got out of the car. He said your packages from Danny are making him consider incarceration as an alternative retirement plan."

"What is that supposed to mean?"

"I think it means he'll shoot you before he ever delivers anything that smells this bad again."

"What are you doing here?"

"None of your business."

I hated that I was still in love with his long legs and his near-sighted squint, not to mention the way his mouth always seemed about to curl into a smile. My body lusted for all of it. He handed me the package, "Wait 'til I leave before you open it. The damn thing might explode."

Nothing gross bothers Steven, but I held the stinking mail by one corner while he thrashed around his bedroom and the kitchen and the boys drooled and jumped for joy. Even Prudence was a traitor and twitched her ears. Steven finally found whatever he was looking for and, still dripping guck, I watched him back down the drive and screech away. I could have stood on the porch for hours – holding Danny's package – but thin, brownish ooze dripped steadily onto the rug we used to wipe our feet.

I contemplated throwing everything into the coffin freezer, but I could imagine the FBI actually getting that warrant and rummaging through three months' worth of priority boxes and manila envelopes with weird but true return addresses. Whatever Danny was trying to communicate would be interpreted through the suspicious eyes of gun-toting government agents. They were, hopefully, sane and he wasn't. How accurate could they be?

A dozen frosty pieces of mail (and one still steaming from the warmth of a sunny spring day) rested quietly on the kitchen table as I carefully printed three headings on a sheet of ruled paper: date, return address, contents. I am, you remember, a scientist and have been trained in the collection and interpretation of data.

Next I put the animals outside. Except for Prudence. It is not good for rabbits to be in a fenced yard with predators, even ones who have half-filled food dishes with their own names on them.

I rummaged through my closet and found, along with a dusty wedding album, a map of the United States. I took the map into the living room where the light was better and unfolded all fifteen square feet of it. There, marked in black permanent pen, was our honeymoon road trip. Fuck that. I was almost positive we were getting a divorce the very next time Steven came home smelling of Marissa the Slut.

I opened the spice cupboard where I keep the 1 oz. and 2 oz. bottles of booze from the fancy hotel Dad put us all up in last Christmas. (That's his idea of holiday cheer. He flies everyone – ex-wives, step and half siblings, the whole enchilada – to Las Vegas for two nights at the Bellagio.) The selection was lush but limited: Amaretto, Coconut Rum, and Baileys Irish Cream. I twisted the top of the Baileys and poured it directly into my mouth instead of a glass.

There are three reasons Steven might actually agree to the divorce. First, he doesn't like the way I drink: not the amount, not the content, and not the method. He's a beer man specializing in frozen steins and creamy red or brown ale so thick you have to spoon it into your mouth. Second, we fight all the time about our research. This is, of course, the scientific method and could be seen as positive, but it is hard on relationships. Third, I refuse to even consider having children.

"We're scientists for crissake," I screamed during our latest, worst, argument. "You can't ignore the genetics of the situation."

"There's adoption —"

"I'm not just talking about OUR children turning into little schizophrenics," I yelled. "It can strike up to age forty. Didn't you read anything I gave you? I could flip out at any time!"

"Shay, my heart calls for children." That's what he called me when he was feeling affectionate. Not Sharon but Shay.

I had been starting pitcher for my high school girl's baseball team and when I threw the tiny bottle of Cognac at his head, it split the tender skin just below his eye. I drove him to the Emergency Room and watched while Marissa (who was the nurse on duty) flirted and gave him comfort. That's when they met.

The packages and manila envelopes were starting to defrost and water was leaking through the center crack of the kitchen table. I couldn't put it off any longer, so I put on my own latex gloves. I opened everything in no particular order, filled in the blanks on my sheet of lined paper, and looked for a pattern. The contents were mostly fauna with the occasional flora thrown in. There were broken wings from the Tiger Swallowtail (*Papilio trolius)* along with the Common Wood Nymph (*Cercoyonis pegala.)* Besides the pine needles there was also some rotting vegetable matter that might be pot and some desiccated mushrooms that might be psychedelic. There was the flattened armadillo resembling southwest leather. A rabbit foot with leg attached made me think of my own sweet bunny, but I pushed on until Danny's travel itinerary became clear.

I marked a star over the bend in the road that indicated Humptulips, Washington. Instead of driving 168 miles south to the assigned destination, Danny (and most assuredly my mother) had piddled eastward on Interstate 90 until they bumped into Chicago. From there they dribbled south to Nashville and after seeing the forty foot high replication of the goddess Athena at Nashville Centennial Park (where he obtained a desiccated squirrel's tail and a garish postcard), they mostly trudged westward on Interstate 40 until reaching Bakersfield and were, I gathered, working their way home on Interstate 5. My mother and little brother had turned an afternoon jaunt into a 5,540 mile Odyssey.

It was the same route our mother took (after kidnapping ninth-grade me and fifth-grade Danny) to clear her mind and recover from my father's devastating divorce. Those were her words. Especially poignant was the "clearing her mind" part as she'd taken a sidetrack south to Roswell, New Mexico, and joined the Memorial Day parade which would be, in Danny's and my minds, memorable beyond all others. Not only because of her nudity (which was complete except for White Shoulders perfume) but because she'd gotten arrested and our father flew us home to Seattle, first class. That was back when first class meant something and my older brother was forever jealous which was satisfying in a way few other things were at that time in my life.

I stared at the last package (the one Steven had handed me) and knew with a sinking heart that in spite of the stench I would have to open it, too.

I covered the table with a clean black garbage sack and began snipping at the packing tape with kitchen shears. I don't know what I expected that last parcel to contain: A flat cat? A flightless crow? A dozen fragmented eggshells with yolks run amok? It was none of those. Packed among Styrofoam peanuts and wrapped in a leaky plastic bread sack (that took some doing to untie) was what appeared to be rotting testicles. I went to the kitchen sink and threw up every morsel of Lean Cuisine.

After the nausea passed, I rinsed out my mouth and gave myself a first class pep talk. What the hell was wrong with me? It *couldn't* actually be Danny's manhood. Probably he'd taken a side trip to Las Vegas and they were oceanic raw oysters from the menu of the

Ballagio. He'd been fascinated by them last Christmas and eaten half a dozen while my father told several ribald jokes. I digress. As to the oysters *cum* testicles, why hadn't Danny kept them in the Good Humor truck, frozen? What message was he trying to send me? How did he arrange to have a gathering of short brown hair congregate in the corners of the bread sack? And had he never heard of Overnight Express?

FOLIE A DEUX

Folie a deux is a fusty psychiatric term used to indicate two people who share the same delusional belief system. At least that's what the glossary of my undergraduate abnormal psychology text said. In my opinion, my mother and my baby brother, Danny, were deeply involved in a *folie a deux*.

When they forgot to take their medication, they both believed they were chosen by God to save the earth – not for humans or animals or even insects. No, they were going to save it for the Aliens; the ones circling Alpha Centauri or someplace even further out. They could talk for hours about crop circles, Stonehenge, and coded messages in the telephone book. Also, sometimes Danny built bombs.

I stripped off my gloves and washed my hands. Then I dialed the number on the business card the female agent had left on the stove. She answered before the first ring ended.

"Dorsey here."

"Okay, you guys win. I'll give you my mother's cell phone number and she'll tell you where to find him."

Silence met my capitulation.

"Seriously, I think Mother can help you."

There was some throat clearing and general unease. "I don't think you understand the situation."

"Okay." The word came slowly out of my mouth, like I was on drugs and couldn't get my lips to synchronize with my voice box. "Enlighten me."

"We're parked across the street. Why don't you come join us?"

I went to the living room and peeked out the front window. Two navy blue Buicks sat, nose to tail, at a 75 degree angle from my front door. How could I have missed them? "Enlighten me, first."

Voices muttered in the background. "We are unclear about the details, but we think she's with your brother."

"She usually is."

"We think this may be a kidnapping."

"By my, uh, kid brother?"

"Yes."

"How did you arrive at that conclusion?"

"Come outside." Dorsey was calm. "You can ride with Agent Ramirez or with me, your choice."

"I'll take you."

"Fine."

"Where are we going?"

"Mr. Lambini is out of the hospital now."

My mouth went dry. "What was he in for?"

"Now that he's home, we're having trouble reaching him."

"I'm sure you are."

"But he can explain it better than we can."

"Slime mold could explain it better than you guys."

"We didn't know if you were part of the plot."

Part of the plot. Great, now the FBI was talking like my mother and Danny. I could hardly wait to hear what else they had to say.

HUMPTULIPS, WASHINGTON

Humptulips is located along Highway 101 south of the deepest patch of rainforest on the Western Washington peninsula. It rains three hundred days a year there and has a population of one hundred twenty during hunting season. Also during trout season. The rest of the time it's eighty-three souls waiting to die while listening to my mother talk about Aliens. I'm sure her impromptu lectures at the post office and mercantile have speeded a few citizens on their way. Then, again, hamlets are notorious in their support of an eccentric populace. Nevertheless, what the hell was Earl thinking when he spent my Mother's and Danny's disability checks on a Good Humor truck?

We turned north at the twin cities of Aberdeen and Hoquiam with Ramirez in the Buick following us close. In ten minutes we'd be out of range of any cell towers. "I need to make a phone call."

"Why?"

"Someone needs to feed the animals."

Hamilton (the tough guy) was sitting behind Dorsey. He grunted and handed me his black and silver cell. My darling Ex picked up on the second ring.

"It's me," I said, "I'm going to be out of town for a while and you'll have to take care of the animals."

"How long is awhile?"

"I don't know."

"Overnight? A week?"

"I said I don't know."

"You're going to be gone longer than a week?"

"There will be plenty of time to get a divorce when I get back."

"You're the one who keeps talking about divorce, Shay. You've never heard me say the word."

"I'm not sharing you with Marissa."

"Marissa is old news. You've locked me out and I don't have anywhere else to stay."

"Stay with my father. Stay with Ralph. Stay with anybody besides an emergency room nurse who wants to fuck your brains out! She probably fucks everyone. Get tested for AIDS for God's sake." My hand shook when I gave Hamilton his phone back.

"I didn't know scientists talked that way," Hamilton said.

"Don't be an idiot," Dorsey and I said in unison.

EARL LAMBINI

Earl had black eyes, black hair, and Irish white skin that never tanned. He wore torn camouflage pants with a stained tee shirt and behind his three day stubble, he was lean and handsome in a Brad Pitt sort of way but taller. He met my mother in a Greyhound bus station in Portland, Oregon ten years ago. He used to be a follower of the Prophet Ramtha and I suppose to someone like him, my Mother (with her jangle of earrings and her constant chatter about the end of the world) didn't seem that far off center. Besides, she still was pretty, especially if you were one of those guys attracted to women who weigh a quarter of a ton. Maybe Earl could see past all that to her clear skin, shiny hair, and straight teeth.

However, I'm a scientist and I believe the world is split into two camps: predator and prey. Earl took one look at her disability check and knew his life could be forever easy if he'd just be nice to Danny. All he had to do was not look funny when my little brother started talking about using bombs to make room for the Aliens.

"Turn here," I said and Dorsey swung onto a rutted road tucked between two dairy farms. The pastures were dotted with cows and calves, all of them brown and white Guernseys. It looked pastoral and clean but it smelled like cow shit. Such is the way of the world. Half a mile in, the pastures gave way to scraggly Maples and third growth Douglas fir. As I rolled down my window, the crack of a rifle echoed, as I'd known it would – two warning shots. Dorsey stopped the car fast and the trailing Buick, with Ramirez driving, rammed us hard. Everything was suddenly quiet except for the sound of agents unsnapping holsters and releasing the safeties on their guns.

I unlocked the car door and jerked away from Dorsey's restraining hand. "Earl!" I shouted. "You've got company! Put the goddam gun away!"

"Hey kid, that you?"

"He shoots rabbits," I said, "and squirrels. He's harmless."

Earl Lambini wasn't harmless, but he wouldn't kill us outright if he knew it was family. We entered the dirt-packed clearing (me walking upright and the three agents sidling in a crablike crouch) and right away I could see that things were going to be different. The tar paper shack with its cracked windows and sagging roof was gone. Instead, a brand new doublewide trailer was jacked up on cement blocks. Earl was in his favorite spot, a ratty lawn chair between the garden and the outhouse. Earl had two black eyes, what looked like a broken nose and his non-shooting arm was in a sling.

"Hey, Sharon," he said.

"Hey, yourself," I replied. "You look like shit."

"Don't hold back, Sharon. Let it all hang out."

"Blow any bunnies to smithereens recently?"

"You know them little crappers will eat a garden flat in less than a week." In a gesture of uncharacteristic hospitality he lowered his rifle to his knees, barrel pointing at the chicken house. "I see you brung friends."

"That I did."

"You going to tell 'em who I am?"

It was the classic comment of a consummate Narcissist. He didn't care who they were, it was only important they know who he was. Several descriptors ran through my mind including Asshole and Dumb Shit but I played it straight. "FBI, this is Earl. Earl, this is the FBI."

The rifle barrel shifted in his lap, but the agents instantly responded in what could only be described as a Mexican Standoff. Finally Earl put the rifle on the ground and everyone relaxed.

"Nice house," I said. "When did you get it?"

"A couple months ago. I got a real good deal on it."

"Where'd the money come from?"

"I got a little business on the side," he said. "You know I'm not one to just sit around."

I knew him to be exactly someone who just sat around. "What business? Please God don't let it be your family's secret recipe for white lightning. You damn near killed half the town council with that last batch."

"Where's your wife, sir?" That was Agent Dorsey.

"She isn't his wife," I snapped, "they're not married."

"We're common law," Earl said, "so she counts as my wife but Danny ain't my son. She got him on her own."

"Where are they, sir?"

"That's what I called you idiots for. I want all the money I paid in taxes put to use. You find them and get them back here."

"Do you have any ideas where they might be, sir?" Ramirez put a twist on the 'sir'" and Hamilton's fingers twitched. They wanted to take Earl down. (He had that effect on people.)

"It's been weeks. Everthin's gotta be melted by now and, Jesus, how much gas do you think they're goin' through? It don't come cheap, ya know." He glowered at the three agents. "An' what the hell you been doing besides sitting on your fat asses while my profits is going down the drain?"

While Earl was doing his best to bring Ramirez, Hamilton and Dorsey to a frothing rage, I stalked into the house and spent a good five minutes trying to find the battery-powered telephone. It was tucked behind the flour and sugar canisters on the counter between the stove and the refrigerator. I read the recipes stuck to the freezer door with kitchen magnets while waiting for her to answer. Everything was low-cal or Atkins or South Beach. My mother was perpetually on a diet, all quarter ton of her.

She answered on the twenty-third ring.

"Is this Claxon?" My Mother's whispery soprano faded in and out. "We're on our way to the landing site, but traffic has been horrible." She sounded like she was talking to me through a long metal pipe.

"It's Sharon, Mother. Where are you?"

"I can't talk long, dear. Premier Claxon from the starship Exxon will be calling soon." I listened to her counting under her breath. My whole life she had counted.

"Let me talk to Danny."

"He doesn't like to talk to you, Sharon. You intimidate him."

"I do not." There was only so much time before Mother reached one hundred. Then, as directed by the Aliens inhabiting her mind, she'd hang up. "Why did you stop taking your medication?" I asked.

"As soon as Claxon and the others from the outer world arrive we're going to Alaska. The Spaceships are waiting for us there."

"Alaska takes a lot of money, Mom."

"Earl has a new business."

"Please tell me he's not running drugs. Shit, that's it, isn't it? He's using you and Danny to funnel drugs from one place to another. I fucking can't believe this guy! He's such a loser, Mom. How in god's name did you get caught up with such a —"

"Oh, no, Sharon, it's not drugs. It's beef."

My mother's logic defies rationality. In junior high I wasn't good enough with math to step into that particular world of certainty, so I did the next best thing and took every science course I could. Logic is my guide and I cling tightly to it. "I think people can get beef at a store, Mom. It comes wrapped in plastic and is approved by the FDA."

"Not this kind, dear." A giggle echoed through the static. "It's all because of that Mad Cow." She had already counted up to ninety-one. There wasn't much time left.

"I don't know what you are talking about." It was probably the first sentence I spoke as a baby and I had to be up to a hundred thousand repeats since then.

"Earl saw it on Emeril," she whispered in her little girl voice. "Or maybe it was another show. It doesn't matter; Earl goes to the farm next door and gets them."

Mother hung up and I tried to figure out what the hell she was talking about. The only non-dietetic recipe on the refrigerator was right in front of my nose and seemed eerily familiar. A dim memory from the French restaurant my father had taken me to for my 16th birthday. The menu held a delicacy called calf fries (with chanterelles and asparagus) and it had brought forth a spontaneous gag reflex. A simmering bubble of vague recollection from that 16th birthday menu melded with the ingredients in front of me and everything erupted into a full boil. I stormed out of the doublewide and would have shot Earl with his own rifle but agent Dorsey wrenched it out of my hands. I satisfied myself with kicking at his lawn chair until it collapsed under him.

"You asshole! You total dumb shit. You put my mother and Danny on the road hawking calf testicles."

"Those little shits don't need them, Sharon."

Ramirez and Hamilton broke their FBI stares long enough to shift and wince. Dorsey did neither but stared at Earl like she had just discovered a new and disgusting species.

"Nuts On Ice," Earl said, "that's our motto. Rodeo houses and fancy chefs will pay a fortune for them." He held up his cast. "'Course they weren't that easy to collect."

"Have any actually been sold, Earl? Have Mother and Danny sold even one illegal piece of possibly Mad Cow infected gland?"

"I don't know. Your mother keeps hanging up on me. That's why I called the FBI. She's got my merchandize and there's a rodeo shindig in Portland that wants a bunch for a tub o' what they call bull butter." He leered up at me. "Them cowboys want the real goods."

The agents perked up at that and I could practically read their minds. Finally, something they could sink their teeth into, so to speak. The transportation of illegal bovine body parts across state lines. Surely they join forces with the FDA throw him in jail for a few nights.

Things went downhill from there and Earl fired off a few shots (mostly as warnings because they only pinged into the doors of the first Buick and he could shoot the eye out of a sparrow from a hundred yards if he wanted). The agents used their official satellite car radio to call for reinforcements while I jogged to the nearest neighbors who drove me to the Greyhound bus stop which was, actually, in the middle of nowhere. It was just like high school when I escaped from home (usually with Danny) at least four times a year.

The smell of the Pacific Ocean swamped the twin cities of Aberdeen and Hoquiam and three cell towers came into view. I called Stephen. He didn't answer, so I called the TA office. Ralph, the loathsome piece of crap who shares space with us, did.

He also drove down in his Jeep. I figure he averaged eighty-five miles an hour which is no big deal in Montana but in other states (including this one) it can get you jail time.

HOME

There was another manila envelope waiting in the mailbox. It was (surprise, surprise) from my brother. I could not imagine what it might contain because it is indisputably true that a younger sibling will always know an older sibling better than the other way around. Inside was a folded piece of paper with an intricately drawn happy face that almost filled the entire page.

As I looked closer, I saw that many of the features were my mother's including the eyes, the double chin, and even the delicate mole that accented her upper lip. At the bottom of the page was a lightly traced panel truck with Good Humor (all in caps) on the side. Blue drops of water cascaded from the small van. Each drop metamorphosed into a butterfly that flitted and soared all across the back of the page.

Danny was at the wheel, smiling and waving. I knew it was him because his name was written in block letters in the balloon above the head.

He had driven all over the country until the ice melted, I thought. He wasn't making bombs, he was saving our Mother. That's the part of a *folie a deux* I had forgotten. Love was always in charge.

Maybe Danny was taking his medication and maybe he wasn't. It didn't matter because he wasn't making bombs and for the first time in my life, in spite of everything, I envied my schizophrenic brother. He wasn't the crazy, unpredictable predator the FBI thought and he wasn't the helpless prey I had imagined. He was the driver and, in this life, how many of us can say that?

CALF FRIES

Milk (.95 liter)
Beaten egg
Calf Fries (.675 kilograms)
Cracker meal (11.5 grams)
Flour (157.2 grams)
Sesame seeds – enough to make it gritty
Fresh ground pepper, a pinch
Salt and nutmeg, a pinch each
Oil (.9 kilograms)

Sterilize hands. Mix egg and milk. Combine dry ingredients. Close your eyes and clean your fries. Send the little jewels on a round trip journey through the dry ingredients with an intervening milk and egg bath. Submerge the little steers in sizzling oil until amber. Drain, and serve with booze.

CANDYMAKING

THE APPRENTICE

Everything Ralph knew about cooking he learned from Addie, the *chef de cuisine* across the street. He could roast a turkey, cobble together parsley-sprigged Eggs Benedict, and use cilantro on dishes from two continents and one sub-continent. None of this was any use in the Army where he learned how to eat bugs and stew snakes and drink seven shooters in a row. In spite of his homophobic uncle's predictions about men who cooked, it wasn't stuffing poultry as a civilian that was his undoing. It was the shooters.

THE COOK

Addie's hair was orange and she wore purple (or lime green) workout duds which would have been stylin' but not for someone who got senior discounts at Denny's Diner. She lived at the Happy Trails Retirement Home and, whenever possible, played bridge or pinochle but mostly ended up sitting around a table of Gin Rummy – which wasn't as trying on some of the residents' short-term memory circuits.

Two days after the Spring Equinox, before the leaves started to flare up and really do their thing, Addie put on her backpack and hiked the six blocks to Ralph's house. When he opened the door she said, "I need a case of Goo Goo Clusters because the Happy Trails gift shop quit selling them. And so did 7-Eleven and QFC."

Ralph was thirty years old and could do one hundred pushups in a row. He had a careful smile and shrapnel-pocked skin thanks to one and a quarter tours of duty as a Ranger. "Would you like to come in?"

"No."

"So this isn't a social call."

"Friday is my birthday and the girls are giving me a surprise party so get the candy, okay? And some trick candles. Pink." She handed him a gallon jar of pennies. "I took up a donation."

"That doesn't look like a donation. It looks like the Gin Rummy pot."

"Half the people I live with can't remember to use silverware so we both know the surprise part of my party will be that it actually happens."

He hefted a jar which weighed close to twenty pounds. "You pack this all the way here?"

She stood on tiptoe and kissed his cheek. "I'm on my way to Gold's Gym and don't want to spend time farting around the mall looking for treats. Help me out here."

"You usually make your own candy."

She gave him a dark look and plodded off to work on staying fit for another couple of decades. Addie was determined to live long (if not well) and eventually have a centennial birthday gala which would get written up in the paper. Also, she'd heard the president wrote personal letters to everyone in the country who successfully completed one hundred years and she only hoped they didn't have another bunch of idiots at the helm when hers finally rolled around.

After her workout and a smoothie for lunch, she planned to send out party invitations and then play a cozy hand or two of Five Card Stud with the new bookkeeper. Addie had been slowly setting him up over the past month and Ralph figured she was going to shake Mr. Accountant down for fifty or sixty dollars before he wised up and quit socializing with the residents. That's what she'd done with the last one.

She'd do it to the next one, too. In the senior care services business there was, Ralph thought, always a next one.

THE APPRENTICE

Ralph was an orphan who had known Addie for over twenty years. She was the only woman who had ever baked him a birthday cake or given him cookies and cocoa on a snowy winter afternoon. They were bound together in a way that wouldn't be broken except by his death or hers.

Ralph spent the afternoon rolling pennies. He was about to climb onto his trail bike and pedal the three miles to the mall when the phone rang. It was Addie. "You're right. I shouldn't let one bad experience keep me from doing what I love. I'm going to rustle up a batch of almond toffee and maybe some fudge. You know what to get."

"You still want the clusters?"

"You can never have too much candy."

At the mall's Specialty-Food-Arama a tired brunette rang up the bill and said, "I see Addie's back to cooking. Didn't I read something in the paper about that a few months ago?"

"Give me a case of Goo Goo Clusters," Ralph said, "and the Fire Marshall didn't actually close her down. He and Happy Trails came to an understanding."

"What kind of understanding?"

"She won't cook candy to the hard crack stage on a hotplate in her room. But I'm thinking she might climb back on that horse and work her magic at my place."

"I suppose you know that sounds dirtier than it is." The clerk began ringing up the butter, confectioner's sugar and dark chocolate.

"Don't forget the Goo Goo Clusters," Ralph said.

"We're all out."

"But the old ladies love them."

"Yeah, they like Cherry Mountain Bars, too, and Idaho Spuds but the kids won't eat that retro-candy and so it's off the shelf." The clerk chewed her gum viciously. "Word came down from high."

"From God?"

"From the regional manager."

"Okay, I'll special order two cases."

"No special orders."

"That's a crappy way to run a store."

"Hey, I feel your pain."

Ralph spent the rest of the afternoon biking from store to store, but Clusters seemed to be a thing of the past. He surfed the net until midnight with the vague uneasy feeling he got whenever he tapped into *Google*. It was all the fault of the Patriot Act, but none feel quite so guilty as the innocent. It was with relief that he found three actual websites that not only didn't have pictures of dandruff-shouldered old men handing lollipops to little boys and girls, but actually featured such items as banana pops, licorice nubs and red cherry lips. He went to *Candy7.com* and *Monstermarket.com* and but they could only supply Goo Goo Clusters on a backorder basis. That wouldn't work. Addie's birthday was in three days.

CandyDirect.com was the only site that could, for an extra seven bucks, rush an order which brought the cost of each Goo Goo Cluster to three bucks. He ordered five cases. Like Santa Claus, Addie could dispense sweet treats to the nice residents of Happy Trails.

The last place Ralph stopped was the liquor store on the corner of University and 42nd where he bought dinky bottles of dark rum, Kahlua, and Cointreau. The ancient clerk (the one with hair growing out of his nose and ears) rang everything up and said, "Last year you bought fifths."

"Last year I wasn't on the wagon." Ralph stuffed the tiny bottles in his backpack. "These are for Addie. She's making candy."

"Sure, Kid." The clerk laughed, rang everything up. "See you tomorrow. Or maybe later on today."

THE COOK

Addie piled pots, pans, double boilers, glass bowls, two marble slabs, three candy thermometers, two stainless steel knives, and three spatulas into the back of her old Pontiac. She added spoons of metal, wood, and even a glass beaker with a glass stirring rod. She covered it all with her candy-making apron – a brilliant white jacket (not unlike one worn by a doctor making rounds) which had the tri-colored Dutch flag and *Droste School of Chocolatiers, Amsterdam, 1958* stenciled on the pocket.

Addie was ready to roll.

At Ralph's apartment, she went through the supplies he'd bought: sniffing chocolate, crunching almonds, holding unsalted butter in the palm of her hand.

"You did good, kid," she finally said, "except for the stove. I need a gas stove to do the job right."

"No gas but I do have a new fire extinguisher."

She frowned at him. "I, for one, would like to not have a repeat of last year. I can't control electricity like I can the gas. That's why the hotplate was such a problem."

"Roger that," Ralph said. "I'll get down my camp stove."

After he'd wrestled it from the attic, dusted it off and hooked up the propane tank, Addie handed him a knife. "I want the almonds chopped fine but not turned into powder, understand?"

Thus it began.

Addie worried about the fact that the fudge wouldn't have time to age properly, but she worried about that every year. Dark rum and almonds went into the toffee base which was kept at a rolling boil until she dumped it onto one of the marble slabs. Kahlua went into the fragrant milk chocolate topping that waited in a double boiler. Addie added bits of this, lumps of that, muttering constantly.

"Okay," she finally said, "It's ready."

Ralph breathed deeply of the Cointreau and then dumped the

entire 2 oz. bottle into the creamy mixture, then poured the black-brown satiny mass onto the lightly buttered marble slab. He used spatulas to lift and stir, working the gloss out while shaping the fudge into an oval sheet about an inch thick. After it cooled a bit, he scored the top and garnished each square with an unbroken walnut half and a tiny orange peel curl. "I probably should taste this."

Addie slapped his hand. "It has to cool first. You'll fuck up the sugar granules if you mess with it."

"Fuck?" Ralph raised an eyebrow. "I didn't know candy makers swore."

"The good ones do," Addie said.

Ralph gathered up the little bottles, dumped them in the garbage and turned to begin the dishes.

Addie spooned Kahlua-scented chocolate over the pan of almond rich toffee, then reached for the grater and block of Dark Dutch. A frown of concentration was etched between her eyes as the rich bits sifted down. The table was too high for her to get a good angle, so Ralph dried his hands and finished the job before pressing a knife into the still warm candy, making diamond-shaped pieces beautiful enough to wear threaded on a necklace.

THE APPRENTICE

The towel around Ralph's middle looked like it had been in a confectionery explosion, but Addie's white jacket was still pristine. She sat on the kitchen's only chair. "Are you quitting the booze?"

"Yes."

"Quitting has to be hard for someone like you."

"Quitting is easy," Ralph said. "I've quit three times and it wasn't hard at all."

"Is it going to work this time?"

"I hope so because I can't stand any more smirks from the weasel-faced clerk at the liquor store."

"Is going to that Vet's group helping?"

"Not exactly." Though Ralph knew that was part of it.

"What then?"

"You could have died in that fire, Addie, and I was passed out in the corner, too drunk to help."

"Is that what the Fire Marshall said?"

"Several people said it." He carefully wiped the knife clean. He saw her face. "Don't get all worked up. I just keep you around for the candy."

Addie blew her nose. "You can always buy candy."

"I hate that commercial stuff. I don't know why you get all excited about the Goo Goo Clusters when you make candy fit for the gods."

"Life isn't all about quality," Addie said. "You got to have quantity, too, or you lose perspective." She shifted her shoulders under the weight of eighty-three years of taking both the long and the short view. "Stay sober for five years and maybe I'll give you my fudge notes."

"And the toffee?"

"You get that after I kick the bucket."

They went into the living room and sat on Ralph's ragged couch, nibbling pieces of love and talking about soft ball firmness versus the hard crack stage of the alchemy that had turned a young man and an old woman into something like a family.

It wasn't as dirty as it sounded.

GARRET'S LAMENT

Garret MacDowell and I played football together at State U. before my reserve unit got activated. I left in mid-season and he took my position as quarterback. He made some decent passes but set the conference record in getting sacked because he couldn't figure out how to step away from a tackle. While Garret was eating turf, I wore extra strength military ear plugs and tried to avoid land mines outside of Kabul. After ten months of insomnia, a piece of shrapnel the size of a pack of cigarettes took off my leg at the knee.

A year later, after graduating with a BA in English, Garret got hired at the land office where his uncle worked while I practised the art of screwing on my prosthesis and swearing under my breath. Garret told everyone the job was temporary until he finished his novel. He spent his days pissing and moaning about the workload, whining that most of the surveyors were fat old farts who'd been goofing off for twenty years while he could lift eighty pounds of gear and walk five miles uphill without stopping.

Garret may have been a pain in the ass but he was a wizard at working any landscape; high, low, or densely vegetated. Which, according to half the town, was the only reason (uncle or not) he kept his job.

Time passed, as it is wont to do, and Garret sat at the bar of my father-in-law's tavern and told everyone how supremely excellent he was on shitty old equipment that was so rusty that he was the only employee in the world who could read the gauges accurately. Then somebody wrote a grant and, in the blink of an eye, the old compass was replaced with one so sensitive it responded to magnetic lines in the earth which varied from day to day and hour to hour. Boundaries in the county were no longer based in numerical certainty but in a geometry that was affected by sunspots and changes in the temperature. Long held easements and access to water became a multimillion dollar bombshell and everyone who knew loud-mouth Garret understood surveying had become a job for which he was no longer well-suited.

Garret said it wasn't his fault that gravity called to headwaters of the Cascade Mountains. Not his fault, he muttered, that misty rain and melting snow met and married and, in a lust of motion, dripped and slipped, pooled and plodded, rushed and raged from clouds to earth to ocean in the most inexact way. Cliffside fence lines disappeared only to reappear somewhere else. It had been going on forever but now, after a housing boom and bust, there was no wiggle room in agreed-upon easements. The results of Garret's work changed from day to day and he wouldn't (or couldn't) keep his mouth shut.

"Lakes, rivers, soccer fields, all of it a big fucking mess because the goddam boundaries won't stay put." Garret often muttered into his beer. It was a metaphor for his life, I suspect. Nothing in it had stayed put either. My sister divorced him, his parents moved to Florida and he saw his kids every other weekend.

One night, after the hundred-year flood, when the brown water had finally seeped somewhere else, Garret moved his glass of Red Hook and spread a map over a battered and scarred tavern table. He ran his calloused thumb along a thin line marked Blue Stilly River like a man would trace the curve of a lover's hip. He spoke carefully chosen words but I didn't know it was poetry. I thought Garret was just bitching like he always did when he had to check property lines to find out who was supposed to pay for the road repairs. I thought it was only the angst of more borders that wouldn't stay put.

Only the English graduate student, who sidled in after her night class, could nail it down with the right label. Poetry. That's what she called it and she should know, right? The woman is brilliant in most things.

This is the beginning of Garret's lament. "A map is a river in retrospect."

Garret was not an ignorant man. He used words like *retrospect* and other words too — *morose* and *circumnavigate* and all kinds of polysyllabic words with equal ease. Also, when he swore he said things like *wretched asshole* which I've never been able to do with a straight face but Garret sat at the bar one night and actually said his uncle was a wretched asshole. No wonder the graduate student wanted to fuck him. That night she wrote his words on a sheet of lined paper in her precise and even hand.

GARRET'S LAMENT

A map is a river in retrospect.
Beer is grain and water and hops, in retrospect
Oil is a dinosaur and two million year's of trees and lush grasses and
insects and birds and reptile slime, all mixed together
in retrospect.
A mountain is an earthquake in retrospect.
An eagle is an egg in retrospect.

"Dolly the cloned sheep was once a petri dish in retrospect," I said. "Do you want another beer?"

"Sure," Garret said. "Grab me a bag of peanuts, too."

The graduate student's hair had come undone and her face glowed. She removed the half-glasses she used for reading and writing and said,

"A poem is a jar filled with words
grabbed in bunches or plucked one at a time
shoved into an order that freezes on the page.
A poem is pain, in retrospect."

The graduate student and I have separated after four years of marriage. Neither of us seems to know why. I flushed lager into a glass the shape of a nuclear reactor. Golden liquid slopped a little over the brim of the glass.

"A divorce is a marriage, in retrospect," I said.

My wife lifted the dripping glass, a glass that couldn't hold its cargo, to her ripe red lips and said quietly, "A marriage is simply a plodding kind of longitudinal love. It strays like a river. It doesn't always stay the same."

It hit me between the eyes with the force of a well-aimed aluminum baseball bat, like the one I keep under the bar for troublesome times. Metaphors and similes. That's what comes of loving a woman in love with words. Words. The goddam things are everywhere. They mix and mingle and the meaning of a sentence doesn't stay put, either.

Garret tore open his bag of peanuts and poured some in her palm. His shoulder touched hers, all those silent gestures while he kept on complaining how he hated putting a pen to paper in the certain knowledge that wherever the lines were placed, in however measured a fashion, it will be a lie the next day. "As a cartographer," he said, "I know that crumbling grains of sand, shifting tectonic plates and slippery erosion join with tides and time. It all takes a toll."

The graduate student moaned when he said that part.

"I thought you were a surveyor," I said. "Where did this cartographer shit come from?"

"It's upgrading," Garret said. "But you wouldn't know about that. You're just a bartender."

"I'm more than a simple bartender," I said. "I'm partial-owner of this place."

"Partial owner, huh?" Garret put his hand on my wife's knee. "If there's one thing my job has taught me it's this: ownership is a fleeting thing."

I called him a wretched asshole and everyone in the place laughed because I'm not the kind of man who uses fancy words. That doesn't mean I don't understand them. It doesn't mean I don't feel them. It doesn't mean I can't use them when the occasion calls for clarity.

"Marriage is a promise," I said, "tides and time and slippery erosion be damned. It's a fucking promise to hang on even if the Moon falls from the sky or writing a doctoral dissertation on Sylvia Plath breaks your spirit. You don't walk away from love just because you're tired and you're afraid that you've spent three years concentrating on the wrong thing."

It was late when I locked the door, cashed out the till, and swept out the toilets. The graduate student had moved from the bar to the corner table. She was correcting papers and humming an unfamiliar tune and I thought that, in some ways, Garret was right. Everything does change. In the blink of an eye, a river's current can shift away from the old channel, then rush back to reclaim the defining lines of history and habit and healing.

As for love? Who can tell what will alter the boundaries of a woman's affection? I can't tell and apparently the surveyor-turned-cartographer couldn't either but something broken had been repaired. All I know is that it was a cold wet night and the surveyor-cartographer went home alone.

That's Garret's real lament, in retrospect.

DRIVING SHARON CRAZY

The list of men who were driving Sharon crazy wasn't all that long. It didn't even fill the first page of her diary.

1. *MY FATHER THE ALCOHOLIC*
2. *EARL THE ASSHOLE*
3. *STEPHEN THE WHORE*
4. *RALPH*

The first three names on the list were in black permanent marker. Sharon hadn't decided about Ralph, yet, so his name was lightly sketched in pencil. She began the list at the suggestion of Marie, the woman who led group therapy sessions at the rehab facility. With a voice like a fog horn and the lines of a million cigarettes on her face, Marie gave every recovering alcoholic a journal. "Good luck," she rasped and they were supposed to pick up their lives and get back to normal, whatever the hell *that* was.

Most of the journals had a brown leather cover and thick, creamy pages. The one she gave Sharon had a polished aluminum surface with hinges that looked like they would squeak but didn't. It was the perfect gift since Sharon taught anatomy dissection at the University of Washington and was bad at keeping cat guts and eyeball slime off anything of importance. Plus, the polished aluminum looked professional to the anatomy students.

Sharon understood that looking professional (and not quirky or weirdly gruesome) was important because of her crooked nose and the pinkish four-inch scar along her jawline, not to mention the thick puckered tissue that bunched between her shoulder and her elbow. It, like a fierce comet, possessed a jagged tail visible at the neckline of all her shirts and dresses.

Those scars were given to her by two of the crazy-making men in her life. Her other scar, the scar from a broken heart, was given to her by her husband, a man known throughout Seattle as Stephen-the-Whore. Ralph, last on the list, was in pencil because he hadn't wounded her, yet. Sharon figured it was only a matter of time.

HER FATHER THE ALCOHOLIC

One fall day (just before guiding thirty University of Washington juniors through the intricacies of a feline central nervous system), Sharon called her father, the plastic surgeon. His scrub nurse held the cell phone to his ear while he lathered up for yet another combination butt lift, breast augmentation, and tummy tuck.

Sharon tried to keep her voice steady. "Stephen and I aren't doing so well."

"I'm sorry to hear that." There was the squishy sound of soapy fingers and her father murmuring for the nurse to get her head out of her ass and open a fresh pack of surgical gloves.

"I need to borrow some money," Sharon said. "It's just until I get a new roommate."

"How much?"

"Six hundred."

"Ouch."

"I feel really bad about this, Daddy."

"Sure you do. We all do. My colleagues tell me it's damn near impossible to find a son-in-law who's likeable. Are you sure you can't work this out?"

"He's screwing the Dean's daughter. So will you loan me the money?"

"Just a loan," he said. "How's Stephen doing for cash?"

She threw her cell phone against the far wall and biked to class. The rest of the day was spent deep in the bowels of Marisa, the class's demonstration cat. When she extracted the heart, Sharon found herself calling the gutted feline *Dear Old Dad*. Some of the students squirmed but fuck it. Her father was supposed to be on her side.

It was almost dark when she left Hartzell Hall and the Seattle skyline was bright with a reflected sunset of red and orange. It reminded Sharon of her twelfth birthday. It was a midnight flight on her father's float plane but they missed Lake Union and crash-landed on interstate 5 just north of the Mercer Exit.

When the state patrol showed up, Sharon's father climbed from the cockpit and refused the Breathalyzer. The officer arrested him anyway, not only for reckless endangerment but for scaring the shit out of the mayor's wife who was motoring home from a fund-raising function at the Yacht Club.

Sharon's recollection of that night was spotty because of the concussion and for years she suffered nightmares of the pavement rushing to meet them while her thrice-divorced father incessantly whistled the childhood ditty, "Happy birthday to you, happy birthday to you."

She did remember the Emergency Room doctor who stitched the gash along her jaw. And she remembered the pain of her broken nose and swelling eyes and hiding her face in the crook of her arm as the wheelchair headed down a hallway that smelled of antiseptic and urine. Bottom line, a seventh grade girl will never accept attending school while looking like a raccoon. Her mother understood completely and sent her to live with crazy Uncle Harold in Idaho. Probably Earl, her mother's newest boyfriend, had something to do with that decision but Sharon wanted to think her mother had, for once, thought of her daughter first.

CRAZY UNCLE HAROLD

Uncle Harold, the survivalist, believed in God and in the importance of camouflage. He was a man who took his home schooling duties seriously and every morning he marched Sharon out to the shooting range behind the barn. In the afternoon, they built pipe bombs and estimated the time it would take for a public building to burn to the ground. Sharon realized, years later, that Uncle Harold hadn't made her crazy. Instead, his peculiar teaching methods had whetted her appetite for science and self reliance. She was grateful for both.

Nevertheless, after six months, Sharon was desperate to get back to civilization. Fortunately, she started her period. Uncle Harold put her on the next bus home. To her dismay, she discovered that home was no longer Seattle but a mossy hamlet fifty miles into the Olympic Mountains.

When she stepped off the bus, the first words out of her mother's mouth were, "What happened to your hair?"

"Don't you like the semi-bald look?"

"And your fingernails! My god, didn't you ever clean your nails?"

"I've been learning how to eat grubs. They don't come in nice little plastic-wrapped packages."

"Don't talk back, young lady."

"You left me with someone who thinks insects are a basic food group," Sharon said sullenly. "What the hell did you expect?"

Sharon's mother reached into her purse and pulled out a scarf. "Put this on. We'll tell everyone you had cancer."

They had a major fight, in front of the post office, about whether or not Sharon was going to school on Monday.

Sharon won that fight and spent all spring and summer sleeping in, reading every book she could lay her hands on, and taking showers. By the time fall rolled around she'd grown the requisite hair, boobs, and attitude plus she tested into high school. She graduated at age sixteen.

EARL THE ASSHOLE

Earl was the man who put a bullet through her shoulder.

It started out with a fight about drying the dishes and ended with Earl snarling, "Tomorrow you stop sassing your mother and start earning your keep." Before dawn, he threw back the covers of her twin bed, shoved boots on her feet, zipped her into his camouflage jacket and goose-walked her to his rusty pickup.

The Sun was still struggling to reach the rim of the world when Earl stopped the truck and grabbed the heavy elk rifle he kept racked on the truck's back window. "Stay here. You can help me carry the damn thing out later." He left her in the cab of the truck – cold and alone except for a thermos of whiskey-laced coffee. Fuck this, Sharon thought, and decided to walk home. She planned to keep in the tire tracks and not veer into knee-deep snow but she recognized a shortcut and decided to take it.

Half a mile later, she fell sideways into a sparkling drift and lay there, trying to figure out why. One arm was heavy and wouldn't obey when she began to sit up. Only when she saw the blood did she begin to scream, first in disbelief and then in pain. "You shot me! You stupid sonovabitch, you shot me!"

When Earl showed up, face sweaty and hands rough, she kicked out against the memory of the way he'd looked months earlier when touching her newly budded breasts. Her heel jammed against his crotch and he dropped like a sack of sand onto the snow beside her.

When he finally got his breath he took out his skinning knife. "I told you to stay in the truck! I thought you were a deer!" With shaking hands, he sliced the sodden coat from her shivering body. "Stupid bitch."

It took no time at all for Sharon to figure out that any kind of motion made her want to throw up. Her lips barely moved and her face was so pale that the freckles stood out like nutmeg on skim milk. "I hate you," she said through gritted teeth. "Only an idiot would mistake me for a deer."

"Fuck. Your mother is not going to understand this."

"I hate you, I hate you," Sharon sobbed all the way to the hospital in Olympia.

After what became known as *the accident*, Earl never again took her hunting and he didn't even raise his eyes when she sunbathed on the front porch or went from the bedroom to the outhouse in her baby doll pajamas.

The following spring, after months of physical therapy, Sharon notched an arrow into Earl's new hunting bow just as he stepped around the corner, arms cupping a load of kindling for the kitchen cook stove. When he froze, panic on his face, she released the bowstring, smiling as the arrow sliced off the top part of his ear.

"I guess I owe you that," Earl grunted through gritted teeth and walked on up to the cabin.

Neither of them spoke of it again but in rehab group, years later, Sharon tried to explain how sorry she was that she'd only nicked him.

STEPHEN THE WHORE

Sharon was at her kitchen table, eating from a carton of three day old Pad Thai, when the college custodian (a man who didn't get paid nearly enough for cleaning up cat guts, shark slime, plus all the other acrid, foul messes to be found in the biology building) rang her doorbell. The dogs tripped all over themselves to be first to yelp and slather at his feet. The custodian was in his mid-forties with thinning hair, a florid complexion and a little beer belly. "I should have known you'd have animals that drooled."

He handed her a sealed 9 by 12 manila envelope.

"What's this?"

"I found the photos on the school website and the credit card bill was in the waste basket by your husband's desk."

"I'll be sure he gets them."

"I think you should look at them first."

"Why?"

"I could make a great deal of money off these," the custodian said with a trace of impatience, "but I deleted the file and I'm turning the evidence over to you because you're the only one in the Science

Building to apologize for the mess in the anatomy room and you ask about my cats."

"How are the little dears?"

He sighed. "Meeny is fine but Moe ate a bad bug and is at the vet's right now."

The manila envelope smelled like disinfectant and contained half a dozen color photos. Some were of Stephen, smiling rakishly while fondling a tattooed breast. The breast was not Sharon's. There were also images of the Dean's daughter peeking through tousled hair and sucking her middle finger. Except for the tattoos, the Dean's daughter looked about twelve but Sharon knew she had reached the age of consent. Stephen had always been very careful about that. As for the Visa card, it was clear before the end of the first page of bar bills and hotel rooms that Sharon may have been trying to stay married but Stephen wasn't.

Head down, Sharon trudged to the hardware store on Aurora Avenue and changed the locks to the small house she and Stephen were thinking of buying. *Had been thinking*, she scolded herself. I can't keep forgiving him or ignoring the facts or living with a man who has the morals of my father.

Between unscrewing of the face plates and inserting the new lock mechanism, the cold dull pain of a broken heart became a poker hot rage and, after checking that the mechanism really did work, she headed for the metal box on the top shelf of her closet. It held the nifty little .32 her father gave her when she went to college. "Keep it handy," he'd said. "Keep it loaded."

She spent three hours crying on the bedroom floor and an hour thinking at the kitchen table. By midnight, she figured out that Stephen wasn't worth doing time for. She put her gun back in the closet and thought about getting drunk. Her personal journal was on her desk, under a stack of entomology term papers comparing the collective behavior of fire ants with that of wasps. The phone number for the alcohol and drug rehabilitation facility was stamped inside the polished aluminum cover. She picked up her cell phone and called wizened, wrinkled Marie.

RALPH

An hour later, Ralph showed up at her door, a backpack slung over his shoulder and a vegetarian pizza in his hands. The backpack was filled with catnip, raisins, doggie snacks and half a dozen bottles of homemade root beer. The pockets of his cargo pants were stuffed with Seasons Six and Seven of *Buffy the Vampire Slayer*.

"Maria sent me."

He fired up the DVD while the animals (a rabbit, two dogs and two cats) ecstatically gobbled the treats he'd brought. Sharon got a bottle opener from the kitchen.

Ralph was a part-time biology instructor working on his doctorate – exploring the mitochondria of sponges. Immature undergraduates of both sexes avoided his classes even though he was tall and strong with russet brown eyes and auburn hair that was prematurely fading to white. They avoided him because of the scars. He had taken a face full of shrapnel in Afghanistan and had lost a leg while pulling a buddy out of a tank in Iraq. Tenured Literature professors (of both genders) saw the man underneath the warped flesh and propositioned him in emails filled with sonnets and the occasional haiku. Sometimes they brought him warm Krispy Kremes in the morning which he shared with the Biology Department's adoring secretaries.

Sharon had met Ralph at the rehab facility. They were in the alcohol dependency group together and he knew too much about her, but that was a knife that cut both ways because she knew too much about him, too. Sharon didn't need a man like Ralph in her life – a man who was going through rehab for the third time.

Ralph bit into his pizza. "I heard the custodian declined to do his blackmail bit on you. Lucky you."

"What's that supposed to mean?"

"Half the faculty makes monthly payments to him."

"Do you?"

"Not any more. How do you like the pizza?"

"It's vegetarian. I believe in meat."

"I also heard you needed a roommate."

"I don't want to talk about that right now," Sharon said. "I want to get stinking drunk."

"Me, too. Have a root beer, instead."

They spent the next three hours watching Buffy beat the shit out of all the monsters in Buffyville. Sharon fell asleep in the middle of episode seven, the cats piled on her lap. Ralph stopped the DVD, turned off the lights, put the rabbit in its hutch, the dogs in the backyard and covered Sharon (and the cats) with an afghan. He let himself out the front door, testing to see if it had latched behind him.

SHARON

It was two weeks since her phone call to her father and Sharon still hadn't gotten a check. She awoke to the dogs' barking because Stephen was drunk and pounding the front door with his fist, jiggling the doorknob, and also kicking the metal strip along the bottom. "Boysh will be boysh, Shay. We can't help it." There was also a muddled cry about, "They're my dogs, too, dammit." He promised to do better but, when she pulled back the drapes to look at him through the glass, he threatened to do worse.

I can't live my life this way, she thought. I'm going move past professional and smack into crazy if I don't find a way to stop taking him back. She picked up the phone. This time she didn't dial the suicide hotline or speed dial Marie. This time she called the cops and after they took Stephen away she called Ralph.

"It's two in the morning."

"I know," she said. "This is the deal. You get the front bedroom. You will never, ever come into my room. And you can't watch reality programs in the den."

"I love reality programs."

"Watch them when I'm not home."

They discussed the electric bill, how to divide the refrigerator, and what day he could do laundry. She was about to hang up when Ralph said, "I'm a good guy, Sharon. Don't confuse loathing with embarrassment."

There was no smile on her face when she hung up. It was serious business, this living with a man and not lusting after him or hating him, either. She hoped she was up to it. With a sigh, she pulled out her journal. Ralph had his own demons to quell but he really wasn't one of the men driving her crazy.

The last thing Sharon did before going back to bed was erase his name from the list.

SIBLING RIVALRY

LOVE AND FAMILY

There are many kinds of love, but Sigmund Freud was mainly concerned about the kind between parents and children. Carl Rogers was concerned about unconditional love. And Timothy Leary, between LSD flashbacks, talked about self and experience. Those three giants of psychological theory neglected siblings entirely. That fertile area was left to the minor researchers and only recently have studies shown that in any family (biological, blended, or beaten into submission) the connection is strongest between identical twins, because of the genetic component. Without that link, you may as well be born into a family of complete strangers.

That was according to the article in the *Journal of Family Dynamics* that I was reading just before going to sleep. I love reading in bed but Steven the Whore, my estranged husband, doesn't. So logic will tell you it was another night alone for me. I must have dropped off halfway through the article because I awoke with a lone pen mark scrawling off page 15 like the wake of a rudderless boat heading for the rocky shore. Somewhere my cell phone was ringing.

It continued ringing before going to voice mail and then starting up again. You would think there would be a mercy block after a four minute continuous cycle of jangling and silence but apparently not, so I tore apart my bedroom, kitchen, and living room only to find the little darling in the bag of dog kibbles on the back porch. I have animals who like to chew and hide things but this was the kind of joke Steven played.

I wiped Purina Dog Chow crumbs from the cell phone and headed back into the house. "H'lo."

"You always did sleep like the dead." The line had a tinny quality with a hollow echo and I knew right away it was Bruce, my oldest brother.

I looked at the digital clock on the kitchen stove, "It's three in the morning here."

"Whatever."

There was some kind of chatter in the background, but I couldn't make out the words because Bruce had put his hand over the mouthpiece. When he came back on the line he sounded annoyed. "Constance wants me to tell you hello."

"Who's Constance?"

"My wife."

The pause stretched past the point of politeness because it took me a long time to find my voice and when I did, it squeaked. "I didn't know you were married."

"She's a flutist."

"Peachy. How long have you been married?"

"Almost a year."

"You've been married a year..."

"Almost a year."

"...and you never, even once, thought to bring that fact up? Not even on Facebook?"

"You don't have to shout."

"I thought you were gay. We all did. We were comfortable with that. We thought you went away and never came home because you were gay."

"I went away and never came home because Marjorie is crazy and our father is an asshole." Bruce had started calling our Mother by her first name when he was in the eighth grade. Now he was thirty, and according to his Facebook photo, with thinning hair and a slight paunch. And he'd never once even hinted he was married. I closed my eyes and counted silently to twenty. Married happier than me, I hoped, even if he had made a lifetime commitment to sounding annoyed about everything.

"Congratulations."

"Thanks."

"When are you coming home?"

It was his turn to pause before saying, softly and precisely, "I *am* home, Sharon. I like it here. Come to France. Stay as long as you want. I think Constance would like you and I'm pretty sure you would like her. But you can never, ever, bring Marjorie or Danny with you, understand?"

He hung up without saying goodbye and I was about to throw my cell phone against the wall when the damn thing rang again. "I almost forgot," Bruce said. "I got a message from Oklahoma City patient services saying Margery had a heart attack and is in University Hospital, in the Cardiac Care Unit."

He had to say the last part twice before I got it and then I stammered for a bit but managed to get out two words. "Is she...?"

"No."

"Why didn't they call me?"

"That would have been far too easy."

Then Bruce hung up once-and-for-all and I did throw the phone across the room. That felt so good I let lamp fly and my alarm clock, too, before going to answer the door because whoever was pounding on it sounded determined to knock a hole through the hollow core center.

It was my father. "There's a ticket waiting on Continental," he said. "Get dressed."

"Why the hell did the hospital call Bruce?"

"Damn, I wanted to get here sooner but the lights were against me and I can't afford another DUI." My father shrugged out of his windbreaker. "Bruce called me to find out if it was true. I didn't want you to hear this over the telephone."

I could hardly get the words out. "What happened?"

"Heart attack. She's got to lose weight."

"Wh-why call Bruce? Why not me?"

"Bruce was on her insurance coverage."

"Bruce bought Mother medical insurance?"

"Supplemental. For her Medicaid."

We stared at each other – my father in gray stubble, gray sweats, and a red Nike windbreaker, and me in my ratty tee shirt and bikini panties. Mother was on Medicaid because she was a schizophrenic who forgot to take her pills, thus disabled.

"I was sleeping," I said. "I just got the phone call."

My father, Dr. Peter Hansen, is a well-known plastic surgeon, not to mention womanizer, binge alcoholic and three-time loser in the marriage lotto. My mother was the first wife and bore Bruce, Danny and me before the house of cards came tumbling down.

My father strode to my bedroom and pulled underwear, jeans, socks and a shirt from various drawers and hangers. He was disconcertingly familiar with where each item belonged but perhaps that was because of the wives and how women tend to sort their clothing. Or perhaps it's because I've always kept my bras in the top drawer and my jeans in the closet and for years he was the only parent who was there for us, my siblings and me, every Christmas, Easter, and for the boring weeks of summer break.

"Where's Danny?" My voice had the high tremor that marks anxiety. My pre-veterinarian students had it just before making their first incision into the bowls of a cadaver.

"Your wacko little brother is with your mother, as usual." He saw my look. "At the hospital, waiting."

"Don't call him *wacko*. You're a doctor. You should know better."

My father, the plastic surgeon, understands sags and wrinkles better than schizophrenia. He looked at his watch. "We need to get going."

"Why me? Why do I have to be the Go-To-Girl?"

My father unzipped my suitcase and pulled the handle up with a snap. "Because Danny needs you. Because you are, in spite of your attitude, a genuinely nice person."

"What's wrong with my attitude?"

"Hurry up, Honey. You need to make that flight."

I didn't like it, but it made sense that Bruce talked to our father, the man who hadn't lived with Mother for almost twenty years; the man who changed wives and girlfriends with the regularity that I changed my sheets; and, to be fair, the man who got out of his own warm bed to put me on a plane not because he loved his ex-wife but because he loved his children. Bruce would have called our father because he wanted approval and perhaps even advice. Father would have said, wait. He'd take care of it.

But Bruce had called me right away – in order to play the one-upmanship card. It was a template from our past. It was life with an older brother.

There was a lot to do before my father drove me to the airport.

I got dressed and packed my clothes while he shoved my toothbrush, hand lotion, and hair goop into a zip top plastic bag. He also scooped up my birth control pills and a bottle of vitamin C before giving me a long look. "What about the animals?"

"Steven has them this week." I shrugged into a light jacket; Oklahoma City would have warm days but cool nights. It was that time of year. "We're trying for joint custody."

"How's that working out?"

"The dogs and the rabbit are okay with it. Kit and Kat are having a hard time."

"Cats," my father said.

"Yeah, cats." I drank a glass of orange juice. My voice was under control, finally. "Do we have time to stop for a beer? Maybe a wine cooler?"

His laugh was abrupt. "I paid several thousand dollars to get you on the wagon and I'm not going to help you jump off."

LEAVING SEATTLE

There was plenty to worry about that didn't directly include my father or my mother. Who, for example, would take over the teaching of my anatomy classes at the University of Washington, where I was paid to discourage pre-vet students from naming their cadavers while exploring the digestive system of a small mammal? Of course some insisted in naming these cats "Kitty-kins" or "Peabody" or even "Gray Lady" while putting washrags over the furry faces so the eyes wouldn't stare out accusingly.

My father and I didn't speak for the next two hours which was the time it took to get from my house to Sea-Tac Airport and into the jaws of the security check. Two uniformed guards poked and prodded my boobs and crotch because my father had mistakenly included cuticle scissors when packing my carry-on. I should have laughed, it was funny in a metaphoric way, but I was thinking about life without my mother and who the hell was going to take care of my little brother? Me. That's who. There were no other choices.

On the other side of the x-ray machine I forgave my father for being an easy target for my anger and also for not stopping to buy me a double vodka and turned to give him a small wave and smile but he had already gone.

When I opened my purse to pay for the kick-start triple shot nonfat mocha latte at the Starbucks kiosk it became immediately apparent that he'd slipped a handful of one hundred dollar bills into my checkbook and added an updated charge card to the one he gave me the last time there was a family emergency. It was the only way my father knew how to say "I love you" and frankly, I was weak with relief that he had, again, figured out that part.

I sipped my latte and called my advisor's work phone. I left a slightly garbled message only because there was no way to know how long I'd be gone or, even, if I'd ever be back. Life on the edge, I thought. Life with a crazy Mother and wacko brother. I would never have children, I promised myself. I'd jump off a bridge, first.

The plane was packed with business types and the man sleeping against the window took in huge gulps of air and let them out with little putt-putts broken up with an occasional nasal whistle. It reminded me of Steven's snore and that reminded me of how much I missed his quick wit and the way his lips felt along my throat and his laugh. I especially missed his laugh. Damn him.

Five states later, the 747 circled Will Rogers World Airport amid sporadic thunder showers and wind hiccups. We landed just before dinnertime. Along with the rest of the airsick passengers, I staggered to the central building where I rented a SUV because, if Mother got out of the hospital, I would need something big enough to carry five hundred plus pounds of weight packed onto a five foot seven inch frame. Then I grabbed a McDonald's Burger with fries and a diet Coke. It's Oklahoma so they didn't ask if I wanted it super-sized. They just did it. I also got a Big Mac and a Cheeseburger with a chocolate shake and a large fries. All of it to go. Then I drove to the hospital.

OKLAHOMA CITY

Danny was in the cardiac intensive care waiting room. I handed him the sacks of food and he spread everything out on the low table in front of us which also held old magazines and a stiff plastic plant. He smoothed the napkins, unsheathed the straws, wadded up the empty sacks and stuffed them into the waste basket by the nurses' station. Then we ate together, like old times, except we aren't fighting over the best fries or grabbing each other's straws, but sitting elbow to elbow and squirting the ketchup onto the lid of the Big Mac because you never squirt it directly onto the fries but dip them, one at a time into the red paste. Here, in the silence of the waiting room, we took a kind of bovine comfort in the closeness and warmth of each other. Humans are, except for the occasional vicious rogue, herd animals with the most complicated of pecking orders.

A young man in scrubs and booties came out to tell us we could see our mother, one at a time. I chatted with the nurse (and gave them my cell phone number) while Danny went to see her and pat her hand and, probably, make robot noises. He came back looking like someone had hit him with a two by four.

I took a deep breath and went to spend my own five minutes watching Mother's heart monitor blip and beep and also the blood pressure monitor try to make up its digital mind. Her green eyes were closed and her naturally ash blonde hair was a rat's nest of sweat and something that look suspiciously like vomit. She looked smaller, somehow, in that bed, though god knew she wasn't a small woman. She looked entirely too much like the cat's back at the University of Washington's pre-veterinarian anatomy lab and I understood, for the first time, the need for some students to put a washrag over their cadaver's face. For my mother, though, I would choose an embroidered handkerchief or a veil of delicate lace. She was crazy, but she always loved beauty and thirty years ago she had possessed that quality in such abundance that my father had dropped to his knees in front of her (a complete stranger) and begged for her hand in marriage.

That was before she gained three hundred seventy-five pounds, all of which she blamed on her children.

When I got back to the waiting area, Danny was sitting on the floor, facing the wall and rocking like an overzealous metronome.

"Get him out of here," one of the nurses whispered to me, "before he deconstructs entirely."

I told them we wouldn't be back for twelve straight hours and I thought the surgically-uniformed group clustered in front of the heart monitors would weep in gratitude. Danny had that effect on people.

OKLAHOMA CITY – VIEW OF BRICKTOWN

There are millions of people who use the word *Mother* as a sign of affection. That wasn't the case in our family because tenderness wasn't Marjorie's strong suit. Neither was generosity. When she was crazy she was, well, crazy and when on her medication, her strong suit was a fierce competition for attention and because she was older and wiser she got it all – or most of it – until Bruce and I garnered some of our own through accomplishments in academics and music and athletics. Danny got his attention for being a willing slave, which shows how early his pathology showed up.

I called my mother by her first name when I was angry. Since Bruce was probably one hundred percent angry at her one hundred percent of the time he always called her Marjorie. Danny never called her anything but Mommy. I don't know if it was his inability to individuate from her or if it was simply habit or, perhaps, it had become less a label to him and simply a code word for the woman who owned him lock, stock and barrel.

You think I am being unkind. I am. There was no other way to survive.

Mother and Danny lived on the fourth floor of a seedy hotel wedged between the freeway and the railroad track. Facing north, it overlooked the Bricktown Baseball Stadium which would have meant nothing to my mother, but Danny knew baseball statistics the way a meteorologist knows weather. Imperfectly but with conviction.

The elevator was located in the middle of the building and didn't quite make it flush to any floor on the way up, which must have given Mother some precarious moments when driving in and out on her battery-powered wheelchair – the preferred mode of travel for the morbidly obese.

The hallway smelled of Pine Sol, cigarette smoke, and scorched barbeque sauce. Danny worked his way through the three sets of locks on the door and led me into their room. There was a lumpy stack of black plastic garbage sacks by the door, an electric wheelchair by the closet, a television set bolted to the wall and a sagging La-Z-Boy which Mother apparently used for sleeping, eating and wiling away the hours. There was a two-person kitchen table and two wooden chairs which showed signs of being painted nine or ten times. There were ceiling fixtures and a standing lamp, but the light bulbs were thirty-five watts or less and for a minute I thought I had gone blind.

I went into the bathroom to check out the medicine cabinet while Danny opened the drapes and window, allowing a fine silt of red dust to sift onto the stained carpet, and allowing the entrance of freeway and train noise from outside and also the erratic flash of the flickering sign of the Naughty Lady XXX video store next door. The theory was for the cool evening air to change places with the air in the stifling room. Unfortunately, there was no fan to help with the exchange. I made a mental note to buy one before going to bed tonight. I made a second mental note to forget that and simply use my Father's credit card and get a motel room with air conditioning, clean sheets, and my very own shower.

Danny began to channel surf, looking for the Sci-fi channel or possibly the Discovery channel while I checked the only bedroom. It was Danny's room and held a double bed with a lumpy mattress, a battered chest of drawers and several Star Wars posters tacked to the walls. A cheap card table faced the only window and the view was of half the stadium including the pitcher's mound, second and third bases, and a major portion of the outfield. There were a variety of objects on the table including an Exact-o knife, airplane glue, a plastic space ship (the third or fourth edition of the Enterprise) with decals and a scattering of dynamite caps, timing devices and something that looked like beige Play dough.

Perhaps you already know that C-4 plastic explosive looks like white or light brown Play dough.

I didn't exactly yell, but my voice was forceful enough to capture Danny's attention one room away. "What the hell is that?"

Danny doesn't respond well to confrontation and his reply came in the form of garbled words, along with a series of clicks and whirrs. Danny worked hard to move, talk, and think like a robot. No emotions for him. His Mensa level intelligence figured out at an early age that emotions were not worth the effort – which explained his prior drug use and also his adolescent psychotic break. He was a sweet boy, but puberty hit and he was a goner.

"I mean it, Danny. What the hell is in your bedroom?"

He came to look. "P-P-Play-dough."

Okay. He was making models. Pretending. The only problem was that Danny's imagination had the ability to morph into reality.

"Have you been taking your anti-psychotics?"

He nodded.

"Every day?"

His green eyes were wide and a sheaf of blond hair fell over his forehead. He looked like an angel – a grownup angel filled with goodness and innocence.

"I m-might have f-forgotten today."

"And yesterday?"

He twitched his shoulders and made little clicking sounds with his tongue. "M-Mommy didn't feel good yesterday."

"And the day before?"

"I don't remember." That part came out perfectly clear.

"You have to take your medication, Danny. You can't wander around with voices telling you to blow up every Porta Potty you see. Do you hear voices now?"

"J-just yours."

I opened his prescription bottle and shook two pills into my palm. "Take these now. And take another one before you go to bed. We'll get you back to normal, okay? Mother is going to start feeling better and she'll come home and everything will be back to normal." Which was probably the biggest straight-faced lie I had ever told because, between the two of them, normal wasn't ever going to happen.

I went to the refrigerator and poured myself a Pepsi. I poured Danny a Pepsi, too, and made us a snack of Oreo cookies and big bowls of strawberry ice cream with Smucker's fudge topping. That's how living with Mother went; there might not be enough beds, but, by god there was enough food.

I went next door to the Naughty Lady XXX store to rent Danny diversions. The woman behind the counter had gray hair, brown eyes and looked like the Hollywood version of "Best Gramma of the Year."

Her voice was whiskey low with a three pack a day habit. "You related to the kid next door?"

"How did you know?"

"It's the facial structure and the coloring plus I've got a gift for that kinda thing."

"You saw us drive up together, huh."

"That, too. How's the Big Lady doing?"

"I'll tell you tomorrow."

"Fair enough."

"What's he into?"

"Star Wars: The Next Generation."

"Do you have that?"

"I've got everything including G-rated animation."

I looked at the artificial penises hanging from the ceiling plus the nipple clips, video crotch shots and DVD butt bangers. "Who buys Disney?"

"Parents who want an evening alone."

"Give me what he likes," I said.

She handed me four seasons worth of inter-galactic science fiction and told me to bring everything back in five days. She squinted at the Visa. "This your charge card, honey?"

"Practically. It's my father's."

"Close enough," she said and turned away to help three Hell's Angels who were arguing with a couple of gun-slinging cowboys as to whether the latest pseudo-snuff film was realistic or not. The smell of chocolate cookies permeated the store and somewhere in back an oven timer dinged. Porn in Oklahoma City, I'd never get used to it.

Danny helped me set up the DVD player. Galactic adventures

would keep him occupied until dawn if he didn't fall asleep once his second dose of meds hit.

"I'll be back in the morning," I told him. "We'll have breakfast and then we'll see Mother. She'll be lots better, Danny. It'll be okay."

He nodded absently, too far into 'Revenge of the Sith' to really hear me, but I made him come and set the door locks. He went through the pattern, top to bottom and bottom to top, four times until he was satisfied. As the metallic bolts slid open and shut until his compulsive cycle was completed, I wondered, am I my twenty-three year old little brother's keeper? Or is he mine?

COMMUNICATION IN OKLAHOMA CITY

The shower in Motel 6 was shaped like an upright glass coffin and I tried not to think about Snow White and other Grimm tales while shampooing and body washing and crème rinsing. My cell phone rang while I was drying off, but when I got to it the caller had already hung up. It was Bruce. I had no desire to rack up a call to France on my student teaching assistant wages. If it was important, he'd call back. God only knew if he thought our mother being in the hospital was important.

I feel asleep watching the Food Channel and woke up to my cell phone. It was becoming abundantly clear that I would have no inter-personal life at all if it wasn't for my smart phone. It was Steven the Slut.

"I don't want dog custody anymore," he said. "I'm going on vacation."

"It's two in the frigging morning," I said. "Couldn't this wait?"

"It's not even midnight." There was a pause. "Shay, where are you?"

"I'm in Oklahoma. Two time zones away. My mother's had a heart attack."

"And you didn't think to tell me you'd be gone?"

"We aren't living together, Steven."

"But the dogs were driving my newest, uhm, roommate crazy and we're going camping on the Peninsula this weekend. I've already dropped everybody off at your place. Now what am I going to do?"

"What's her name?"

"Just because I have a female roommate doesn't mean..."

"Fuck you!" I said and turned my cell phone off.

It was another hour before I fell back to sleep. By morning there were several messages in my voice mailbox including three hang-ups, another from my father rambling drunkenly and one from Ralph, the teaching assistant who shared my office.

"Steven, your jerk-off husband, called," Ralph said, "and I've got Stinky and Silky. Kit and Kat are at your place and I'll stop by every day to feed them. Prudence is nibbling grass in the back yard, so she'll be fine. How are you? How's Danny? How's your mother? I'm so very sorry. If I can do anything else, let me know." There was a pause. Ralph and I had gone through rehab together. "Don't have that first drink, Sharon. I know you want to but don't do it."

I erased his message and wondered how it was that Steven, the man I was still married to, hadn't thought to say any of that to me.

Morning sun was already working to heat things up when Danny went through the locks and opened the door for me. I didn't step inside. "Did you take your medication?"

"Yes." His voice was less like a robot. "I'll have to take care of Mommy when she gets back and so I'll need to be, like, clear."

"You're a good son," I said. "Let's take the videos back to the porn shop and we'll go McDonald's for breakfast."

"Granny doesn't like it when you call it a porn shop."

"What does she call it?"

"Home."

I remembered the cookies. "I suppose she does."

Bruce called while I was eating breakfast special #1 and Danny was eating Specials #3 & #4 and looking like a starving Adonis.

Constantly having the jitters kept the weight off.

"I was going to call you after I talked to the doctor," I said.

"Sure." There was the sound of a flute, clear and lovely, running scales in the background.

"Tell Constance hello," I said. "It would be good to meet her sometime."

"Thank you," Bruce said and sounded like he meant it. The flute changed to a staccato piece like birds in an echo chamber. "Uncle Harold put some money put aside for Marjorie."

"How come you're the expert on Marjorie's finances?"

"I'm the eldest son. People tell me things."

"Uncle Harold is certifiable."

"Yes. But he's put aside a shit-load money and if Marjorie needs anything not covered by the insurance there's cash in a savings deposit box at the Bank of America on the west side. Danny has the key."

"The west side of where?"

"Oklahoma City."

"What will happen when Marjorie and Danny move to Denver or Anchorage?"

"One of Uncle Harold's friends takes care of things."

"His friends are criminals."

"Whatever. Uncle Harold worries about Marjorie. She's his baby sister."

The eating area was filled with the scent of phony syrup and the static of country western music. Danny gathered up our empty containers and napkins and went to wash his hands. McDonald's hadn't turned on their air-conditioner yet and my hand on the cell phone was sweaty. I wiped it on my pants and thought about cold beers and icy martinis. I had to ask it. "I'm your baby sister. Do you worry about me?"

"Always."

"What about Danny and Mother?"

"I'm the oldest," Bruce said, "and I've been dialing your cell phone for five hours. What the hell do you think?" Then he hung up.

THERE ARE NO HALF SIBLINGS

Dr. God was a short, pudgy bald guy with hairy ears and thick glasses. He was really Dr. Godlinskiyetski but hospital staff had shortened it to something pronounceable and easy to remember. It was spoken, I noticed, with a mix of admiration and sarcasm, depending upon the medical specialist; the neurologists were sarcastic and the surgical residents were admiring. Most patients called him Dr. G.

Mother was out of intensive care but still on the cardiac wing. Her hair had been washed and her bed cranked to full sitting position. She was still wired to a platoon of digitally blipping machines and when Danny and I walked in the room, Dr. God was hunched over her massive breasts, murmuring earnestly. "Must lose weight" was one phrase and another was "darn lucky this time." We shook hands all around and the great man walked me to the elevators.

"I'm going to be blunt." He punched the down button and waited, arms crossed over his paunch and rocking back slightly on his heels. "She needs to loose three hundred pounds or she'll be dead in a year."

"I don't know if that's possible," I said.

"She tells me she used to be a model."

"That's right."

"Somewhere in all that lard there's a body image for slimness. She just needs to find it again."

I looked at his soft waistline and sagging jowls. "Easier said than done as you probably know."

"I had my stomach stapled a few decades ago. You should have seen me before that." The elevator doors opened. "Your brother's an enabler. You have to keep them apart for awhile for this to work." The doors closed, then opened again and Dr. God took my hand, standing half in and half out of the elevator with an empty gurney in the back and two bored LPNs leaning against the brushed aluminum walls. "She's your mother. You have a chance to save her life. I'd suggest you try or, take it from someone who knows, you'll be left with sour regrets and nasty memories."

Then he was gone.

When I got back to the room, Mother was on the telephone ordering an extra large pizza with everything-on-it and Danny was nowhere to be seen. Getting her some candy bars, she whispered, and racing down some donuts and salted peanuts. Whether psychotic or medicated, she sounded like a young Marilyn Monroe.

I ripped the receiver from her hand and cancelled the order. "Didn't you hear the doctor? You could be dead in a year!"

"He didn't really mean that."

"Yes. He did."

"He practically wallowed in my boobs." She held one up and flipped its pink nipple nose at me. "Guys always go for big boobs. You should do something about yours. If you spent half as much money on your looks as you do on your graduate tuition, Steven would stick around longer."

"Listen to your doctor," I said. "If not for yourself then for Danny. You'll die and he'll be lost without you."

"But you'll be there, dearest. Of course that's what's really bothering you, isn't it? Once I'm gone, you'll have to carry the load."

She could always defeat me with guilt. Danny came in with three Butterfingers and two Snickers. "I'll bring donuts tonight," he said.

I went out to the parking lot and telephoned Paris, France. "Help," I said.

"Did you know I'm not your full brother?" Bruce's voice was thick with sleep.

I said the only words I could think of. The ones I had said most of my childhood. "Fuck you."

"You were conceived when our parents were separated. Danny and I are full brothers but you're not our full sister. I envied you," Bruce went on. "I thought you were going to make it out of the insanity of their lives. But it's got you, hasn't it?"

I could hardly get the words out. "You're going to walk away because I'm a half-sibling?"

"There are no half-siblings," Bruce said. "Look it up in the dictionary. There are half-brothers and half-sisters but there's no such thing as a half-sibling, so stop crying."

"I'm not crying." My voice was the top string of a badly-played violin. "Does Dad know?"

"He never cared. You were his favorite." Bruce sighed. "Go count the money in Crazy Uncle Harold's safety deposit box."

"I'm not on the signature slip."

"Danny is. And stop crying, dammit. You're not alone. We're all in this mess together."

I wiped my eyes and blew my nose and went back upstairs to get Danny. "We have to go to the bank," I said. "We have to take care of business."

"The food in here stinks," Marjorie whispered as we were walking out the door. "Be a good boy, Danny, and bring Mommy some KFC chicken strips and some Reese's Pieces."

She was Mother when I came and she was Marjorie when I left. Why was I not surprised?

A QUARTER OF A MILLION GOOD FEELINGS

Bank of America was on the west side of Oklahoma City which meant it was surrounded by Hispanics and African Americans. The lines were long because the clerks were so nice. They wanted to know how everybody was and they were willing to remember names and faces. Danny sat on a padded leatherette bench by the door and I stood in line with the bronze key with a number on it. When it was finally our turn, Danny came over, signed the book, and followed us into the vault. The double width box was in the row that was second from the top and the middle-aged clerk and I had to take turns climbing up on a stool to get the keys inserted.

She locked us in and went to help someone at the counter while Danny and I flipped back the lid to find the thing was packed with stacks of William McKinley's. I did the math (five hundred times five hundred) and realized, with a jolt, the bank box held a quarter of a million dollars. I guessed that would take care of whatever Bruce had planned.

Crazy Uncle Harold sold guns and other weaponry inside and outside the country. I hoped none of the money I stuffed into Danny's jacket and my purse was going to land us in jail. We could claim ignorance, I thought, but, just in case, I had our clerk run some of the numbers through her computer and she confirmed everything was real and legal. I told her it was an inheritance and she said something silly like, don't forget to pay taxes. Then we all grinned and she went back to the counter and the line of people that snaked around the inside of the bank and on out the door.

When we got to the car I called Bruce. This time it took forever and I finally left a message on his answering machine. "A quarter of a mil. Now what?"

An hour later, Danny and I went to the Bricktown Stadium for a double header with real seats behind the catcher and real food like hot dogs, garlic fries and frothy root beer. In game number one the Oklahoma City Red Hawks were beating the snot out of the Kansas City T-Bones and everything was fine until Dr. God's assistant called my cell phone to tell me Marjorie's condition had deteriorated and she was in surgery getting a five way by-pass. They weren't sure if she'd make it.

That's when I remembered the good times, when she was crazy and counting everything from freckles sprinkled over my nose to the number of times my father used the preposition "from" in a sentence. In between times, when she wasn't counting, we'd build tree houses or go ice skating and spend the week before Christmas turning homemade marzipan into an edible crèche. Easter meant silly hats and eggs dyed to match the furniture with the trio of plaid eggs her finest endeavor. That's when I called her Mother and loved her with all my heart. It was during medicated sanity when the bitch came out. She hated herself and made sure everyone else hated her, too.

We were resigned to sanity because the bitch wasn't going to get locked away for taking her clothes off and marching down Main Street and the bitch took care of Danny and, Marjorie-Mother was right, neither Bruce nor I wanted him. Neither did our father. So it was a conundrum.

"What's wrong?" Danny handed me greasy napkins to blow my nose and wipe my hands. "It's Mommy, isn't it? Is she dead?"

"No."

"When can we see her?"

"It'll be hours, Danny. They'll call and tell us. Nobody wants us hanging around right now." I didn't tell Danny that the Critical Care staff, including the chaplain, had begged me not to bring him.

Danny's voice trembled. "I have to get the donuts and stuff."

"Not today."

The Red Hawks won the first game and the T-Bones won the second. The cell phone rang on our walk back to the apartment. It was Bruce. "Dr. Godlinskiyetski called. He said Marjorie's through surgery and they don't think it went well. I'm flying in. I'll be at Tinker Air Force Base at 6:00 in the morning."

"That's quick."

"Constance has connections. Her aunt is assistant attaché to the French Ambassador."

"Will Constance be coming, too?"

"Yes. Heaven help her."

"You can stay with me at the Motel 6. I have two queen-sized beds and my very own hair dryer."

Bruce the perpetually annoyed was back. "We'll be staying at the Marriot."

He hung up and I was left with a coldness that didn't belong in Oklahoma City in late spring. Things were out of season with me. I hadn't talked with my oldest brother for years but now we were having daily chats. It was unnerving. He wasn't gay. He didn't hate me. Who the hell was he?

THE FAT FARM

Bruce and Constance walked into the cardiac intensive care waiting room a little after seven in the morning. They brought coffee and Krispy Kremes. The first thing I noticed about Constance was that she had blonde hair, green eyes, and creamy skin. Not only that, she was the same height as Mother and her nose was the same shape. She was the *doppelganger* of our mother only thirty years younger and thin – except for her belly which I took to be somewhere in the second trimester of pregnancy.

Bruce handed me a coffee. "Don't say it."

"What? What would I say?"

"You could mention Freud. Father did when he came to Paris last time."

"Father met her?"

"Yes."

I looked at Constance and sadly understood why my father hadn't mentioned her to me. Probably because pre-conceived notions based on past experience would have made him anticipate that someone who looked almost exactly like out mother could not avoid the Schizophrenic scorpion.

"I'm not into Freud," I said. "I'm studying butterflies and teaching anatomy and sometimes, for fun, I'm reading up on family dynamics."

"Ever the brain."

"Somebody's got to do it."

We stood there, watching Danny dig into the donuts. "I love her," Bruce said.

I couldn't decide if he meant Constance or Mother. It didn't really matter much. The important thing, from my totally sober and selfish point of view, was that my big brother also loved me.

Dr. God scuffed into the room, still wearing his scrubs and looking like a garden gnome with steamed-up glasses and rosy cheeks. "I've been on the telephone with your father," he said. "He's found a Fat Farm that also specializes in psychiatric care. If your mother makes it through the next few days, and it's looking like she might, then she should go there." He grabbed up one of the donuts and took two small bites before throwing the rest of it into the waste basket.

"We have the means to pay for that," Bruce said, "up to a point. How long will she be in there?"

"At least a year."

Danny started to cry. Not just little whimpers and beeps like he'd been doing in the rental on the way over. This was the wail of someone who'd had an arm and leg ripped off without anesthetic.

"You'll stay with me," I whispered. He liked whispering better that yelling. Why couldn't I remember that when I was upset? "It'll be fun. We'll go to the Seattle aquarium and look at the fish. You'll love the octopus. We'll go to the space needle and the museums. You'll like it, Danny."

"Constance and I will stay with you," Bruce said, "until Marj-Mother gets out of the hospital. "Later, after we'd each had our five minutes in intensive care, looking at the woman who had grudgingly borne us, we went to Bricktown to eat at the Shrimp Shack and figure out the details. Danny told them about his Star Wars posters and Constance told us we would have a nephew sometime in September.

"It's going to be a boy," Bruce's voice cracked but he carried on, much as he always had. "We've had the genetic tests. So far, so good."

After dinner, while Constance was letting Danny feel the baby kicks under her smock, Bruce and I stood in the parking lot and I had to ask. "At the hospital, when Danny was crying, you called her Mother."

"So?"

"You never call her Mother. Not since you were thirteen."

Bruce said, not sounding a bit annoyed, "I can't keep carrying a grudge. Sometimes she'll be Marjorie and sometimes, like now, she's Mother. I can't explain it any better than that."

He put his arm around me. I hadn't felt it lazing over my shoulders in years. His voice was thick with emotion. "I get to do the easy stuff. I know that. I arrange the finances and talk to the doctors. You'll have to put up with him for a fucking year. I don't know how you'll do it."

"I love you, too," I said.

We smiled at each other, goofy, as if we were still seven and ten. Who would know the dictionary was the source of such a deep and vital truth? There were blended families and step-siblings and half-sisters and full brothers but a parent's connection with a child trumps all of that. Webster got it right, beating out Jung's archetypes and Maslow's hierarchy. Leave it to a wordsmith to establish the true boundaries of commitment and family. There were no half-siblings.

SEX AND MAPLE BARS

Joe Ballinger gave up sex at the age of forty-three years, two months, and twelve days. It was after a Saturday quickie with his wife, Sally Ann, while a sheen of perspiration stuck them together in ways both humorous and uncomfortable. High noon in July guaranteed that sheen. That itch. That air so scorching hot a person couldn't seem to suck in enough oxygen no matter how many cubic centimeters of filtered coolness the window frame swamp box blew into the room. That's the way it was in Spokane, Washington. Probably in Seattle, too, though maybe not. Joe had never lived anywhere but in the place promoters called the Inland Empire.

Joe unstuck himself from Sally Ann and settled against the Early American headboard. He'd given up smoking so the post-coital cigarette wasn't going to happen and post-coital chewing gum didn't have the same class though he found himself wishing he'd kept some in the drawer of the little stand that held the telephone. He wanted something to prolong the past six minutes and mark it as special.

The stand at his elbow held Kleenex and also some kind of stupid knickknack that tipped over most nights when he reached to turn out the light. This, he understood, was the chief difference between men and women. The male need for clutter was manifested through dirty clothes and empty food containers. The female need for clutter always involved double-ply tissues and something breakable.

From downstairs came the sound of Nintendo madness and also the sound of rap music and water running. Eleven-year-old Bobby was annihilating his friends in the den and Joe Junior was washing the Blazer in the driveway. He'd damn well better not do a half-assed job like last time or he wasn't going to get it for the dance. He and his hot date from the community college. Joe Ballinger watched the ceiling fan slowly turn and tried to figure out how he'd come to have the best sex of his entire life at forty-three years of age with a woman who was sixty pounds overweight and had a voice that could cut glass. He'd had the occasional red-hot sex during his two years at community college and he'd had close to kinky sex with a prostitute, a package of wieners, and a can of pork and beans on the night of his bachelor party. But nothing matched the bliss he'd just experienced. It was damn near a miracle and Joe Ballinger couldn't figure out why it had happened. Forget trying to figure out how. Why? That was the real question.

If Sally Ann was telling the truth it had been the best for her, too. The woman was distressingly honest – a trait that was refreshing in the beginning and annoying as hell later on – so he had to believe her. Well, that tears it, Joe thought. We've reached sexual perfection and there's nowhere to go but downhill. They'd been married twenty-two years and had another thirty-five to go. At least if you went by how their own parents were chugging along. Downhill for three plus decades was more than anyone ought to have staring them in the face.

While Sally Ann cleaned up in the bathroom, he rubbed himself dry with his tee shirt, then stepped into his size Medium chinos and alligator shirt and went downstairs to preview the Blazer and unclog the kitchen sink before handling the one-to-nine shift at the hardware store.

After he replaced the rusted out gooseneck and ragged at Little Joe to put away the hose, he popped a beer and chug-a-lugged it. The belch was full and throaty and made Joe smile in spite of the fact that this was his last day for having sex. Ever. Because perfect sex was something a person could have only once in a lifetime. All the rest was just picking at the leftovers of a dinner he'd already eaten. Take turkey. The golden bird was rescued from the oven, carved, and gobbled down with gravy and mashed spuds and stuffing and all the rest of it. Salad and candied yams and two kinds of pie and gobs of whipped cream. The whole shooting match.

A person ate that sumptuous meal and sank groaning into the

recliner in a stupor that lasted into the next day. After an experience like that, two weeks of turkey leftovers became punishment. Joe didn't want sex to be punishment. He wanted only the finest memories of his last encounter.

He wasn't sure how to explain this to Sally Ann but Joe figured the subject would come up. The only question was how long it would take his wife to notice.

• • •

It took three and a half weeks. She put the moves on him twenty minutes before the alarm rang, hanging onto his morning hard-on as if it were a life preserver and she'd just been dumped from the Titanic into an ocean strewn with ice. She'd prepared ahead for this moment of mid-summer passion by wearing her nicest nighty and setting the air conditioner too high. He felt goose bumps break out when she threw back the covers to run her Ruby Red manicure (with its 'rose of summer' design) over his chest and belly.

When he didn't respond right away, he expected her to sigh and climb out of bed and get ready for work while he made breakfast which wasn't more than putting out four bowls, a carton of milk, and three boxes of cereal.

Sally Ann didn't sigh, though. Or climb out of bed. Or even let go. She cuddled closer, threw a fleshy thigh over his lean one, and worked at his hard-on. She let him feel how gentle but nimble her fingers could be. It surprised him and made him smile at the vision of her decorated fingers on his undecorated self. Then he remembered his vow.

"No." It came out wrong – like a peevish bully – so he felt compelled to soften things a little. To explain. "I gotta pee."

After his urine steamed into the toilet he took time to examine his bald spot, wash his hands, check his teeth. When he left the bathroom, his manly vigor had gone the way of all fleeting and transient things: The last spring frost. A full head of hair. The luster of a brand new car before bugs and gravel and god knew what other shit got to the finish.

Sally Ann was still in bed. Waiting and watching. "It's me, isn't it?"

"No. It's not you."

"Are you 'impudent'?

Another trait once cute and now maddening. The woman couldn't talk. Joe Junior took after her in that way. The oldest, Megan, was a B+ student at WSU and eleven-year-old Bobby had a poem published in the student section of the *Spokane Review*, but Little Joe and his mother were always coming up with the wrong word at the wrong time. Joe used to think they did it to be funny, but the school guidance counselor called it a minor learning disability and said lots of brilliant folks had it. So he couldn't even think his wife and son were stupid or lazy or purposely trying to drive him crazy.

"*Impotent*. And no I'm not."

"It's nothing to be ashamed of. It happens to men your age. Bob Dole even went on TV to talk about his 'Erector' Dysfunction."

"*Erectile* and if I was, I couldn't get it up at all. But I can. I just don't want to do anything with it right now."

"You don't want to?"

He probably should have explained to her right then and there but the truth was too damn complicated. Which was the problem with truth most of the time. It was hard to defend something that couldn't be put into a simple sentence. The ad makers were right about that one.

"Joe?"

He rummaged through his underwear drawer gathering jockey shorts and socks before heading to the closet.

"So it's me." She got out of bed, stuck her feet in flip-flops, and reached for the housecoat to cover her boobs and belly. "I'm too fat."

"That's never bothered me." It was true but it came out wrong. "I didn't mean it that way."

"You meant it exactly that way."

"I like you the way you are. I just don't want to have sex with you."

"Because I'm fat."

"Being fat has nothing to do with it!"

That's when she reached for the Kleenex and headed down the hall.

Well shit, she *was* running heavy, but he liked the soft feel of her against him and the little mewling noises she made when he... no. He wasn't going to make love to his wife. Not after the perfect sex of July. He should have told her that his lower back was out. Next time the subject came up – and he was positive it would – that's what he'd say. That he couldn't have sex because he threw his back out loading some dumb piece of shit into a customer's pickup.

Joe put out the breakfast bowls (and made toast to prove there were no hard feelings on his part) while Sally Ann woke up Bobby. He showered and shaved while she had a screaming fight with Little Joe about what was appropriate body jewelry for someone who was living at home. He rattled the paper and drank his coffee while she was running the hair dryer and electric curling iron and by the end of the sports section decided a peace offering was in order – maybe some of those maple bars she liked so much. He'd pick half a dozen up after work.

Joe worked sixty hours a week but, to be fair, Sally Ann put in long hours, too. She was a bookkeeper for the oncology clinic that crouched like an ugly toad across from St. Elizabeth Hospital. Counting her medical coverage and three weeks of paid vacation, she made more than Joe, but he didn't like to linger on that fact. Not because he was sexist (okay, he was a little, but when you got right down to it, who wasn't?), but because nothing counted unless you deposited it in the bank. That was his philosophy. He sure as hell didn't count the tongue and groove he brought home to turn the carport into a garage. Or the grade B decking and ten pound bag of nails for the patio in back.

Joe had worked as a Floor Manager for the hardware store for ten years and before that he'd worked in the warehouse. He had a reputation for being a steady and loyal employee who could be counted on to hold down the fort while the big money General Managers came and went like fleas on a dog. Joe didn't have what it took to be a General Manager because he only had four quarters of English Literature and Ancient History at the community college. Completely useless stuff that had, once upon a time, made his heart pound and his eyes gleam.

Joe ate a late lunch at Pete's Place, the combination Deli and lunch counter across the street. Getting away from the store helped clear his mind and kept him sharp, plus it was good business to support the merchants in the area. He'd gone to high school with Pete who handed him a ham and cheese on rye the minute he walked through the door.

"You want a pickle with that?"

"I been eating here for twenty years. How come you always ask?"

"I figure you'll wise up eventually."

"No pickles," Joe said.

"Hold the dill!" Pete yelled to his daughter, then brought his coffee mug to sit with Joe at the booth in the back of the shop and watch him eat. Usually Pete talked non-stop about politics, golf, and fishing. Today he was silent. After fifteen minutes, Joe couldn't take it anymore. "Okay," he said around the last bite of sandwich, "spit it out."

"I hear you ain't boinking your old lady like you should."

Joe choked, but managed to keep his lunch in his mouth where it belonged.

"I only bring this up because Sally Ann told Myrna. She's worried you got 'prostrate' problems."

"Pro*state*." Joe said the word slowly, emphasizing the last syllable. "Like Washington *state* or *state* of the Union."

"My old man died of it," Pete said. "Cancer's a helluva way to go. I don't like nobody sticking their finger up my ass, either, but it's better than the alternative. Believe me."

"I believe you."

"So get it checked out."

"I will," Joe said.

"When?"

"I will!"

"You're like a brother to me." Pete leaned across the table and cuffed Joe on the ear. Man-to-man. "Don't fuck this up. You die of 'Prostrate' and I'm never going to forgive you."

"Prostate."

"We're talking the Big C. You don't want it."

Joe felt tired. "I'll get it checked out. I'll make a doctor's appointment as soon as I get back to the store."

Pete handed him a scrap of paper and a cell phone. "Do it now." He left the table then, to work on some last minute orders, but he cocked his finger at Joe and winked so Joe would understand he had to dial the number and do the deed.

As luck would have it there was a cancellation. Two hours later Joe was bent over a sanitized table pondering how the esoteric call to spiritual perfection had resulted in a prostate massage.

"Seems okay," Doc Brannard said. "We'll do the blood work and if anything shows up I'll call."

"If I don't hear from you, everything's okay?"

"No news is good news."

"Great." Joe unbent and reached for his pants. "I'll see you next year."

"Not so fast." Doc Brannard finished writing notes and leaned against the wall.

"I got to get going, Doc." Joe's shoes were hanging up in the leg openings. "Summer is the busiest time of the year and not just because of the weather. Seems like everybody in Spokane is either remodeling their kitchen or putting in storm windows."

Doc's tone was bone dry, lacking every bit of the jovial good humor he usually displayed. "I think the store will have to do without you for a few more minutes."

Joe felt his stomach drop and ran a quick mental check. Blood pressure okay. Weight okay. The occasional migraine but everyone on his side of the family got headaches. Maybe it wasn't him. Maybe it was Sally Ann. One of those female things she was always complaining about. It didn't have to be anything special. Half the ads on TV were for irritable bowels and hot flashes. That was it. Sally Ann was going through the change. Or maybe it was one of the kids. Maybe Little Joe had knocked somebody up and he couldn't face telling his old man. Probably that girl from the college. Cute kid. They could get married. That's what he and Sally Ann had done and it had worked out okay.

Doc Brannard put the file on the counter next to the glass jar of long-stemmed Q-Tips. He took a while getting his pen in the pocket of his white coat and then polishing his glasses. When everything was to his satisfaction, he folded his arms and addressed the magazine rack beside Joe's head. "Sally Ann was in for her annual physical this morning."

Joe felt his knees go weak and he sat down, hard, on the little stool with his pants still around his ankles. It was her. That was why they were so hot to see him. She couldn't be pregnant. Maybe it was breast cancer. Lop it off, he thought. Take both of them. He didn't care. Take everything. Uterus. Ovaries. The works. But leave him his wife. Then he rallied. They'd made it through plenty of tough times and they'd make it through this. His mother could come down and help out. It would be okay. It had to because, frankly, he didn't think he could live without Sally Ann. Not when you got right down to it. Shit, shit, shit.

"She's worried that you're having an affair."

Joe sat, stunned, trying to make sense of Doc Brannard's words – which weren't anything like what he'd expected – then he put his head in his hands. After a long while he was able to mumble, "I'm not having an affair."

"It up to you, Joe, you're an adult male and adult males have urges, but there are potential problems you may not have thought about."

"I love my wife. Sure, we don't always get along but nobody gets along one hundred percent."

"The world isn't the same as when you were a kid. Love isn't free anymore. You could bring something home. Did you think about that?"

"Jesus, Doc! I've been almost a hundred percent faithful!"

"I'm not judging you, Joe. I just want to be sure you understand the possible ramifications of your behavior."

"There is no behavior!" Joe ran his hand through thinning hair. "That was one stupid mistake nineteen years ago. I'm past all that."

Doc didn't say anything, but there was a lift to his right eyebrow.

Joe understood, then, that no matter how hard he protested – maybe because of the intensity of his denial – Doc wouldn't believe him. Maybe because Doc was on his third marriage since every time he went to a medical convention he met a pretty young thing who screwed his brains out. Joe knew this because of Sally Ann's job. Two of the ex-wives worked in the oncology clinic and all the juicy gossip got passed around a dozen times – maybe more.

"I can't tell you how to live your life," Doc said, "but for God's sake be careful. At least use a condom." A sudden vision of Doc Brannard (the man who'd just given him a prostate massage) rolling on a French tickler flitted past Joe's eyes and he lurched up to stand, red-faced and sweating. He jerked up his pants, mumbled something vague like, okay, sure, thanks Doc, and beat it the hell out of that cubicle.

On the way back to the store, in the safety of his Blazer, Joe couldn't decide whether to forget the whole thing or to be furious about Sally Ann's blabbing. Not ordinary blabbing about his mother's meddling or Little Joe's grades or how much money they lost in that dot.com stock market investment, but blabbing about sex. Their sex. Or lack thereof. He pulled over to the curb, shut off the engine, and gave into a shaky kind of laughter that didn't mean he found anything funny nearly as much as it meant he was helpless to shape the forces against him.

He'd talk to Sally Ann tonight. After dinner.

• • •

Dinner wasn't quite what he hoped. For some reason it became a somber affair with half a dozen maple bars in the garbage under the sink. Joe and the boys ate pizza in a kitchen silent as a tomb. Little Joe glowered all through the eating of five pieces, then barked that he was going to his girlfriend's apartment to study. Anatomy, Joe figured. Or Sex Ed.

"What's your girlfriend's name?"

"Why?"

"You're spending roughly forty hours a week with this person. What's her name?"

"I don't have to put up with this bullshit!" Little Joe kicked over the kitchen stool on the way out the door and left in a cloud of exhaust and burned rubber. He was driving Sally Ann's Camry.

That's when Joe knew things had gotten completely out of hand. Sally Ann loved her sedan and had made it perfectly clear that she'd let her oldest son drive the car somewhere around the third coming of Christ. Now he was clearing the exhaust system on his way to his girlfriend's. Joe closed the kitchen door and sighed.

"Dad?"

Bobby's leg was jerking and twitching like a bed vibrator at a cheap motel. Joe knew about those because of the cheap place he and Sally Ann had stayed at on parent's weekend at WSU last year. They'd gotten the giggles and had just about perfect sex then, too, though not as good as what they had on their own non-vibrating bed almost a month ago.

"Are you and Mom getting a divorce?"

"No. Of course not." Joe went to the refrigerator for another beer. He got Bobby a Dr. Pepper. "Is that what Little Joe thinks?"

"I dunno."

"Is that what you think?"

"Maybe."

"Why?" Joe straddled the stool, legs sticking out like a grasshopper on a narrow blade of grass. "I mean, why would you think your mother and I would get a divorce?"

"Because she's been crying all afternoon and that's what Mary Beth's mom did before her dad left to live with that cheap little whore over in Seattle."

"I don't like you talking that way, Bobby."

"That's what Mary Beth's *mom* calls her." The cheese on the pizza congealed and Bobby picked at a drying spot the color of old snot. "Mary Beth hardly ever gets to see her dad anymore."

"Who the hell's Mary Beth?"

"She sits behind me at school. She cries all the time. Just like Mom."

"Your mother and I are not getting a divorce. You may not have noticed, but women are always crying about something." Joe took a long swallow. "It's one of those... *female* things."

Bobby picked at the spot of dried cheese until it peeled loose. He put his paper plate in the garbage and his pop bottle in the blue recycling bin, then headed for the television set in the den. End of conversation, Joe thought. He went to the den, too, and together father and twitching youngest son watched the Mariners lose, 13 to 1. The score was oddly comforting to Joe.

● ● ●

Joe hardly ever went to church, but Sally Ann liked it when he did so there he was – listening to a soloist who couldn't hit the top notes instead of popping a beer and enjoying his only time off. He'd stop by the store this evening – in fact, when you thought about it, the damn store owned him – but Sundays were mostly his own. To spend as he wished. Except for today when he was sitting beside Sally Ann smelling her perfume and noticing how her hair curled so nicely against the clear, smooth skin of her neck and cheek.

The sermon was Galatians. Fifth chapter; Fourth verse. "Ye are fallen from grace."

Joe didn't figure a minister could sermonize very long on five words but it turned out Pastor Savage was able to dredge up forty minutes' worth of mind-numbing platitudes and non sequiturs. When you got right down to it, it took a kind of genius to pull that off. However, it was not a talent much appreciated by Joe, nor to any other members of the flock, from what Joe could tell by the bored faces and surreptitious peeks at various timepieces up and down the pew.

Going to church was tolerable when the junior minister – Pastor Gutierrez – was in the pulpit. Sure, he spoke with an accent but his sermons had fire and relevance. This senior guy, Pastor Savage, suffered from a condition Joe recognized. He was burnt out. He'd given up on the dreams of his youth and was waiting to retire. He wasn't even looking for that perfect something on which to build the latter days of his life.

On the way out, as everyone filed through the heavy wooden doors to murmur what a great time they'd had trying to keep from falling asleep, Pastor Savage leaned into Joe's handshake. "Good to see you, Joe. How's it going?"

Joe tried to push past, but the older man's grip was firm. "There's a little matter I'd like to chew over with you."

Oh, shit, Joe thought. Him, too.

"I've got a wedding rehearsal this afternoon, but we could meet after that." The words rolled and thundered over the church lawn and the assembled flock. "Why don't you stop by and we'll get everything settled quick as the shake of a lamb's tail."

Face burning, Joe told the first lie he could think of. "I'll be at the store until closing. Later, too. Until midnight, probably, and all day tomorrow. We're doing inventory. For the rest of the month."

"This will only take a few minutes. I'll expect you around four o'clock."

Joe was sure there were men all over Spokane who could publicly turn down a pastor's request to fuck up a day best spent watching the Mariners move rapidly from one infield error to the next, but Joe wasn't one of them.

The Sun was well into its slanting descent and the Mariners were winning the first game in two weeks when Pastor Savage ushered Joe into the musty church office. It smelled vaguely of mouse droppings and some kind of floral air spray. The older man moved a pile of hymnals from the stained floor and motioned for Joe to sit on the cracked leather couch backed against the wall.

"I don't have much time," Joe said.

"This won't take long."

And it wouldn't have except the mother of the bride stuck her head through the door with new questions about the seating of ex-relatives and the father of the groom had serious reservations about the church's firm stand on no booze in the reception punch. Then there was a telephone call from the church treasurer. It was almost five o'clock before things settled down enough for Pastor Savage to hem and haw around about the weather and the tithe campaign and how good it was to see Joe in church. Since the man wasn't making any headway in getting to the point, Joe took the matter into his own hands.

"I know why you called me down here," Joe said, "so let's cut to the chase. I'll give you my side of things. Okay?"

Pastor Savage blew out a big sigh and nodded.

"I have never messed around on Sally Ann. Okay, that one time after Megan was born and she went into postpartum depression for six months, but that was a one night stand and not even a full night at that. More like four minutes in the broom closet. And it sure as hell wasn't worth it. I haven't done anything near as stupid for nineteen years..."

Pastor Savage brushed at his lined face as if he had walked through a doorway webbed with spider silk. "Joe," he murmured, "confession's good for the soul but –"

"I'm a good father. Ask anyone. Ask Little Joe – okay, he's not the best one to ask because he's pissed at me right now – but ask his older sister. She'll tell you I'm a good father. Bobby will, too."

"Listen, Joe, maybe we could back up a bit and –"

"I know Sally Ann thinks I don't love her, but I do. It's just that I don't want to have sex with her. I'm trying to work on my spiritual side. You should be able to understand that."

"Slow down, Joe, we're getting –"

"You're a minister. You deal with ideas and perfection. If you can't understand what I'm trying to do then what kind of religious leader are you because –"

Pastor Savage's face flushed seven kinds of red, and air whistled in and out of his veined and bulbous nose. "For God's sake, Joe, let me get a word in edgewise!"

Joe sucked in a deep breath and locked eyes with the senior pastor. The man's face was purple and he had the crazed look of a trapped squirrel. Joe hoped like hell the old fart wasn't heading into a stroke or going to keel over with a first class heart attack, because Joe didn't feel like doing mouth to mouth resuscitation on him. Not today, anyway.

"This is the thing," Pastor Savage said through gritted teeth.

"God might care about what goes on in the bedroom between you and Sally Ann but I don't. I've got problems of my own."

They stared at each other, exhaling and inhaling like opposing bulls in a pasture. Joe knew how to deal with cranky customers and panicky General Managers. Pastor Savage looked both cranky and panicked. Joe swallowed hard. "Okay. Fine. What exactly was it that you wanted to talk to me about?"

"I want you to see the parsonage kitchen and the primary school bathrooms," Pastor Savage said. "I was hoping you could get us a good deal on linoleum."

"Linoleum," Joe said.

"Or tile."

"Tile."

"Either one."

Joe could feel his own blood pressure backing up and his fingers twitched with the need to curl around a saggy, mottled neck. "You could have called me at the store. On a weekday. You didn't have to drag me down here in the middle of the Mariner's game. A game they might even win." His voice didn't break until that last part.

"Now Joe, there's no need to get upset."

"Sure there is! I'm spilling my guts while you're trying to wheel and deal some fucking great price on *flooring!*"

"It's not just flooring, Joe. Have you been inside the parsonage lately? Have you tried to walk from the stove to the sink without tripping? My wife has to do that. Her eighty-six year old mother has to do that. The Ladies Aid society has to do that. Some of those women are wearing three inch high heels." It started out soft, in an earnest whisper, but by the end Pastor Savage was giving it a first class revivalist walk-to-salvation bellow. "And another thing, Joe. Have you been *inside* the primary church school bathrooms? Have you *inhaled* the dry rot and mold? Have you *seen* where those little kiddies have to go pee-pee?"

Joe wrenched himself free of the cracked leather couch and

stumbled to the heavy wooden door that led outside. He turned the knob and stepped into air the approximate temperature of a flame-thrower. He stumbled to the Blazer, climbed in, and started the engine, the radio, and the air conditioner, in that order. He sat, waiting for his hands to stop shaking, then drove to the hardware store, stopping completely at every yellow light and using the turn signal with every lane change and at every corner. It was too soon to congratulate himself for not flattening Pastor Savage. If he held off until next Sunday, Joe figured he'd be over the urge.

The hardware store was quiet – like a tomb. The crew was clustered around a portable television one of the warehouse guys brought in. Joe didn't even ask how the Mariners were doing. He walked to the back and locked himself in the office. He emptied cold coffee from a cup labeled THE BOSS and poured three fingers of Scotch from a bottle the General Manager kept under "E" in the file cabinet. E for Emergency. Which this was. He downed the Scotch and poured three fingers more. After an hour of sipping and thinking about the perils of perfection, Joe stuffed the bottle into file "C" – C for Crisis or maybe Chaos or even Too Damn Complicated. He sent everyone home and switched on the pink CLOSED sign. If the General Manager didn't like it, well fuck him. Fuck perfection and fuck trying to find a reason to make the last part of his life anything but the long, slow downhill slide of every other poor sonofabitch over the age of forty.

It wasn't even seven o'clock when Joe locked the back door, set the security codes, and headed for the parking lot, but took a quick detour to Pete's Place instead. To pick up a six pack of beer and some maple bars. When he got home, Sally Ann was making iced tea in the kitchen, stirring a pound of sugar into a pitcher of dark blue glass.

"I brought you a present," Joe said. He put the bag of maple bars, oily, dense, and weeping beige frosting, on the counter. He put five beers into the refrigerator and began work on the sixth.

"What did the pastor want?" The metal spoon clicked against the sides of the pitcher as the granules of sugar slowly dissolved.

Joe took long swallow. "How come you never eat the maple bars I bring?"

"They're stale."

"That never bothered you before. I thought you liked maple bars. New or old. That's what you said."

"I do like them."

"So how come you're not eating them?"

She stood at the sink window, wearing his favorite sun dress while the spoon dripped onto the counter and the Sun sent golden rays skimming over the lawn to gild her face and hair.

"I was helping out at Bobby's class after spring break and one of the kids brought this whole big box of stuff from the bakery next to the post office."

Joe nodded to show he remembered the hole-in-the-wall bakery with greasy windows. He settled into the kitchen chair to wait out whatever the hell she was trying to say. No matter how long it took. And god knew Sally Ann could beat around an acre of brush before finally getting to the point.

"There were a couple of glazed donuts and a few apricot danish and some of those french 'curlers'..."

"Crullers," Joe said. "They're called crullers."

"... Anyway the ones your mother likes and there was a maple bar. It didn't look very special. The frosting had smeared on one side and there were some almost burned tags along the bottom." Tears trembled on her eyelashes. Joe pulled another swallow and waited. He figured he had thirty or forty years of waiting to go before he died and got planted. "But you know, Joe, it was the best maple bar I'd ever eaten. It was..." She hesitated, her eyes crinkled and her forehead bunched, and her mouth pursed.

"Perfect," Joe said. "It was perfect."

"Yeah. Perfect. And I don't want any more. I know it's silly but ... I just don't want any more."

"This isn't some new diet is it? Like the time you only ate mangoes and ended up in the Emergency Room?"

"No, it isn't a new diet."

"Because you're not too fat," Joe said. "I've always thought you were just right."

"You've been drinking."

"Some."

Sally Ann put the pitcher of tea in the refrigerator and got herself a beer. She poured it slowly into a glass so that the foam didn't end up on the table. She looked good enough to eat in the dress the color of peaches and cream.

"You closed the store early." It wasn't a question.

"No customers." He drew a long swallow. "May as well let the floor crew go home and..." He was going to say something like "go home and screw their wives" but that wasn't where he wanted to go. Not yet, anyway.

"So," she said, "you don't have 'prostrate'."

"No."

Her fingernails were blue with sparkles. They curled around the glass of beer in a way that was reminiscent of languorous mornings and tousled sheets. "No," he said again.

"And you aren't using the broom closet?"

"I told you a long time ago. No more closets."

"What did Pastor Savage want?"

"Linoleum."

"Linoleum?"

"Or tile."

The glass of beer slopped, just a little, on the table when Sally Ann laughed. She had a nice laugh – quiet and sweet – it was the reason Joe had noticed her all those long years ago. He laughed, too, and when they fell silent the kitchen had lost the stiff, tight awkwardness of the past month.

"I want to go back to school," Joe said. "I want to do something besides work at a hardware store my whole goddam life."

"Okay," Sally Ann said.

"Okay? Just like that, okay?"

"Sure. Why, not?" Foam bubbled on her upper lip and Joe wanted suddenly, urgently, to lick it off.

"But the money..."

"We'll manage. We always have."

He leaned back in the chair, watched his wife's fingers stroke the glass of beer and felt desire slowly make its way from the far corners of his body. Making his throat tight and his fingers tingle. Making his thighs tense and his palms sweat and making it hard to suck in enough breath to ask, "Where's Little Joe?"

"At his girlfriend's."

"And Bobby?"

"He's spending the night next door."

"Ah."

Joe snagged the greasy bakery bag and set it on the table. "I've been thinking about sex," he began. "Perfect sex."

She didn't cave in quick – that wasn't Sally Ann's way – but she did break off a corner of maple bar. She licked congealed frosting and nibbled stale crust while Joe Ballinger explained how a sane man could, one smoldering Saturday in July, forget his dreams, lose his mind, and slowly find his way back home.

THE YARD SALE

CLARICE

Judge Nathan Curtis, the alcoholic idiot who lives across the street, has shown his true colors and decided to kick Ralph out of the servant's apartment above the garage. This may have something to do with the phase of the Moon as it sucks back the tides or it may simply be the $105,000 Jaguar XK the Judge recently bought. Apparently, a vehicle that seats two needs to be protected from the elements and, somehow, the Judge has decided that his nephew does not. Narcissists are like that, thinking only of themselves and not of the impact their behavior has on others. I know all about narcissists, being related to several at the nuclear family level.

The Judge wants to get the garage remodeled by Christmas so when Santa comes calling, Ralph will be homeless. A decade ago, when he was in high school and going steady with my sister, Ralph practically lived at our house and, because there will soon be an empty bedroom, he probably still could live there. In a perfect world everything would balance out. But the world isn't perfect. Time plays its weird accordion allowing the home of my memories to stay the same while wrenching those exact same elements into a new, up-to-date, out-of-whack, shape. My parents divorced. The cook retired. Ralph went to war. My sister, Leslie became a lost cause.

Ten years ago, Leslie was sleek with porcelain skin and glossy black hair. Now, the neighbors don't recognize her. She moved back home last month in order to write a tell-all book about her life as a loser. Back in high school, that wasn't what she expected and probably not what she deserved. Except that, now, she works assiduously at that identity, keeping it alive for all to see. After a month of watching her hair fall out, I applied for work in Alaska, where none of my relatives lived and also where, I was led to believe, the elk and the antelope played.

My new employer said I would be teaching two dozen students, kindergarten through eighth grade, and sent a brochure showing a log cabin framed by mountains. Thankfully, there were no pictures of mushing Huskies or polar bears snagging salmon out of holes in the ice. Seattleites, like myself, do not appreciate cold or slush in any form except, possibly, in a tall mocha Frappuccino or a salty-rimmed margarita.

This is what happens when you leave home out of desperation; you end up buying all your clothes at REI and L.L. Bean.

In order to pay off my charge cards and get a little grocery money before my first Icicle Canyon paycheck, I put up signs for a garage sale. My boyfriend, Joseph, was supposed to assist with the move but, the minute we stepped into my childhood bedroom, he slipped his hands under my sweater and began nibbling my neck which was pleasant but not helpful in dismantling the singlewide bed or getting the nightstand down the stairs and into the front yard.

I pulled away, regretfully, and gestured toward the three boxes stacked in front of the closet. "The stuff I'm taking with me is on that side of the room. The rest goes downstairs."

"November isn't the best time for a garage sale," Joseph murmured.

"The weatherman said it's supposed to be sunny this weekend," I replied.

"The weatherman is having a brain fart and my back is killing me."

I kissed Joseph's chin and handed him my ruffled Disney lamp. "Maybe I should ask Ralph to help."

"Ralph the drunken war hero?"

"He's sober these days and can bench press an eighth of a ton."

"That's only 250 pounds."

"How much can you bench press?"

"I'm getting a MSW and a MBA," Joseph said. "I don't have to lift weights. I lift books. I crack them too and burn the midnight oil. Does Ralph do that?"

I pulled away from the soft kisses. "Ralph does a hundred one-armed pushups all on the same day. In spite of his injuries he's strong as an ox. Plus he lives across the street." I stressed that last part.

"Will that help with the chest of drawers?"

"God, I hope so because what I need is someone who doesn't distract me with all this great smooching."

"Then get his ass over here," Joseph said. "I'm going to be in traction if I have to carry your crap downstairs all by myself."

Joseph is short and compact and has clever hands but very little brute strength. I walked across the street, darted around Ralph's mountain bike, climbed the fifteen steps and knocked on the apartment door.

Ralph had just gotten out of the shower and had a towel around his waist. He was drying his hair with another towel and the steam rose from his body into the cold air like fog drifting from a mountain. He leaned against the doorjamb for support.

I gave him my best smile. "I need help."

"Everybody does," Ralph said. "It's a stressful time to be alive."

"I'm having a garage sale before I leave for Alaska."

"So the neighborhood rumors are true. You really are leaving."

"I need someone to help with getting my stuff down to the driveway."

"Out with the old, in with the new."

Tears stung my eyes. "I'm tired of watching Leslie eat one rib of celery then race to the bathroom to barf it back up. Plus she's flirting with Joseph. It's pathetic."

He stopped running the towel through his hair and began sopping droplets from his chest. "Anorexia is a horrible disease."

"My whole family is in denial. They eat it for dinner. They breathe it for dessert."

He gave me a lopsided grin and raised an eyebrow.

"Okay," I said, "maybe not the best metaphor."

"Do you think Alaska will be far enough away?"

"Probably not," I said glumly, "but it's a start."

"Your father will miss you."

"I doubt that."

"Sure he will." Ralph's hair stuck up in all directions. "You're very entertaining, Clarice. He'll probably even notice you're gone in a couple of weeks."

"No, he won't. He's watching television and drinking beer."

"That's because it's football season."

"Before he lost the election, my father used to be a Johnnie Walker man. Now he's wearing pajama bottoms. He's belching and passing gas."

"It's unpatriotic to drink anything *but* beer while watching pro sports," Ralph said. "Ask anyone."

"My boyfriend watches sports and he doesn't drink beer."

"He watches golf?"

"Poker."

"Ah. That explains so much."

I was halfway down the stairs, in a bit of a huff, when Ralph added, "If I help out will you let me join your garage sale? Sharon's ex-husband has a ton of shit she wants to ditch."

"Who's Sharon?"

"The woman I hope to marry."

I had always looked up to Ralph. Not simply because he was smarter and older and wilder but because his heart was true. I hoped Sharon, whoever she was, would treat him kindly.

"I don't care what your girlfriend brings over as long as you help carry my bed and chest of drawers downstairs."

Ralph winked and went back inside to get dressed.

RALPH

It was before he met Sharon but after his second round of rehab that Ralph learned the hardest part of being raised by Uncle Curtis wasn't the man's violent, drunken rages or being sent to boarding schools. The hardest part was learning not to blame the Judge for everything.

"Sanity is an uphill struggle," Sharon said, "but I've been told it's worth the effort."

"We'll have to try it sometime," Ralph replied and they both laughed.

They had just had a weekend marathon of sex and were settled back onto Sharon's creaky double bed. The top sheet had bunched at their feet so Ralph's broken body and Sharon's scarred wrists and shoulder weren't hidden away like something sinful.

It was cold outside but they were sweaty with the aftermath of lust. Ralph, without his appliance, hopped from the bed to the kitchen and returned, with cereal bowls in one hand and a pint of Ben & Jerry's in the other. He made it through the hallway and past the bathroom, leaning against the walls for support, but the open doorway defeated him and he crashed into the bed, spilling spoons, bowls and smashing the unopened carton against the headboard. Sharon pried the lid from the Butter Pecan. "Where's the chocolate sauce?"

That was why he loved her. She acted like a one-legged lover was up to whatever he attempted. And if he fell across the bed, well, Ralph was pretty sure that plenty of males with both legs had wanted to perform that little trick, but he was the one she wanted to spend time with.

He crawled all the way onto the bed. "I'm done. Your turn."

Sharon leaped out of bed and dashed, buck naked, to the kitchen and grabbed a plastic bottle of Hershey's double thick topping. She grinned at him poured it over herself and her ice cream in thick, gloppy swirls.

Ralph leaned to lick sweet goodness from her breasts. Afterward they put the empty bowls on the floor and lay in a delicious tangle of thighs and arms, her belly pressed against his belly. She smelled like pecans and chocolate. Her tawny hair fell like a silken curtain over Ralph's scars.

That's when he asked if she would marry him and, although her answer was muffled, he still understood the "yes" part of it.

After dinner, Sharon graded papers and Ralph worked on a series of graphs for his dissertation. Kit and Kat purred on the sofa and the rabbit was in his hutch on the back porch. If I believed in heaven, Ralph thought, it would be this.

Sharon closed her Macintosh grading ledger. Her voice was soft but seemed to fill the room. "Tell me something you haven't told me before. Tell me something that will make me cry."

Ralph felt the sudden cold of panic and focused on the monitor in front of him, with its graphs and numbers and letters. "You know me better than anyone. I don't know what else there is to tell."

She sat by the cats, petting first one and then the other and still he couldn't figure out what to say. Finally, exasperated, she snapped, "Just make it the truest thing you've ever said to me."

Ralph stayed in the chair behind the desk and told her about his Aunt. "It was right after my parents' car wreak and a few months before Aunt Ellen committed suicide. She took me to Hawaii. Her eyes were red from drinking," Ralph said, "and she couldn't stop shaking because of the cocaine but she took me snorkeling and showed me the most beautiful, silent world under the warm ocean water. Later, after Afghanistan and Iraq, I went to Mexico and watched men harvest sponges and I thought how lucky they were to be working where the silence was profound and everything moved in slow motion. One of the men, a boy really, saw me standing there on the dock and tossed me a sponge, still dripping and smelling of fish and seawater.

"I squeezed it as hard as I could and when all the wetness had poured over my face and chest it went back to its original shape. I couldn't hurt it. You can't know how that felt, Sharon. To know I couldn't hurt it. It was the first time I'd felt that way since..."

He swallowed and swallowed again and still couldn't finish the sentence.

"Since the explosion?"

"Before that. Since I shot that kid."

"You saved an officer's life."

"He wasn't worth it." After a while Ralph said, "I'm not superstitious and I'm not religious but it seemed like a sign. In Mexico, at that moment, it seemed like I could keep on living and not feel every breath I took was a sin."

"It isn't." Sharon rose from the couch, scattering the cats. She was there, at Ralph's side, in less time that it had taken him to fall onto the bed all those many hours before. "Oh, God, it isn't."

CLARICE

I poked through Ralph's apartment, checking out the contents of the kitchen, bedroom, and living room. The saleable stuff consisted of half a ton in weight-lifting equipment, an ancient Hasselblad 35 mm camera, and the best computer Army disability could buy.

"I'm taking that to Sharon's," he said, "along with my mountain bike. "You can sell everything else."

Everything else consisted of a lumpy futon trailing cotton batting, three boxes of water-stained baseball cards, half a dozen boarding school yearbooks, and a box of medals from Afghanistan and Iraq.

"Probably you should keep the medals," I said.

The look he gave me was fierce, so I went back to mentally pricing the pots and pans along with mismatched silverware and a blender that worked only on the low setting. A vintage black &

white television was on an ancient card table. His sheets were faded and the elastic corners were frayed. He apparently ate off paper plates and drank from a plastic cup. This made up the contents of Ralph's apartment.

I folded my arms across my chest. "I hope your girlfriend has some saleable stuff because everything in your apartment is crap."

JOSEPH

Joseph Takemura sipped a beer and thought about his view of the world in the third person, which was how he'd survived most of his childhood and was also what had burned and buried his first marriage but, fuck, life was too hard to take head-on. In spite of his inability to form a first person life, he had to make this work because Clarice was smart and funny and mostly sane and his parents liked her. That alone was a miracle.

Clarice brought an armful of sundresses from the back of her closet and dumped them across his lap. "I didn't know you drank beer."

"I'm slumming." He drained the can and missed the shot at the Cinderella wastebasket. "You didn't tell me he looked like that," Joseph said. "If you had told me I wouldn't have made such an ass of myself."

"You did okay."

"I gulped. Guys notice when other guys gulp. And my voice cracked. Plus he's wearing shorts. Who in the hell wears shorts when the temperature is in the mid-forties?"

"What should I have said?"

"That half his face is gone."

"But it isn't."

"His eye droops, his nose is broken, and his mouth doesn't smile on both sides at the same time."

"It doesn't frown on both sides, either," Clarice said evenly, "unlike mine which is frowning across my whole face right now."

"You know what I mean." Joseph's palms were damp even though it was almost freezing. "He has shrapnel scars on his arms and part of his leg is missing."

"Ralph doesn't notice his appliance. He runs marathons on it."

"You could have said something."

"You're going to be a social worker, Joseph. I thought you'd be used to disfigurement."

"I probably should be," he said, "but my MBA part slipped out. It happens when I least expect it."

Clarice kneaded and rubbed his back and arms until his breathing slowed and the rabbity look around his eyes went away. "It's okay that you aren't perfect, Joseph. And it's great that you don't try to be all blustery and superior when you don't know your ass from your elbow. That's one of the main reasons I love you."

His third-person voice was husky. "Thank God because it's true, Joseph Takemura is really bad at that ass-elbow thing."

SHARON

Sharon got to the garage sale in time to see Ralph and a stunning brunette wrestle a child's desk set across the lawn to the curving driveway. Ralph carried the desk and the woman carried the chair. An Asian male, on a lawn chair, sat huddled under a beach umbrella. She parked beside him and rolled down the Jeep's window. "I'm Sharon. I'm with Ralph."

"I'm Joseph Takemura."

"Where should I put the stuff for the sale?"

"Anywhere you want but most of the big items are going closer to the house. I'm in charge of the miscellaneous section."

"I've got plenty of that."

He followed her to the Jeep and lifted a bin of porn from the backseat. He set aside the Babes in Boyland DVD and also the Behind the Green Door. "There's some amazing shit here."

"I don't watch those. They belong to my Ex."

"Yeah, that's what I tell everybody, too. How much do you want for them?"

"You've got to be kidding."

"What about a buck each?"

"You can have them for free."

Across the yard, Clarice put down the chair she was carrying and wandered over to pick through the boxes. When she realized what Bambi and The Three Little Piggies really meant her face flared red.

"Hey, that's a classic," Joseph said. "We could do some research tonight – for that paper I've been thinking about writing."

"Men," Clarice and Sharon said in unison.

Clarice stuck out her hand. "I'm hosting this garage sale. Think of me as Ralph's non-genetic sister."

Joseph lifted more boxes from the Jeep. "You have a wine making kit in here. How much do you want for it?"

"It's free," Sharon said. "I'm in AA. It's how I met Ralph."

Joseph put the copper tubing and glass bottles on the curb next to a pile of DVDs. "This will be a good Alaska activity. I can bring it up when I visit."

"I'm not watching porn with you," Clarice said.

"No problem," Joseph said. "I'll give these to my old man for his birthday. Shit, he'll probably cry and call me his number one son."

"I thought you were Japanese," Sharon said. "The son thing is Chinese, isn't it?"

"Yeah, but everybody knows we Asians are all like."

"You're making fun of me, right?"

"I'm perfecting biting sarcasm," Joseph said. "I've been told I'll need to be nasty for the MBA program."

He put the porn in a paper sack and started going through the rest of the box. "There's a lot of good stuff in here."

"Don't take this personally, but none of that is good stuff. It's mostly jock-a-rama crapola full of loud explosions and pointless violence."

"All non-jocks like me crave excitement in the form of Halo and Grand Theft Auto 3." He stuffed the plastic cases into a paper bag. "It reminds us of our fallibility, not to mention the humiliation of our adolescence."

"Porn and pointless violence can do that?"

He smiled at her. "Asian guys try to be well-rounded, but it's an uphill battle because the qualities of nerdy and brilliant are at cross purposes with hunky and popular. If it weren't for Tai Kwon Do and inscrutable faces we wouldn't have anything going for us at all."

Sharon paused in clearing out the Jeep's backseat. "Don't worry. I don't think the MBA guys will give you any crap."

He pulled an athletic bag from under the front seat and unzipped it. "Is this yours?"

"No," Sharon said. "My ex-husband left a bunch of junk behind in his rush toward freedom. I haven't gone through it all."

Joseph tilted the bag so she could see the plastic sacks of pharmaceuticals. "I think everything in here is illegal."

"My ex-husband thrived on excitement."

"Apparently he also thrived on Percodan and OxyContin," Joseph said. "I'm no expert but a garage sale isn't the best place to move this kind of product."

Behind them, Ralph staggered out of his apartment and down the stairs with a rack of bar-bells on his back. The Jeep sank five inches when he dropped the weights behind the front seats. He looked at the packaged pills and raised an eyebrow.

The three of them looked across the lawn where Clarice was folding old sweaters and lining up old sandals.

"Clarice," Ralph called, "could you come over here for a moment?"

She listened carefully, poked the packages, and it didn't take her long to decide. "Keep Halo and the Grand Theft Auto series," she said firmly. "That's all. We'll wipe the fingerprints off everything else."

"Wipe the fingerprints?"

"I watch reality TV," Clarice said. "I know these things."

They spent half an hour wiping the remaining DVD cases and each pill baggie. Then they stuffed the athletic bag behind the spare tire of the Judge's Jaguar.

"He's bound to get tagged," Joseph said. "I mean, driving a Jag is just begging to get caught speeding. And if they search the car..."

"Poetic justice," Clarice said. She and Sharon grinned in unison.

CLARICE

I was hauling a bin of my sister's junior high school scrunchies across the street when Ralph's girlfriend picked up all his medals.

"How much for these?"

"No charge," I said.

"Are you sure?"

I nodded and she stuffed them into her purse.

"It seems like they're finally in a safe place," I said.

There was a kind of earnestness about Sharon, but a smile flashed free and you'd have thought she won the Powerball Sweepstakes or found her one, true, love. "I'm pregnant," she said.

"And that's a good thing?"

"Yes."

"And you're getting married?"

"Yes," she said again. She was, as the romance novels say, radiant.

"Excellent," I replied.

Only one neighbor came over and that was mostly to gawk. Ted MacDowell (a newly retired county worker) tried to look manly while holding the leash of a yapping Pekinese in one hand and a bulging plastic bag of dog excrement in the other. "November's too late in the year for a garage sale," he said.

"I'm moving up to Alaska and if Nipper so much as lifts his leg on that Disneyland nightstand it's yours for $30."

"Get back here, you little fucker." He jerked the leash and Nipper yelped. "The wife's in Spokane at a nurse's conference. She's staying with a chum from high school." He tightened Nipper's leash with another loop around his hand. "Woman's husband sounds like a real loser. Worked at a hardware store for years then quit to write books or some damn thing. Anyway, their daughter, Megan, is going to college. The kid might want some sheets and shit for her dorm room."

"When's Mrs. MacDowell coming back?"

"Next Wednesday."

"The sale will be over then. I'm serious about Nipper, so maybe you want to pull him away from the desk."

He dragged Nipper to the center of the sidewalk. "Will Ralph be mowing lawns this summer?"

"He's almost finished with grad school," I said. "He's probably moving on."

"He does a damn fine job with the lawns. Hate to lose him." Then he waddled off, dog and doo-doo in tow.

Joseph looked up from the girly magazine he'd filched from Clarice's box of porn. "If I ever turn into an old fart walking a yappy dog, just shoot me."

"You got it," I said.

Ancient vans and beater Chevys had begun to line up at the curb, but nobody exited. They just sat there with pinched faces behind steamy windows.

"So far I'd made exactly zero pennies not to mention dimes, quarters or dollars. "This garage sale is a bust."

"There are customers at the curb."

"They're waiting for the price to come down."

"Slash everything forty percent. That's what the stores do."

"I don't care what the stores would do. I just want to get rid of this crap and I'm not paying waste management to take it. Do you know how expensive that is?"

"So give it away."

Ralph and Sharon were sitting in the Jeep, with the heat on. Every once in a while they would kiss. I wondered how it would be to kiss someone whose mouth both smiled and frowned; like kissing Buddha or Jesus or one of the other holy guys with faces that held sorrow and joy all at the same time.

My father strolled over, a sweatshirt over his pajamas and a Heineken in his hand. "The Seahawks lost," he said. "Jesus, it's cold out here."

A few minutes later, Leslie came out to tell him that Mr. MacDowell phoned to say that according to the neighborhood covenant garage sales weren't allowed.

I tried to not stare at her pinched face. "Eat something," I said.

"Leave me alone," she replied.

"I'm leaving soon," I said.

My father and sister looked dumbfounded, as if I hadn't told them about Alaska, emptied my bedroom, or rented the U-Haul while living in the house where he drank and she put on layer after layer of clothes.

"Right," my father said. "Will you be back for my birthday?" His birthday fell on Thanksgiving this year.

"No."

Confusion battled with disapproval. "Will you be back for Christmas?"

"Yes."

The temperature had dropped to freezing and the street lights blinked on so I wrote another sign, the letters nine inches high, FREE FREE FREE, and propped it against the curb. People emerged from the vehicles like refugees stepping onto the shores of a generous continent. They loaded everything up, even the out-of-date textbooks.

Leslie squinting at each item as it was carted away. She was wearing her Big Sister frowny-face. "Those are my sheets!" she hissed at me. "That's my desk! And my lamps! I love those lamps."

I felt my own frowny face emerge from some distant sisterly fighting closet. "Cinderella has been in my bedroom for fifteen years," I said.

"But I picked everything out for my seventh birthday."

"In middle school you got the Sweet Sixteen bedroom combination with stripes and polka dots and mother gave me your old set."

A Hispanic couple loaded Cinderella and company into the back of a beat-up van. Their daughter's face bloomed like a flower right before our eyes.

"Cinderella was mine," Leslie said. "You can't just give her to complete strangers."

"Grow up," I snapped.

Leslie's face got red and she actually stamped her foot. "You can't give her away! She's mine!" That's when I realized my older sister had disintegrated to the point where she thought she could still apply toddler ownership rules.

Father drank his beer and watched a man throw bag after bag of clothing into the trunk of his car. Everyone else was watching my sister and me.

Ralph stood in front of me, his voice too low for the others to hear. "This one isn't worth winning," he murmured. "Walk away."

"How?"

Ralph handed me the camera, "Distract them. Take some pictures."

"There isn't any film."

"They don't know that. They just want you to pay attention to them. Your real memories, the truest ones, can't be printed into a glossy color photo, anyway."

While the last battered vehicle drove away, I had Leslie stand under the blinking streetlamp. Father stood beside her, beer in hand. I raised the empty camera and made them move closer and closer until his arm rested, lightly, on Leslie's achingly thin shoulders. That's when my father winced and looked down at her. Finally, he saw her bones, her brittle hair, her blotched, sagging skin. He smelled the death that lingered on her breath. Pain tightened his mouth and skittered in his eyes but I made them stand there, touching one another, while I adjusted the focus and steadied the empty camera. I took shot after shot of the most important, the truest, picture I could *never* take.

When they walked up the driveway, my father's arm stayed around Leslie and she leaned into him, shoulders hunched and shaking.

Ralph and Sharon held hands, their faces sad with understanding. My throat ached and Joseph, the complicated man I think I love, turned out to be simple enough to do the right thing.

He pulled me down onto his lap, put his face in my hair and just held me.

SEVEN STAGES OF SIN

"It's important that you not let things get bogged down."

"What's that mean, exactly?" Renae asked.

"It means you can't let them exchange broccoli salad recipes to the exclusion of all else." Dr. Klean pushed four folders across his desk. "The main thing is to be sure they don't try to solve everything by talking about their pets."

Renae flipped through the charts. "Why are they here?"

"They are depressed."

"Why don't they take antidepressants? Don't they know about better living through chemistry?" She looked up from the file folders. "I'm *not* going to be stuck with a lot of midnight phone calls, am I?"

Dr Klean forced himself to relax which, after twenty years of supervising student interns, wasn't the oxymoron it appeared. "Explain to me, again, why you decided to major in Psychology."

Renae wrinkled her brow and sighed heavily. She was very good at sighing. "I'm just so much better with teen alcoholics."

"Someone else is doing that group."

"I'm not comfortable with depressed old women. They remind me of my mother."

"And?"

"And I would like to have some part of my day NOT being reminded of her."

"If you plan to graduate in June and get that promised trip around the world you will stop acting like a petulant twelve year old."

"What makes you think I've been promised a trip?"

"Your college advisor loves to gossip."

She sighed again but they spent fifteen minutes discussing where, when, and what reaction notes she had to take. Dr. Klean withheld comments about her attire, her face jewelry, and her purple bangs.

The women in the support group were depressed. Maybe the outrageous Renae Jacobs would actually jolt them out of their lethargy.

"Each session will be videotaped and I'll review it before I read your therapeutic response. Be sure to write your reaction paper in the third person."

"Why is everything in third person? That's a stupid way to write."

"It keeps things objective."

"Says who?"

"Says me. As well as generations of academics."

"That's a lot of work for six credits. I'm really busy. I need to pick up my mother's prescription for antidepressants and some other junk for her, too. God, you can't imagine the crap she has me doing these days."

"Since I'm the one setting the rules for your internship, therefore the one establishing guidelines for you to receive the necessary credits for graduation, I'm betting you'll find the time to complete your assignment.

"One more thing," Dr. Klean suppressed a smile, "You won't be in this alone. As an undergraduate, the group will be the responsibility of your co-facilitator but I expect you to participate fully."

"Who is it?"

"Joseph Takemura. I believe he was the teaching assistant for your Systems of Psychology class."

The silence stretched to a full minute before she said, "Shit."

Dr. Klean managed to keep his voice from sounding too satisfied. "Joseph is excited to be working with you, too."

GROUP NOTES – SESSION ONE

Joseph Takemura, *Group Facilitator*
Renae Jacobs, *Intern*
Group Participants: *Tyree, Evita, Carole, and Bonnie.*

Evita

(61, Hispanic) took charge of everyone's coat, being sure the buttons were buttoned and that hangers were all pointed the same direction. She printed everyone's nametag in the clear handwriting of an elementary school teacher and insisted they be worn.

Tyree

(48, African-American) brought fresh ground Kona Coffee beans and Rice Krispy bars frosted with milk chocolate. This was the ninth semester in a row Tyree attended a group of one kind or another.

Carole

(58, Caucasian) sat in the chair nearest the bathroom and put a pair of orange-handled scissors and several packets of yarn on the chair next to her, which she began cutting into four inch sections.

The clock clicked to six, the official starting time. Joseph, primary group facilitator, cleared his throat and took the bull by the horns.

"Thank you for coming,"

Tyree nodded and the other women fidgeted.

"I thought we'd begin by introducing ourselves. I'm Joseph Takemura and this is Renae Jacobs. As you all know, this is a caregivers support group. It is mandatory that you attend at least five sessions a year in order for your loved ones to participate in the Alzheimer Day Care program."

The women had settled into their chairs, at least one empty seat between each of them.

"I have an outline." Joseph handed a sheet of paper to each of the women. "The first meeting we'll get acquainted and talk a little bit about what makes caretaking a loved one difficult. The second meeting we'll talk about the hardest part of your day and do some brainstorming about how to get through it. The third meeting we'll talk about your feelings. The fourth meeting you can vote what to talk about. The same for the fifth meeting plus we'll decide whether to continue or not. You've each committed to five meetings so, let me stress, it's important that everyone comes to every meeting.

Joseph liked women and usually they liked him. He was counting on an easy A for six credits.

"I'll begin. My grandfather had Alzheimer's and things got pretty tough for my Grandmother. I wish she'd had a group of women, like you, to talk with."

He smiled at Renae and said, "Your turn."

She gave him a dirty look and said, "I'm Renae. I'm really good with teen alcoholic groups." She folded her arms and admired the far wall.

"Okay," Joseph said. "We'll move to Carole."

Carole's hands shook as she clipped the yarn. Joseph restrained the urge to take the scissors out of her hands. "I'm Carole," she whispered. "My doctor said I should come. I hope nobody minds if I work on my latch hook rug. I get nervous if I don't keep busy."

"Okay," Joseph said. "Tyree's next."

The big woman looked around the group. "If no one minds, I'll bring the treats. It gives me something to do." She plucked another cookie from the plate. "I'm here because of my sister but don't go thinking she's a loved one to me. The nursing home won't take her because she's so mean. Now her daycare is talking about kickin' her out. Sometimes, I wish she'd just hurry up and die."

The group thought about that for a while, then Evita spoke up. "I'm here because my daughter said I should come."

"Your husband has Alzheimer's?" Joseph asked.

Evita nodded. "My mother-in-law does, too. She's sicker than my husband. She just lays in bed and stares at the wall." Evita looked at Tyree. "She's looked at the wall for fifteen years so I wouldn't get my hopes up about your sister going any time soon."

Carol had pulled a half-finished rug from her enormous purse and the sleeves of her sweater hiked up to her elbows. Joseph worked hard not to stare at the bandages that circled her thin wrists. She whispered that she had a recipe for Rice Krispy Treats at home, one that used peanut butter. Tyree said she'd heard of that but had never tried it. Evita took up the torch and said that at Christmas she added nuts and chocolate chips.

After several minutes of discussing the merits of generic store brand rice cereals versus using the original Kellogg's Rice Krispies, a young woman rushed into the room, red hair flying around her face. "Sorry, sorry, sorry," she kept saying. "I couldn't get a ride. The Dial-a-ride driver won't take us anymore."

Joseph looked at the attendance list. There she was. (*Bonnie*, 29, Caucasian) After hanging up her jacket and settling into a chair, Bonnie said that she didn't bake cookies but bought them at Safeway. Date bars were her favorites.

Joseph handed Bonnie the schedule. "Welcome to the group. We're talking about what makes our life hard right now. Renae, would you give Bonnie an example?"

Renae took a sip of coffee and began. "I want a tattoo for my face, something that reflects my life but also with a universal message. You would NOT believe how much crap my father is giving me about it. He is such a fucking loser."

The women sat with stunned smiles on their faces. This was something Joseph noticed about caretakers. They smiled no matter what. It was unnerving.

"I doubt they want to talk about tattoos, Renae," he said.

"Dr. Klean said no recipes, remember?"

"We were talking about recipes in order to get acquainted before we start talking about things in life that are difficult."

"It sounded like recipe talk. Well, I'm sharing something that's personally important so that *they*," she glanced around the circle, "will want to share their own important stuff, too."

"About tattoos?"

"Don't be such an asshole."

The room was silent except for the sound of Carole's scissors, snipping lengths of bright yarn. For the first time, Joseph wondered if getting an A was going to be all that easy.

There were six clumps of color, stacked like a three dimensional rainbow, on the chair beside Carole. "My husband has a tattoo," she whispered. "He was in the Navy, during Vietnam. He has an anchor on his arm."

Evita nodded. "My granddaughter's tattoo is a butterfly, on her shoulder blade. You only see it when she wears her bathing suit."

Tyree sniffed. "Well, I think only whores and drug addicts have tattoos."

The room fell silent again, except for the buzz of florescent lights. It seemed to Joseph that the bursts of silence were the rests in a complicated jazz piece, an irregular drumbeat offset by the riffs of notes and a passionate scat made up of words and emotions. After a couple of minutes, Renae started to talk again.

"The selection of a tattoo is akin to a religious sacrament."

"It's time to move on," Joseph said.

"Move on?" Renae squeaked.

"Change the subject or let someone else talk."

"But nobody else is talking and I'm not finished yet."

"Yes," he said firmly, "you are." He turned to Tyree. "Do you think Evita's thirteen-year-old granddaughter is a whore? Or what about Carole's husband? Is he is a whore?"

Tyree picked up her purse, stuffed the bag of ground coffee into it and collected the empty cookie plate. "I don't know about Carole or her husband. I don't know about any of you. But my sister has a tattoo," she said, "and she was a drug addicted whore. That's why she has Alzheimer's and I don't." She slammed the door on her way out.

"Nice job," Renae said as the rest of the women filed out.

"Fuck you," Joseph replied.

After the group notes were printed out, for Dr. Klean to peruse, Joseph added a personal comment,

Dear **Doctor Klean,**

I feel the personality conflict between Renae and me can only negatively affect the dynamics of the group as a whole. Therefore, I request a new co-facilitator. If that isn't possible then just shoot me because, at this point, those are the only two options I can come up with.

Sincerely, **Joseph Takemura**

GROUP NOTES – SESSION ONE

Everyone showed up. They talked about food. I couldn't get them to change the subject. This is a stupid fucking waste of my time and I hate my co-facilitator.

Sincerely, **Renae Jacobs**

• • •

GROUP NOTES – SESSION TWO

Joseph Takemura, *Group Facilitator*
Renae Jacobs, *Intern*
Participants: *Amazingly, they all came.*

At Dr. Klean's suggestion, Joseph began to think of his co-facilitator as one of the participants. The soundness of this decision was based upon the videotape of the first session. Joseph also wanted to base it upon Renae's newest (and still seeping) tattoo, but Dr. Klean felt that the tattoo was a personal statement and acting like a tight-ass was academic suicide. The two men did agree, however, that putting a tropical jungle (with various birds, insects, and vines) across one's forehead could be seen as a creepy but silent cry for help.

Joseph's goal for the second session was to discuss the reality of taking care of someone with Alzheimer's versus the uplifting magazine articles that came out regularly. 'Silver Linings and Letting Go'. 'Who's the Daughter Now?' 'My Father Took Care of Me – Now I Take Care of Him'.

It didn't seem that the women in the group felt uplifted, blessed, or anything but exhausted by the daily demands of their situation. It had certainly become exhausting for his grandmother, when Grandfather Takemura became unable to tell a car key from a doorknob. Or when the old man wandered from room to room asking, each time he passed through a portal, "Where am I? Where am I?"

After Tyree had made pot of regular Columbian coffee and passed around a plate of banana bread crusted with candied pecans, Joseph began. "Let's talk about your daily routines..."

"Oh, God, now they'll start with the breakfast recipes." Renae sighed heavily and rolled her eyes. "We should be talking about something important."

"Routines are important."

"Routines are little prisons here on earth!" She made a sweeping gesture with her coffee cup, slopping a little on the floor. Evita jumped to her feet, to clean the mess, and after the floor was shiny again, she sat back down.

"Routines are important," Joseph repeated. "Without them things can fall apart."

That is so true!" Evita looked at Joseph earnestly. "Every night, before I go to bed, I drive to Rite-Aide and buy a case of adult diapers. I don't know what I'd do without that routine."

"Sure," Joseph said, "I suppose that's a kind of routine."

"The person who invented disposable diapers is a saint," Evita continued. "Between my mother-in-law and my husband, I go through a case a day. Disposable diapers really cut down on the laundry."

"Your husband should be in a nursing home," Renae snapped.

"My husband is just a little sick. You don't put a sick person in a nursing home."

"If I had insurance, I would."

"We aren't talking about you," Joseph said. "It isn't your turn yet."

"I don't have to do my Daddy's laundry," Bonnie whispered. "He don't have any."

"Of course he has laundry," Carole's bandages were smaller now and the bubble gum pink of new scar tissue showed at either end of the rectangular gauze. "Everyone has laundry."

"Daddy don't."

Carole pulled packets of yarn from her bag. "My Andrew would wear the same slacks for a month if I let him, but sometimes he dribbles around the diaper and you just can't let a man walk around with dribble day after day."

Tyree put down her coffee. "My sister throws a fit when she don't get to wear her favorite pink warm-ups, but too bad. When they get stinky, I wash them." Tyree took a bite of banana bread, chewed and swallowed. "Let your Papa sit in front of the dryer in his robe."

"Papa don't have a robe."

"Well, I suppose wearing his underwear is okay." That was Evita, passing out more napkins. Her uncombed hair was matted and spiked out in half a dozen directions. To Joseph's thinking, Evita had every right to never talk again or to only sob in prolonged bursts, but here she was, picking up after them all.

"Does your Daddy have any favorite outfits?" That was Carole, snipping yarn like crazy.

"No," Bonnie said, "he don't." Her voice was flat and she kept looking at the floor. Joseph felt a buzzing begin behind his left eye. He's heard that flatness in another group he'd co-facilitated. The parolees who'd all been abused as children often spoke in that non-tone of voice when discussing their childhoods. Shit. Shit. Shit. They were out of their depth, he and Renae. They were way the hell up the fucking creek without a paddle.

"Oh for God's sake!" Renae's voice filled the room with distain. "We don't have time for this crap. We're supposed to be focused on depression and not washday woes!"

"Shut up, Renae." Joseph didn't shout it but his voice carried.

But she snapped that laundry talk was a waste of time. Next thing they'd be back exchanging more cookie recipes and showing pictures of their grandkids. Well, she had better things to do than sit and listen to a bunch of silly old women. Joseph wanted to leap up, race across the circle and slap her face but he didn't. He was going to treat her as if she was a group member with inappropriate social behavior. Which she was, actually.

He lifted his coffee cup and drank brown liquid so hot it burned his taste buds. Renae finally paused, to take another bite of banana bread, and in that slice of silence Joseph swallowed hard and asked Bonnie, "What did you want to say about your Daddy not wearing a robe?"

"Nothing. I didn't want to say nothing about it."

Carole paused in her snipping. "Yes, Dear, you did. You were saying your Papa didn't wear anything. He must wear something. I mean, he can't sit around stark naked."

Bonnie's face turned a brilliant pink. They all leaned forward and she finally mumbled, "He don't never wear nothing if he can help it. I'm just so tired of looking at his tired old Mr. Winkie I can hardly stand it."

The room was silent – and Joseph felt the horrible urge to laugh. Or cry.

"Well," Tyree said, "Sis tries to run around without her clothes on but you just can't let 'em get away with it. I tell her, I'm not looking at your twat one more minute so you put your pants on right now!"

"You tell him if he doesn't put wear pajama bottoms you'll strap him on the bed like you do his mother," Evita said. "That'll settle him down."

"Most men don't like being strapped down," Carole chimed in. "They don't like diapers either but you tell him the doctors will lock him away if he doesn't wear something."

In the blink of an eye, it was as if Mr. Winkie wasn't anything to be mortally, frantically, embarrassed about. Mr. Winkie was just one more incident in the life of an Alzheimer caregiver.

That, Joseph typed, *was pretty much the end of Session Two. Carole and Evita folded the chairs, talking about how to pick colors for a do-it-yourself latch hook design. Bonnie and Tyree walked out together, whispering, and he thought he heard a snort of laughter. God only knew if anyone would come back, including at least one of the co-facilitators.*
Sincerely, **Joseph Takemura**

GROUP NOTES – SESSION TWO

Writing everything in third person is stupid. You can watch the video or stand behind the two way mirror if you want to know what's going on. Why don't you give me a group of teen addicts instead of these stupid old women?
Sincerely, **Renae Jacobs**

• • •

GROUP NOTES – SESSION THREE

Joseph Takemura, *Group Facilitator*
Renae Jacobs, *Intern*
Participants, *Evita* and *Carole,* arms bristling with books on latch hook projects, came early. *Tyree* followed them with a Tupperware container in one hand and a bag of finely ground Sidamo beans in the other.

"Bonnie called to say she might be a little late." Tyree scooped almost black coffee into the paper filter. "I made my Seven Stages of Sin cookies and I want her to taste them."

Joseph looked up from his notes. "Seven Stages of Sin?"

Tyree smiled. "Seven layers of calorie laden goodies."

"Do you make them with walnuts and shredded coconut?" That was Evita, reworking the chairs until the circle was perfectly round. "Or do you use almonds and chocolate chips?"

"I have nothing against the classics," Tyree said, "but I feel a person should indulge their own imagination on occasion."

"I like them with cashews and butterscotch." Carole dug through her yarn bag. "I seem to be missing my hooks. Oh, there they are."

A new bandage showed under the cuff of her long-sleeved blouse. It went all the way around her arm. Joseph wondered if Carole was cutting again. He'd have her hospitalized if he had to. He didn't have balls for a lot of things, but he would not allow Carole to drain every ounce of blood from her body.

"We used to have these at Christmas." The words were out before Joseph realized he'd inadvertently joined the recipe club. What the hell – in for a penny, in for a pound. "My older sister used dried cranberries, pecans and crushed peppermint candy canes."

"What a good idea," Carole said. "It's always stressful trying to find a new cookie when the holidays come around."

Later, Joseph wondered how long they could have gone, sharing recipes. If left on their own, they'd move into vacuuming tips or start comparing favorite breakfast cereals. The only bright note was that no one had mentioned pets.

The room was silent as Tyree poured coffee with its dark citrus undertone and Evita passed around cookies made with white chocolate chunks, caramel topping and roasted peanuts.

Joseph took two. He ate the first cookie quickly then slowed down for the second, savoring the alternating layers of crunch between his teeth and melting softness on his tongue and thought that maybe he should research it a bit more and then develop his findings into a paper and submit it to *The British Journal of Social Work*. It would be titled, 'Facilitating intimacy in a Group Setting through the use of Comfort Foods'. It was cutting edge. It was cross cultural. It was inspired.

When he opened his eyes, Renae was slouched in the doorway, purple dreads pulled back into a pony tail while her three color tattoo crawled down her forehead and cheek bones like a miniature Brazilian rainforest.

"I came to say good-bye."

Joseph choked on the last crumbs of coconut. When his eyes quit watering and the mucus from his nose and mouth lessened he rasped, "Good-bye?"

"This gig isn't right for me. Your lives are over. I need to work with people who still have something to hope for."

The circle was silent, even the snip of Carole's scissors was stopped. Then Tyree spoke, "Being bitchy won't protect you, little girl. Take it from someone who knows. Keep it up and your life will turn into pure shit. And, someday you will remember every thoughtless, stupid thing you ever did or said and there won't be any way to go back and fix it. I remember all the horrible things I said to my own father and I can't fix none of it because Katrina got him. My aunt called to tell us the water pulled him right through the window in front of her eyes. That storm is how I got stuck with my baby sister."

"Life sucks," Renae said, "and then you die."

"Sometimes not soon enough," Tyree said and at the other side of the circle, Carole started to cry.

Evita handed her a paper napkin and after a while Carole sighed, blew her nose, and picked up her coffee cup. Tyree passed around more cookies and Joseph took another one. It was the only way he could keep his mouth occupied with something other than shouting at Renae. The women began talking about detergent brands and had pretty much settled the question of which was better, power or liquid, when Bonnie crept in with a black eye and a bruised jaw. There were more bruises around her throat and it looked like someone had tried to choke her.

"Tyree said I had to come." Bonnie's lilting soprano had become that of a seventy-year-old woman who smoked four packs of cigarettes a day. Bruises to the larynx, Joseph thought. Next time it could be a shattered hyoid bone and she'd be a goner.

"Maybe it's time your father moved out," he said.

"No. I-I can't."

"If he's hurting you," Joseph said, "then he shouldn't be living at home."

"My father was a really nice man. He sang in the church choir and drove me to piano lessons. He taught me how to ride a bike. He loved me. He would be humiliated to think he did these things."

"He isn't your father anymore," Tyree said quietly. "He hasn't been your father for a couple years now." She took the empty plate from

Joseph. "As hard as it is for me to agree with someone half my age, Mr. Can't-Get-Enough-Cookies is right. It's time to let your father go."

That's when Evita, sitting across the circle from Bonnie, burst into tears and rushed from the room, leaving her purse (and car keys) on the floor beside the empty folding chair.

Joseph hesitated, crumbs falling from his shirt like dandruff, caught between running after Evita and staying with Bonnie.

"I'll get her," Tyree said. She snagged Evita's car keys and purse. "See you all next week."

Joseph took Bonnie to the Emergency Room leaving Carole to stack chairs, rinse out the coffee-maker, and turn off the lights. Somewhere in the middle of the commotion, Renae had slipped out. Joseph had no idea if it was before or after Bonnie showed up – which made him believe he wasn't paying close enough attention to the group's underlying dynamics. He'd been like all the others in that room, diverted by crisis and not watching for the reaction of the others. That was bad in a group leader and it made him seriously consider leaving social work behind and walking across campus to the School of Business. Surely the financial world wouldn't be quite so fucked up.

Sincerely, *Joseph Takemura*

GROUP NOTES – SESSION THREE

I'm meeting with some street kids who hang around Yesler and First Avenue. The nuns hand out sandwiches and they never know how many will show up but they say it's okay for me to talk to any teens who want to rap about safe sex and stuff. That should be worth six credits. And you can tell my father – the jerk who wants to bribe me into getting this degree but refuses to keep my mother and I on his health insurance – to go fuck himself.
*Sincerely, **Renae Jacobs***

• • •

GROUP NOTES – SESSION FOUR

Joseph Takemura – *Group Facilitator*
Renae – *cameo appearance*
Bonnie – *absent*
Evita – *absent*

Carole and *Tyree* showed up. *Carole* didn't bring her rug and *Tyree* didn't bring treats. The circle of chairs was a ragged triangle and, at the tip, *Joseph* sat holding five blank sheets of paper and five pens emblazoned with the promotional logos of various pharmaceutical companies.

"Where is everyone?" Joseph asked.

"Evita has a bad cold," Carole said, "and Bonnie has an appointment to get her father into an impaired memory facility."

"Today we get to vote," Tryee said. "I been looking forward to this session."

"But there are only two of you. I'm not sure that's fair."

"Sure it is," Tyree said. "We showed up and no-one else did. I vote for a field trip. Baskin and Robbins has this terrific flavor, Love Potion Number 31. I'm going to get a dish of that."

"We're not voting on ice cream," Joseph said. "We're voting on what to talk about today."

"But I didn't bring treats because I thought there'd be ice cream."

"No field trips," Joseph said firmly.

"Where's the girl?" Carole asked. "The one with spiders on her face."

"She isn't coming anymore," Joseph said.

"You never liked her," Carole said, "because of the tattoos."

"She didn't want us to like her." Tyree took one of the squares of paper from Joseph and wrote, ICE CREAM on it with the Blue Viagra pen.

Joseph wrote NO ICE CREAM on his slip and Carole didn't write anything which made the whole voting issue moot since it was, technically, a tie. Next group I lead, Joseph thought, there will be no voting at all for any reason.

"Fine," Tyree said, "I vote we all tell a secret. Something we don't want anyone else to know. They did that in the ice cream group and it built trust."

"Okay," Joseph said, "I'll vote for that, too. You go first."

Tyree closed her eyes and said, "My sister isn't really my sister. She's my daughter and she just wasn't ever right because I drank too much when I was pregnant."

"Fetal Alcohol Syndrome," Joseph said.

"I'm not supposed to be in the Alzheimer's group but the facilitator in the ice cream group said it didn't matter. He said if Labelle was getting lost on the way to the kitchen I should be able to go to any group I wanted."

"Works for me," Joseph said.

Carole pulled a tissue from her purse and dabbed at her eyes. "My secret is that I hate my husband."

"That's no secret," Tyree said. "Everybody knows you hate that sonofabitch. Mother Teresa would hate him."

"But I hate my pastor and the mail carrier and my sister-in-law and the guy in vegetables at the grocery store, too."

"That's a lot of people to hate," Joseph said.

"And I hate my dog, Ruffie." Carole dabbed her eyes and blew her nose. "My stupid-assed husband keeps locking him in the house and now Ruffie piddles and craps all over everything."

"Okay," Tyree said, "I guess hate is a good enough secret."

Carole looked at Joseph. "Please don't kick me out of group because I said 'crap'."

"I believe I've said worse," Joseph said.

"I never used to be like this." Carole's voice was squeaky and her nose snotty. "I just fucking hate everything about my life."

"Girl," Tyree said, "you're on a hating binge, but don't worry about it. Sometimes you just got to hate everyone before you can get around to stop hating yourself."

Joseph felt like he was watching a group dynamics training movie because Tyree was saying all the things he should be saying but sometimes that's the way it was in group. Sometimes the best possible thing to do was sit like a lump and just let things happen.

"I don't hate that girl – that Renae." Carole tucked her tissue into her sleeve. "I kind of wish I was like her. She doesn't take any fucking crap off of anybody."

"No," Joseph said, "I guess she doesn't."

They sat quietly while Tyree drew random designs on her paper, curlicues and loops and a series of boxes within boxes.

"What's your secret, Mr. Can't-Get-Enough-Cookies?" Tyree asked.

"I'm the facilitator. I don't get to have secrets."

"Sure you do. And you voted so that means you have to play."

"Yes, Joseph," a voice murmured coolly and there was Renae, with smudged eyes and a series of short, red scratches on her gothic pale cheek. "Tell us your secret."

"You came!" Carole's face blossomed into a smile.

Renae moved to a seat between Tyree and Carole. Now there were three women at the base of the inverted triangle of chairs and Joseph at the peak.

"You tell your secret," Renae said, "and then I'll tell mine."

"The leader of the ice cream group told a secret," Tyree said.

Joseph had a lot of secrets, most of them not worth much. Mentally he went through the catalogue of minor ones. "Okay," he said. "I married right out of high school and now I'm divorced."

"Big deal," Tyree said. "Everybody got something like that."

"I told about hate," Carole said. "You have to tell about your feelings, too."

"Joseph doesn't have any feelings," Renae said.

"Of course I have feelings," Joseph snapped. He thought a bit longer. "I'll talk about guilt."

"I already did guilt," Tyree said. "And anyway, it's the easiest one."

"I haven't found that to be true," Joseph said and Renae laughed sharply.

The women were silent, waiting. Tyree folded her arms across her massive breasts, Carole tugged at her cuffs and tilted her head, Renae crossed her legs and jiggled her foot.

"We're going for ice cream later," Carole told Renae. "You can come, too."

Joseph glanced up at the two-way mirror. Behind it the camera was recording everything.

"My older sister is a little crazy. She has what we call OCD – Obsessive Compulsive Disorder – and when she takes her medicine she can do things like make cookies that aren't all exactly the same and can get an A minus in PE without trying to kill herself. But when she doesn't take her medicine she's a mess, she can't leave her room because she has to flip the light switch a thousand times before going through a door, literally, a thousand times." Joseph didn't want to be telling this secret but the words tumbled out of his mouth like a pack of wild dogs with the ability to rip apart everything he believed in: Family. Loyalty. His own small cup of self-respect.

"She was okay until she went into puberty and then the OCD got hold of her and just took over. My grandfather didn't understand this. He was ashamed and so he beat her. He started beating her when she was twelve. Everyone stood by when he broke her arm and when he threw her down the stairs. Nobody stopped him. My father just stood by." Joseph could barely get the words out. "... I stood by too."

The room was very quiet except for the sound of Joseph crying.

"You said she was older." Renae's voice didn't have the usual strident ring to it. "How much older?"

"Seven years."

"So you were five when she was twelve."

He nodded.

"I suppose you were big for your age," Renae said dryly. "I suppose you could have taken on a full grown man and knocked him on his ass."

"I... I could have at least tried."

"Jesus," Renae said, "you really are pathetic. You think you could have saved your sister when you were too damn small to even save yourself."

"This is just more of that guilt shit," Tyree said. "We all got guilt so this secret isn't all that special after all."

"What about your parents?" Renae asked. "Why didn't they step in?"

Joseph shrugged. Tears rolled down his cheek.

Carole came over and sat by him. She handed him a tissue. "Do you hate your grandfather for being so sick and so stupid and your parents for not protecting you all?"

"Always."

"Do you hate yourself?"

"Sometimes."

"Do you hate your sister?"

"Once in awhile. When she won't take her medicine. I hate her then."

"Well," Carole said briskly, "I guess it's a good thing you're in this group with us. Since we understand perfectly how you feel."

Except for the squeak of Renae's chair when she jiggled her foot, the room was quiet. Like they were all sitting on the front porch at home, with no breeze, in the middle of a summer afternoon.

Joseph blew his nose and wiped his eyes. "You're all pretty good at this, aren't you? I mean, you go right to the heart of the matter."

"We been in more groups than you and Little-Miss-Jungle-Face," Tyree said. "We know how things go."

"I suppose it's my turn, now," Renae said.

"No," Tyree and Carole said in unison. "Now we go for ice cream."

"But what about me?"

"Joseph is vulnerable right now," Tyree said. "Joseph gets to push all that shame back into the trunk where he keeps his secrets, before we get into whatever shit you want to shovel."

So they all went for ice cream. Tyree had a triple cone of Love Potion #31. Carole had two scoops of Blackberry Swirl. Renae had peppermint sprinkles on Vanilla Yogurt in a waffle cone. And Joseph had Orange Sherbet dipped in smooth dark chocolate and the shell snapped into lovely little shards when he bit into it.

Sincerely, *Joseph Takemura*

GROUP NOTES – SESSION FOUR

Watch the fucking video.
Sincerely, **Renae Jacobs**

• • •

GROUP NOTES – SESSION FIVE

Joseph Takemura, *Group Facilitator*
Renae Jacobs, *Intern*
Participants, *all present.*

When Joseph unlocked the door the chairs were already in a perfectly round circle and Evita was putting out the napkins and paper cups. "How did you get in?" Joseph asked and she just took his coat and smiled.

"When my mother-in-law first got sick, she'd lock herself in the house or forget how to get out of the bathroom. I got good at picking locks." Evita hung his coat on the rack, repositioning some of the hangers so that the hooks didn't touch each other and all faced the same direction. "Carole told me about your sister."

Joseph waited for her to continue, to say how she understood the need to flip a light switch, but Evita went to her usual chair, twitched it into place so that the circle was perfectly round, and sat quietly, waiting.

After a few minutes Carole and Bonnie came, both of them with shaggy rugs clamped under their arms. Carole's was further along with pink flowers and green leaves against a cream background. Bonnie's seemed to be all one color, sky blue, except for a brilliant yellow splotch at the top edge. It held the fascination of a Rorschach Inkblot Test and Joseph made several guesses about what it could be (*The tuft at the top of a clown hat? The sun breaking through the clouds?*) before wrenching his attention away.

Bonnie's bruises had faded and a smile brightened her face. Joseph assumed her father was now housed in the impaired memory program, also called IMP by the state licensing agency. Tyree and Renae came in together. Renae carried a box of Krispy Kreams and Tyree carried a bag of freshly-ground hazelnut coffee.

"I thought we could have donuts," Renae said, "while I tell *my* secret."

The coffee gurgled and perked while napkins were passed around and donuts selected. Joseph lifted a classic vanilla glazed wheel to his mouth while the women went for pink sprinkles or chocolate icing. Finally, everyone in the group settled their faces into a kind of bright anticipation, as if waiting to hear a piano recital by a precocious grandchild or well-loved niece.

As was so often the case with therapy, everything made sense in hindsight.

Renae sat beside Joseph, so close their knees almost touched.

"I'm dealing with cancer."

"What kind of cancer?"

She lifted the hair at the back of her neck and the other women crowded around to see something that resembled a pale blue flower invaded by a white worm.

"I'm focusing on the anger," Renae said. "It makes me feel alive."

"You... you have cancer?"

She brought a packet from the pocket of her black velveteen jacket. The papers had been folded into an uneven square, as if she'd begun a complicated origami but given up halfway through. "I brought lab reports."

Joseph slowly unfolded the lab reports and saw they described adenocarcinoma of the pancreas. And they were for Renae's mother.

"These aren't yours," Joseph said. "What the hell are you playing?"

"The tattoos are a symbol. You're supposed to be a smart guy. Don't you know anything about symbols?"

The women in the group were silent, swiveling their heads to look first at Renae and then at Joseph then back at Renae. There was only the buzz of the neon lights and the ping of the heating system as he read the reports of a Stage Four malignancy, plus morphine dosages and X-number of months to live which had dwindled down to next-to-nothing.

"I'm never growing up," Renae repeated. "In her mind I'll always be this mouthy teenaged bitch."

"How long does she have?"

"The doctors say she's terminal."

"Sooner or later we're all terminal," Tyree said.

Renae's eyes were bright with tears that wouldn't fall. "I've been such a shit to her."

Joseph wanted to say no, that was only guilt talking but Renae had been perfectly awful to everyone. Odds were she was awful to her dying mother, too.

Tyree was relentless. "So that's your big fat Krispy Kremes secret – that you've been a shit to the only person in the world who can stand you?"

"Stop it," Renae said.

"We've all been shits," Tyree said. "You still have time to change things if you want. It's too late for the rest of us. Their minds are gone and they can't remember anything but the bad stuff."

"Tyree," Joseph said quietly, "this isn't about you."

"The hell it isn't! It's about all of us here!"

Carole put down her latch hook and picked up Renae's hand. "How long does she have?"

"Three months. Maybe. Most of the time she doesn't even know I'm around they keep her so doped up. But she wanted to die at home. So every day I wake up to a hospital bed in the living room and a bald mother who drools out of the corner of her mouth."

"You don't have to act so tough all the time," Joseph said. "It's okay to cry."

"No. It isn't. If I start I'll never stop."

"You'll stop," Evita said. "Then you'll start again and things will go that way for a couple years. Eventually you'll only cry for a couple minutes on special occasions. Like holidays or when you see a red dress that reminds you of her."

Bonnie handed a pink sprinkled donut to Renae. "Even though it feels like you're all alone, you're not."

Joseph stared at his coffee cup and when he was finally able to look up, he saw that Carole had pulled Renae onto her lap and was rocking the girl as if she weighed twelve pounds instead of ten times that.

"It's okay, sweet baby," she crooned. "We'll take care of you."

"I won't take care of you," Tyree said. "I'm all tapped out with my daughter."

"I'm tapped out, too," Evita said.

"I'm not," Bonnie said. "I'm full of energy and I need someplace to put it. I'll be there for you."

"I will too." Carole's voice was loud and firm. "I need someone to hug and someone to hold. I'll be here for you this year and next year and the year after that. I need a future to work on."

That's when Renae pushed her tattooed face into Carole's plump shoulder and cried. First it was a burst of wracked sobs that settled into a kind of soft weeping and ended with a series of gasps and drawn out sighs. All the while Carole rocked and crooned and held her. It took fifteen minutes and was, Joseph thought, worth every painful, awkward minute.

"Okay," Renae finally said. "Okay. I'm ready."

"For being alive? For being an adult?" Tyree asked.

"Stop it, Tyree," Evita said. "You don't always have to act so tough."

"Yes, she does," Joseph said.

Bonnie knelt on the floor and put her arms around both Carole and Renae. "What are you ready for?"

"I'm ready for another donut."

So we ate all the donuts, Joseph wrote. And then I drove Renae to see her father, the Head of the Department. I told him his daughter was about to collapse from exhaustion and she needed him to step up and help with his ex-wife's care. When he resisted, I told him if he didn't at least handle the funeral, I'd take out an ad in the campus newspaper so everyone would know what an asshole he was.

The group voted to keep going indefinitely. We're bonded now and I think Renae and I will manage to do this for the rest of the school year.

Sincerely, *Joseph Takemua*

GROUP NOTES – SESSION FIVE

The Alzheimer's group is probably better than the downtown-scary-kids group where I almost got raped. Thanks to my brass-toed boots, that homeless fucker won't be screwing ANYONE for a while.
Sincerely, *Renae Jacobs*

· · ·

Dr. Klean sat at his desk, entering final grades into the computer. The Dean, of course, wanted Joseph thrown out of the program. But the Dean was an idiot and an asshole. Sometimes he managed to be both at once. To Dr. Klean's mind, Joseph had followed protocol most of the time and had earned an A.

As for Renae, Dr. Klean thought she'd come a long way over the semester and she would need a free trip to Europe after her mother died.

He gave her a P, for Pass.

· · ·

SEVEN STAGES of SIN

Melt:
1 stick Margarine in a 9 x 13 pan
Sprinkle over it, in following order:
1 Cup graham cracker crumbs
1 Cup coconut
1 small pkg. chocolate chips (or white chocolate)
1 small pkg. butterscotch bits (or crushed peppermint)
Drizzle over this:
1 (15 oz) can sweetened condensed milk (Eagle brand)
Sprinkle:
1 1/2 cups chopped nuts... any kind including salted
Bake in a 350 degree oven for 30 minutes. Cut in small squares.
Do not over bake.

CHANT OF SURVIVAL

MAC

"I understand that you want to do this on your own," Mandy said, "but we're going to have a baby and, when the time comes, I need you absolutely clean and clear."

"I know."

"Not just for now, either, but for the rest of our lives."

Mac nodded and finished screwing on his leg.

She handed him the gold-framed wedding picture of the two of them; Mandy in her flowing white dress and Mac in his uniform. "I love you," she said, "no matter what." She tucked the picture into the gym bag's side pocket, kissed him and went downstairs to unlock the door and flip the switch to the open-for-business beer sign of her father's tavern. Mac blinked away the sting of tears and finished packing his gear in the battered and stained Navy duffel.

RALPH

The VA Hospital waiting room was filled with demons and aliens. That's how Ralph thought of them. Hell, that's how he thought of himself. It wasn't just the fact that he no longer needed to shave the half of his face that was pocked and scarred with skin as pink and shiny as half-chewed bubblegum. It wasn't the shrapnel-dimpled torso. It was the lost leg, chopped off six inches above an absent knee. When it came right down to it, he was just one more partial person sitting next to half a squadron of partial people.

The man sitting across from Ralph had the body of a long distance runner and wore blue camouflage pants and a t-shirt with a Navy insignia and the letters EOD stenciled on the front. Ralph knew Explosive Ordinance Disposal would be stenciled on the back. It was a job that demanded steady hands and nerves of steel but Ralph could see that one of those hands only had three fingers. Ralph noticed that because the vet was reading one of the slick advertisements piled on the floor. The colorful brochure said a bionic prosthetic leg system (with a chrome socket design) could be ramped up for hard duty road work but the plastic ball-bearing prosthesis was cheaper and nearly unnoticeable in a pair of long pants.

Ralph was going back into rehab because he needed to sweat off too many months of hard drinking. Plus, half a year ago he'd gone into debt to buy the prosthetic upgrade and he was still learning how to navigate the titanium spring-loaded-stilt. The money for the metal leg was eating away at him because, after all this time, he was still trying to master the skillset of a daily run – which, some days, was the only thing that kept him from putting the barrel of his Glock in his mouth and pulling the trigger.

The navy guy looked up. "Stop grinding your teeth. It's fucking annoying."

Ralph nodded and shrugged. "Sorry."

"Where were you stationed?"

"Afghanistan was the first tour and Iraq the second. That's how I ended up here."

"Army?"

"1st Battalion. 75th Regiment."

The Navy guy nodded. "You were a Ranger."

"I can kill you seventeen different ways with a toothbrush and a rubber band."

"Don't think that will get you in to see the doctors any quicker."

The room smelled of sweat and fear with an overtone of urine. "I'd suggest we go for a run, but that piece of pink plastic you're looking at won't stand up to the pounding," Ralph said.

"In case you haven't noticed, I'm wearing a training blade. This cheap shit would be for Christmas with the in-laws." The shiny brochure in the thick, freckled hands sagged like an upside down pup tent. "I don't need them making nice to the family cripple. My wife doesn't need it either."

"You don't look old enough to be married."

The sailor pulled out his cell phone and flipped it open to show a series of pictures featuring a clear-eyed redhead with the face that could stop traffic.

"Wow."

"I need to keep clean for my wife and for the little angel that's coming."

"You don't want to keep clean for yourself?"

"Right now, I'm willing to do it for them."

"Whatever works, I guess."

The sailor's hands were shaky as he flipped through the brochure's pages. "I've got most of my fingers and an opposable thumb. And I still got my dick. I'm partial owner of a pub and I need those parts."

"It takes a dick to operate a tavern?"

"You bet. That and a baseball bat. You would not believe what assholes some drunks can be."

"I might."

The sailor put down his magazine. "Sometimes life hands you a peach and sometimes it hands you a lemon."

"If you tell me that life is learning how to turn lemons into lemonade, I'm going home to get my gun."

"I sold all my guns. I'm done with explosives. Especially the point and shoot kind."

"Thus the baseball bat."

"And the need for a dick."

Ralph found himself smiling. "What's the name of your place?"

"The Office."

"You're shittin' me."

"Nope. Mandy and I live upstairs and we're buying it from my father-in-law."

Somewhere there was a shout and then laughter echoed down the long, linoleum floor. The two men were silent, watching a young woman wheel across the room, down the hallway and through the slowly-opening sliding glass doors. The chair was automatic because both her feet and her left hand were missing but her smile was brilliant and the toddler on her lap was laughing and saying, "Faster, Mommy! Faster!"

"How the fuck can she smile?" Ralph's voice was filled with awe. "You think it's easier on women?"

"No."

Ralph wiped his face. He hoped it was sweat and not tears. "I just lost a leg and I'm furious most of the time. I don't know what I'd do without both my hands."

"I think having a kid helps. It gives you something to live for. You got kids?"

"No." Ralph cleared his throat. "I'm one of those drunk assholes you were talking about."

"Yeah, that's what I figured."

"It's that obvious?"

"The old brewski aroma gave you away."

"I'm just getting back into rehab," Ralph said. "I've got an AA meeting later."

"Day at a time."

Sounds of a door slamming and shouts echoed through the waiting room. The receptionist and the nurse behind the desk didn't even bother to look up as a loud angry baritone damned the Lord God straight to hell and all the fucking congressional assholes, too.

Ralph sucked in a breath and the sailor across from him squinted, hard, at the floor. After the room relaxed back into murmurs and groans, Ralph cleared his throat and whispered, "I met someone. Is *that* making lemonade?"

"Maybe." The sailor stuck out his hand. "My name's Leonard MacDougal. You can call me Mac."

MAC

The VA doc didn't look at Mac. He looked at the computer. "You know that I can't give you anything for the phantom pain."

"It doesn't feel phantom."

"I'm sure it doesn't but it comes with the territory. Just be glad you look normal and people don't stare when you walk into a room."

"I don't mind my wife staring," Mac said. "Especially when I'm doing my male stripper routine."

The doc quit tapping on the keyboard and smiled. "Get outa here. And no script for Oxycodone. I don't care if it feels like the devil has set your foot on fire."

"I didn't ask for Oxy," Mac said. "I'm done with that. I asked if there was any medicine that wasn't addictive that I could take instead."

The doc's face was sad. "Not that I know of."

Mac hated running, but was good at it. It kept him clear. It kept him clean. Mac didn't do the marathons because he mostly liked to run alone, at night. The VA didn't allow that so he ran with a partner. His old partner was discharged so he grabbed onto the new guy, Ralph, who was horrible at keeping his balance and also abysmal at setting a reasonable pace.

"Fuck," Mac said, "do you want to be dead by the end of the first mile?"

"Yes, I do," Ralph said. "I truly do."

After two miles Ralph had fallen fifteen times and Mac was losing patience. "You're going about this all wrong," he said. "You can't try to run like you did before."

"So, how am I supposed to run?"

"Not like you're dragging a log."

"But it *feels* like a fucking log."

"Pretend like it's a motorcycle," Mac said. "The engineers knew what they were doing. Let the spring-loaded thingamajig do its job.

Don't fight the mechanism. Just trust it and let the damn thing push you forward. Your job is to keep up."

"Fuck," Ralph said.

They ran daily for a week while Mac coached and Ralph swore. Then, something clicked and Ralph made a mile without falling and then he was pushing three miles at a time.

MAC

The rehab group was celebrating Mac's discharge by taking him out for dinner. He picked the Thai restaurant six blocks from the base and the whole crew walked there. They celebrated with sparkling water and four-star hot sauces and laughed their respective asses off. They especially laughed at the VA counselor's suggestion that they start every morning with the chant, "Keeping straight! We'll be great!"

After dinner, Mac headed for the restroom, but the hallway was dark and he bumped into a six foot tall woman wearing a long black coat, three inch heels and not much else. "Mac?" she said in a voice that was more *Basso profondo* than *Contralto*. "Is it really you?"

"It might be. Who are you?"

"Georgette Finelli."

"George? From my unit?"

"Georgette." The baritone was firm. "I'm my own true self now."

"Wow. You look... uh... nice boots."

"Don't be a prick, Mac."

"Give me a minute. I might need a little time to adjust."

Mac hugged her, then, in a purely comradely fashion. George Finelli had saved his life – pulled him from flaming oil-slick water and into a lifeboat and he was pretty sure his folks and Mandy were grateful for that.

"How you doing?" George AKA Georgette asked.

"Good. And you?"

"Day at a time."

Mac nodded.

"The booze never called your name, did it." It wasn't a question.

Mac shrugged.

"You still juicing?"

"I never juiced George... ette."

"Right. I forgot. You were the Ox-hound."

"Was."

"You quit?"

"Yes."

"I got some nice stuff in my bra and I don't mean boobs."

"I quit!" Mac's voice was fierce. "I quit Oxy, Cotton, Kicker, Hillbilly Heroin. Whatever the hell you want to call it! I *quit*, dammit!"

Mac didn't realize he was shouting until he turned and saw that Ralph was suddenly standing beside him.

"I have you recorded." Ralph held up his cell phone to the woman in the shadowed hallway. "You were trying to sell an illegal substance. If you don't get the hell out of my man's face, I'm turning this evidence over to the authorities."

The boots and the wigged figure wearing them pushed out the EXIT at the end of the hallway and melted into the shadows. Mac would have thought it was another hallucination except for Ralph's hand on his shoulder. The rest of the group had headed back to the dorm but Ralph stayed.

"You got to expect that kind of thing." Ralph's eyes were on the streetlamp and anyone watching would think he was talking to himself but Mac was listening hard. "It creeps up on you and *blam*, there you are."

Mac shrugged.

"But you handled it," Ralph said.

Mac shrugged again and Ralph pushed on. "Damn straight, you did fucking great."

"No stupid fucking poetry," Mac muttered.

"Poetry?" Ralph stared at Mac.

"Straight. Great." Then they were both laughing and it was okay, really okay, again.

RALPH

The Saturday after Mac finished his oxy rehab and told everyone good-bye, Ralph entered his first Hero's Half – also known on base as an open-to-anyone 10-K. He came in tenth from last (behind a pregnant stroller-pushing mom but ahead of the three hundred pound grandfather.) Ralph only fell twice so he considered it a personal best.

He called Mac at The Office. "I finished it."

"Glad to hear it." Over the phone, the buzz of the tavern was tinny but familiar and Ralph felt the longing start up – longing for booze, longing for a whole body and – under it all – the longing for the bullet.

"A beer right now would taste pretty damn good."

"Stop it," Mac said sharply.

Ralphs's hand was sweaty and he almost dropped his cell phone onto the sidewalk where he was still sprawled by the finish line. His voice shook. "You talking to me?"

"You know I am."

"Doper."

"Drunk."

It was a supposed to be funny but it held the sour aftertaste of truth. At the VA, they had started every run and workout with it. It was their own chant for survival.

"Call your sponsor," Mac said roughly.

"Is that what you'd do?"

Mac snorted.

"I'm asking," Ralph said. "*Is* that what you do?"

"I'd call my wife, but you don't have one of those."

"Your wife can't be much good," Ralph said. "You went to rehab."

"And I'm keeping clean. Now quit bothering me at work." Mac cradled his cell phone between his shoulder and chin while filling two steins with the house dark ale. Mac looked at the customers lined up along the bar and clotted in the rough wooden booths surrounding the small dance floor. "You still there?" he asked into the phone.

Ralph started to cry, sobs wracked his lean body like a series of seizures. They were so loud that Mac almost dropped the phone. "Where are you?" he asked again.

"F-Finished. At the finish line."

"Don't leave."

Mac shoved the cell into his pocket. "Garret!" He handed his brother-in-law the keys. "The bar's yours for the night. Don't steal anything but beer." Then he limped out the door.

The Hero's Half organizers were taking down the flags, folding up the tables, and loading the pickup parked at the curb. Mac's missing fingers had never bothered him but the stump, where fire and the devil with pitchfork lived, always ached. Booze had never helped but the Oxycodone had. And, he reminded himself, the running helped, too. He figured he would log a million miles before he died.

Mac handed Ralph a Gatorade. "What's going on?"

"I gotta have something to work for. My friend explained that to me. At least I think he's my friend."

Mac sighed. "Of course I'm your friend."

Ralph finished the liter and a half and let loose a rumbling burp. "Maybe I'll get married."

"Do you have anyone in mind?"

"Sort of. A woman in my last rehab group." Tears gathered in Ralph's eyes and rolled down a face pink and pitted with scar tissue. "Maybe, if I keep clean and work hard, she'll notice me and not because of my face and leg. Because of who I'm trying to be."

The wind had picked up and a cold rain soaked his jacket. Mac cracked the plastic lid of another Gatorade and handed it to Ralph. "And who's this person you want to be?"

"Somebody with a future. I've been thinking that I'll go back to college."

"*Back* to college?"

"I'm sorta working on my doctorate. In Science."

"We've run a couple hundred miles together and you neglected to tell me this."

Ralph's head was down. "It's like you said," he mumbled. "I'm trying to make lemonade."

"Fuck lemonade," Mac said. "And fuck life ever handing out peaches but do you remember that woman in a wheelchair, back when we first met? The one with the kid in her lap?"

"Can't forget her," Ralph said. "I keep hearing their laughter."

Mac put a steady hand on Ralph's shoulder. "If a woman in a wheelchair can laugh her way to the door, maybe we can, too."

Ralph nodded and stood up. "Okay. Maybe I can't laugh but I can run and I can go back to college..."

"And you can call me," Mac said. "Anytime."

"It's a start," Ralph said.

"One without that stupid fucking chant of survival," Mac said. And they both laughed.

THIS IS WHAT SHE KNEW

By the time she graduated from high school, Lolita Dorsey figured that God gave Adam and Eve a brain in order to punish them for screwing up in the Garden of Eden. There was no other reason for humans to be saddled with all those impossible ideals and desperate dreams, not to mention calculus and Latin. Her mother, the expert on disarray and destroyed possibilities, told her more than once, "Lolita, baby, you think too much. You'd be a whole lot happier if you just let things happen instead of trying to figure everything out." Of course that was before early-onset Alzheimer's took every shred of thought and language from a woman whose main hope for the future was to play a lot of bridge and enjoy her grandchildren.

Which Dorsey never planned to give her.

In college, Dorsey got engaged and her fiancé's favorite quote was, "Don't worry your pretty little head about it." That meant, don't ask why he was so distracted during sex or dinner or damn near anything that involved face-to-face intimacy, and especially don't ask where he went that one week when it wasn't even fishing season. He finally answered all those unarticulated questions by running off with an airline attendant – who happened to have great abs and a penis.

Dorsey hadn't found a life of fulfilled hopes and dreams in the Army and civilian life wasn't especially uplifting either because working for the government for the past ten years was all paper and scissors and no rocks. Dorsey's favorite part of the job was unsnapping her holster. That was when the adrenaline flushed through her veins and she felt hot all over – like just before an orgasm. She wanted more of that either in bed or out.

Her second favorite part of government work was putting a difficult case to rest. But the case she was assigned last spring was just some nutty kid (though twenty-four wasn't exactly a juvenile) and his schizophrenic mother waiting for the aliens to land their spaceship and take over the earth. Totally off-the-wall crazy shit like that; nothing that called for the unsnapping of a holster. Not to mention the fact that the case had gone nowhere and would never be put to rest or stashed in the completed file. Not until both the principles had died, which would be long after Dorsey, herself, was diagnosed with pre-Alzheimer's and planted in the ground having (hopefully) found the courage and presence of mind to blow her brains out with her handy-dandy little .25 which was the privately owned gun she kept in the trunk of her car.

Of course there was the off chance that the psycho son, Danny, would start making bombs again, now that his mother had gone into the loony bin and wasn't available to boss him around and monitor every waking hour of his day. And if Dorsey got lucky, and the kid started up with the boom-booms, as a female field agent, she could throw herself onto a lump of plastic explosive and be seen as a hero instead of some pathetic creature overwhelmed by the swift progression of a disease that robbed a person of the ability to put one's clothes on right side out. But as Dorsey's own mother had told her, continually, all through elementary school, high school, and community college, "Don't get your hopes up, kiddo." It was the single-most sensible thing the woman had ever said.

In the meantime, Dorsey was going to keep an eye on the potential bomb builder in the Hansen household which meant twice a month she knocked on the door of the little bungalow in Seattle and invited herself to dinner. The older sister, Sharon, was sane and thus the one who held things together. She wasn't that good of a cook so Dorsey usually brought a bag of groceries and fixed something quick like shrimp Alfredo or Thai stir fry or once in awhile she'd take the time to roast a chicken with Mediterranean veggies and couscous on the side and bring baklava for dessert from the hole-in-the-wall

Turkish restaurant on the corner of Broadway and Pine. Or, if Dorsey didn't bring dessert, they'd all have a bowl of ice cream while watching the Sci-Fi channel. Then Dorsey would go home.

Not exactly regulation keeping-an-eye-on-things but it was better than your standard surveillance which meant Dorsey scrunched in the front seat of her non-government issue Mustang, bored out of her mind, eating fast food and wishing she could go pee. It also got nutty Danny comfortable enough to stop doing the stupid robotic beeping and clicking that he usually did when stressed and the sister actually seemed to appreciate the company. Pretty soon it went from twice a month to a bi-weekly party along with a couple of neighbors and Sharon's roommate, Ralph. He sometimes gave Dorsey's food budget a break by bringing Pike Place Market salmon to grill along with corn on the cob and a watermelon.

Except, Dorsey thought. Except last night which was a complete and total fiasco because it was Danny's twenty-fourth birthday and Dorsey had brought a couple bottles of champagne which nobody drank. Since she'd already opened the first bottle, Dorsey polished off the whole thing herself. Before that, though, came the undoing.

"How was I to know you're all on the wagon?"

"It's probably in our file," Sharon said.

Dorsey reached into the cupboard for a wineglass that was shaped like an elongated tear. "Yeah, but I got to know you guys and the file stuff sort of went out the window."

"What the hell," Sharon said, "I'll have some, too. We'll toast to Danny's mental health."

"I thought you were on the wagon."

"I am but, like you said, it's Danny's birthday." Sharon uncorked the champagne which made a fine popping sound and frothed just a little over the lip of the opening. "You only turn twenty-four once in your life. Thank God for that." Sharon had gotten married at age twenty-four. It hadn't turned out to be a good year. She was trying to decide if her husband was worth divorcing or if she should just shoot him. She had discussed this with Dorsey one night during a particularly boring double rerun of The X-Files.

"How many days have you been sober?" Dorsey asked.

"Months and months." Sharon poured liquid the color of aged pearls into Dorsey's glass and reached for her own delicate crystal but Ralph, her roommate, came into the kitchen and exchanged it for a water glass filled with icy lemonade. He was that way, Dorsey noticed. Never finding fault or raising his voice but always making sobriety happen. Well screw that. The last thing Dorsey wanted was a sobriety enabler.

Dorsey took a deep drink and said, "Happy Birthday, Danny. May the force be with you."

Danny turned a fluorescent shade of pink and grinned all during dinner and dessert which included a homemade birthday cake covered with fluffy frosting and enough toasted coconut to look like it had been dragged through a bale of hay. Dorsey wasn't hungry so didn't bother to fill her plate with either dinner or dessert.

Instead, she drank one magnum of champagne and started on the other, which some folks would think meant she should climb up on that wagon along with the rest of Hansen clan but she couldn't let a $35 bottle of good cheer go flat. Nobody could do that. Dorsey was running on borrowed time, looking early-onset straight in the face. She needed all the false courage she could get.

Hours later, they put her to bed on the couch in the living room and covered her with a homemade quilt. She awoke to a silent house and a splitting headache. The clock on the bookcase said nine-thirty which meant she'd been out for twelve hours, missing out on all the morning rituals of showers and breakfast and feeding the pets.

Shit, another blackout.

Dorsey had not planned on turning into a drunk, but the brain, once again, had not cooperated by keeping her on the straight and narrow. It had, instead, colluded with the innermost fear-demons that lived under her heart and wanted in the worst way to get drunk and stay drunk for ever and ever, amen.

She heard the dogs snuffling around the back porch and the cats were curled up in a puddle of sun on the rug. *This is here*, she thought. *This is now*. After the dizziness subsided and as soon as she got her headache under control, she would go to the gym. That was safer than the Dojo which she hadn't been to in way too long and the calluses on her hands were starting to get soft. Also her timing was going and she couldn't remember what the hell she'd done with the white pajamas all Tai Kwon Do students wore. Next week she'd start running, again. Sure, like that would happen.

She threw back the quilt and that's when she noticed her clothes had vanished (except for her sandals) and her nude body was covered with indelible black marker – mountain scenes and raging oceans seemed to the basic theme this time with some nonsensical curlicues twirling around her nipples and twining down her legs to her ankles and feet. The pale thatch of her pubic area was surrounded by birds and bees. Jesus, she really must have tied one on. She hadn't gone with the birds and bees theme for months.

Groaning, she got off the couch, wrapped the quilt around her and scuffed through the house, looking for lost clothes. She couldn't find them anywhere, not even the bathroom, but the washing machine on the back porch was thumping out a spin cycle, so perhaps Sharon-the-Compulsive was doing Dorsey's laundry.

That's when the telephone rang.

"You're up," Sharon said. "There's Aspirin in the medicine chest and a bottle of Tums in my bedroom on the bookcase."

"My clothes are gone."

"You got kind of crazy there toward the end but we're used to crazy so don't worry about it. If you're going to keep stalking us, you might want to cut back on the booze."

"I'm not stalking you."

"Sure you are."

"It's a job, Sharon. It's either me or a bunch of people who don't really give a crap about your family. They are coldhearted mean-assed bureaucrats who only care about getting assigned to Washington DC. I'm not like that."

"So you say."

"Where are my clothes?"

"In the washing machine. You'll have to run them through the dryer; the fabric softener is in the cupboard."

"This is fucking embarrassing."

"Good."

"Where is everyone?"

"Ralph has taken Danny to Science Center. They'll be back before dinner. I'm at work and I won't get off until five."

"I'll be gone before then."

"You promised us a Thanksgiving dinner: turkey, dressing, potatoes and gravy, candied yams, fruit salad, pecan pie. The boys are counting on it."

"I'm sick. The whole idea of food makes me want to puke."

"That's what a hangover is all about."

"I'm not cooking dinner."

"Ralph went to the store early this morning and bought everything you need."

Dorsey didn't want to keep the conversation going, but her brain, that stupid detail-loving entity, couldn't let it go. "Everything? What about heavy whip cream for the salad and pie? It doesn't whip right if you get the thin stuff."

"He got the extra heavy."

"And marshmallows for the sweet potatoes?"

"He got the little ones."

"What kind of cranberry sauce did he get?"

"Both kinds – the jelled and the lumpy."

Dorsey was becoming more and more familiar with defeat. It was around every corner. "Okay, but just this once."

"The boys will be very happy."

"What about you? Will you be happy?"

Sharon's answer was a long time in coming and, when she did speak, she sounded tired. "Yes Dorsey, I'll be happy."

Dorsey ate three Aspirin, drank a glass of milk and settled in to wait for the clothes to get done. That's when it hit her. *They left me here, alone.* Dorsey couldn't believe they trusted her that much. Or were naïve enough to think she'd respect their privacy. Maybe she could toss the place, discretely, and have something worthwhile to tell her supervisor – the asshole who had put her on ninety days of leave – something that would pull the fat out of the fire and get her back to work.

But she wasn't going to do it naked or wearing a quilt. The last thing she needed was Ralph-the-Honorable or Danny-the-Weird to walk in on her. She'd toss the place dressed or she wouldn't toss it at all.

She made ginger tea to settle her stomach and dumped in two globs of honey. After the cup was empty, she transferred everything (khakis, long-sleeved tee, and undies) to the dryer, threw in a sheet of fabric softener and went back to the living room to wait. There was a dog-eared book next to the TV remote titled, 'How to Improve Your Life'. It was the kind of book Dorsey used to read and she flipped through it idly as she waited for the dryer to stop thumping.

The flysheet read, *Daniel Hansen, 2008*, so it was given to him a couple years after his breakdown. Before then he was the brightest star of all, winning early entrance into MIT and scaring the crap out of his older classmates with his quick grasp of mathematical concepts. The spiral downward was quick and complete and his first hospitalization was before he had enough beard to shave everyday. But his brain was spinning like her clothes, except with no fabric softener to keep things from sticking together in the wrong order.

Maybe that's what the year of meth was about – later, when he was released, living under a bridge and trying to keep things from making the wrong connections. Or maybe he just liked the high. Anyway, he was here now, sober and clean, and living with his sister.

Dorsey thumbed through the book and started reading the first place she saw yellow highlighter – which was at the check list a couple pages in.

1. *Pick your goals*
2. *Set your priorities*
3. *Believe in yourself.*
4. *Practise a healthy lifestyle.*
5. *Develop satisfying personal relationships.*

She read the list twice and felt the old twisting knot in her stomach that wasn't a hangover but probably because number five really hit home. All of her personal relationships sucked. Not to mention the fact that her supervisor had always given her crap about number four. Who the hell wanted to practise a healthy lifestyle? Number three was a problem, too, because of her job which she didn't like, really, and not just because she had never believed in herself. If she could figure out how the hell to accomplish one and two – the old picking your goals and setting your priorities that seemed to be in the first chapter of every how-to book she'd every read – she wouldn't have to deal with the rest of the crap on the list.

Dorsey threw the book across the room and went to the porch to see if the dryer had succeeded in getting things damp at least. She could wear damp clothing. Half the things she put on in the morning were damp.

Everything in the dryer was wet because she'd forgotten to set the heat dial. They'd been bumping around in cold air and Dorsey thought maybe she'd just toss the place then drive home buck naked, except for the etching of black marks that covered her body. Truckers could see down into her Mustang. The last thing she needed was some trucker's horn to start beeping out a tattoo of non-Morse code.

She went into Sharon's room and tried on shirts and pants but everything was either too short or too tight because Dorsey was almost six feet tall and Sharon wasn't. Also, Sharon didn't lift weights or crack bricks with her bare hands and Dorsey did. Or had. She'd slacked off the past couple months but muscles didn't wither in that short period of time. Not by much, anyway.

The walls of Sharon's room were littered with nail holes. Dorsey figured they were for framed pictures and she found the stash (along with a white wedding photo album) in the back of the closet, under a sleeping bag and seventeen pair of shoes. Who would have thought that someone like Sharon, someone who never wore a dress, would have that many shoes? Among the sandals and boots, cross trainers, moccasins, loafers and slip-ons, were five pair of four inch satin heels, in brilliant shades of pink, turquoise, navy, green and a scuffed white. Bride's maid's heels, no doubt except the white ones would be from her own wedding where she married the man known throughout Seattle as Steven the Whore.

All of the framed pictures were of the philandering ex-husband. There were pictures of him hiking, roasting marshmallows at the beach, and hoisting a rattler above his head. There was even a fuzzy close-up of him in a Speedo, with a hard-on, sticking out a long (and pierced) tongue. Dorsey took that one to the window, pulled back the curtain and tipped the frame so that light danced off the surface of the glass. The quilt kept slipping so she dropped it altogether. Her pale skin with its tracings of fauna and flora, amid the shadows of the room, looked like an engraved etching by Albrecht Durer. Squinting at the photograph, making sense of the time and place of it, her body went hot all over and she felt a shiver start in her ribcage and work its way downward and outward until she was covered with goosebumps and even her teeth were chattering. *Fuck, I know him.*

That's when the dogs started barking and Ralph, the boyfriend, walked into the house. Dorsey grabbed the quilt, wrapped the faded pattern of triangles and squares around her shoulders, and stood perfectly still, half-hidden behind the bedroom curtains. Ralph clomped into the kitchen, headed right to the refrigerator, took something out and poured it in a glass. He went into the bathroom and peed, the sound of gushing urine loud because he hadn't shut the door. The dogs were going crazy out back, but he didn't join them or yell at them to pipe down. He came into the bedroom, probably to get the leashes that were coiled over a hook by the closet door.

When he saw her, his words were not warm and friendly. "What the hell are you doing in here?"

"Where's Danny?"

"Out back, playing with Silky and Stinky."

"I thought you were going to the Aquarium."

"It's Monday. We forgot that it's closed on Monday. You didn't answer my question."

"I don't have any clothes," Dorsey said, as if that would explain why she was clutching the quilt along with the picture of Sharon's almost-ex-husband. "Mine are still wet."

"I'll get you something," Ralph said.

Dorsey scuffed back to the living room, sinking into the rump-sprung easy chair, holding the photograph carefully. "He didn't have a mustache back then and his head was shaved. In fact, his whole body was."

"What are you talking about?" Ralph was in the front bedroom, opening drawers.

"Sharon's husband. He was a platform diver in college. He could do three half-gainers with a double twist. He went to Regionals. They called him Splash. I didn't know his real name." She was babbling because she had gone from cold to hot and everything came back like someone throwing a bucket of ice water over her head. She barely remembered the event because she was half tanked and her pantyhose were around her ankles as they grappled in the back of his

Escort station wagon. Dorsey was supposed to go to the dance with the football captain (who had a Camaro) but he was in Detox so she'd ended up with the friend of someone's brother, a guy who wasn't in a fraternity. "It was the best sex I ever had."

Ralph came into the living room holding out military sweats pocked with ragged holes and a faded SEMPER FI on the back of the shirt.

Dorsey's head hurt. She'd had over thirty sexual encounters trying to replicate that single orgasmic night in the beater Escort wagon. Fuck, life was just too hard sometimes. "What do you think about sex?" she asked. "Do you think it's the most important thing in a relationship?"

"Are you asking about the biological imperative or are you asking about a one night stand?"

"It's a simple fucking question! Just give me a fucking answer."

"You swear too much."

"And you're an idiot in love with a woman who doesn't even know you're alive!"

His eyes were a flat gray, like the ocean on a cloudy day, or a stone found at the bottom of a river or old ice at the back of the freezer. He sat on the couch, hands holding the sweats loosely. His voice was low and there didn't seem to be any anger in it, only sadness. "This is what I know," he said, "and this is what you know, too, but don't want to face. You can never be smart enough, Dorsey, or strong enough or drunk enough. Your mother has Alzheimer's and you have not been given the gift of denial so you search your mind hourly to see if you remember what a house key is for and where a boat belongs. You know it, your boss knows it and all of us here, in this house, know it. I'm sorry but there's nothing much anyone can do to change that. Maybe there's a cutting edge experiment or gene therapy or maybe a brain transplant available someplace but probably not. The only thing you can do is put one foot in front of the other and try to live a life you're not ashamed of."

Danny came in then, for a drink of water. He saw Dorsey on the couch, tears creeping down her cheeks, and his face turned that brilliant pink. The one she remembered from the night before. Probably he had a crush on her. Or maybe he was shy. Who the hell knew?

"I like turkey," Danny said. Then he went back out to bring the dogs around front.

Ralph dropped his sweats on the couch between them, took the leashes from the Sharon's bedroom and went to join Danny and the dogs. Ralph was working on a half a marathon and Danny was training for a 10-K. The dogs were just along for the fun of it.

Dorsey sank back into the couch and when she woke up her headache was gone and the dryer was silent. She borrowed some shampoo from under the sink and a razor from Ralph or maybe it was Danny's. When she took a shower it turned out the pen's ink wasn't all that indelible. As she scrubbed various images washed down the drain; the birds and bees, the twirls and curlicues, the Webster's Dictionary definition of Alzheimer's written across her belly. After most of it was gone, she washed her hair, shaved her legs and under her arms and dressed in her own clothes.

She wandered into the kitchen where the tang of apples and oranges mingled with the spices lined up beside the stove burners. She checked the refrigerator, the cupboards, the counter, and the drawer under the stove where the pots and pans were kept. Everything was there, waiting. The turkey, the fruit and vegetables, the nuts for the pecan pie, two kinds of cranberry sauce. The roaster pan and fine china. All of it.

Her brain clicked along, figuring out cooking sequences and how to double the recipe for gravy. She found an apron in the towel drawer. She put it on and reached for the oven's temperature dial.

If it wasn't perfect, if she forgot how to make the stuffing or what a potato masher was for, it wouldn't matter. She would ignore the empty champagne bottles languishing in the recycling bin. She wouldn't check to see if an inch or two of flattened liquid remained or to climb into her car to drive to the liquor store. Like the ingredients for dinner, what she needed was already here, in this houseful of sobriety enablers.

At the end of her career, knowing she wouldn't be called back from her furlough, but before early onset gobbled her alive, Lolita Dorsey could put one foot in front of another. She could find affection in the most unlikely of places. She could almost be happy. This was what she knew.

PASSING THE TORCH

December 3rd

Joseph and I are house sitting for my father who has decided that Seattle's icy winter rains are the reason his life is going down the crapper – his words, not mine – so he is currently drinking too much in a time-share condo in Hawaii. My mother and sister are also experiencing sunshine but in the Southern Hemisphere because my narcissistic mother always wanted to paint the Chilean Andes and my anorectic sister would rather spend two months running errands for Mother than eating a decent breakfast with me. Plus my Alaskan teaching position was postponed (first because of the sequestration and then because of the weather) and so I am sleeping on a double-wide blowup mattress in what used to be my bedroom.

I know, too much information, but it seems information *sans* power is all I have these days. My only task is to wince and take straight-in-the-face whatever comes my way.

December 12th

Sharon and Ralph are on their month-long Honeymoon to France so the torch-of-responsibility, so to speak, has been passed onto Joseph and me only because I once lived across the street from Ralph and because Joseph and Ralph are friends. The torch is Sharon's twenty-five year old brother, Danny, who looks sane but almost everyone in my very own biological family looks sane so I know appearances can be deceiving. Danny needed consistency, familiar surroundings and the regular dosage of anti-psychotic medication – which meant he needed to stay where he was and Joseph and I were supposed to provide a kind of respite care. That's what the social worker called it and I can see that most people in the world can use a little respite at one time or another.

I don't mind temporarily living at their place and sleeping in an actual bed and I don't mind feeding the dogs, cats and rabbit. Picking up the poop isn't fun so I arranged to pay the kid across the alley to do that. He was a skinny twelve year old with a Justin Bieber haircut and dorky glasses. "Fifteen bucks a day," he said.

"Not in your wildest dreams."

"There are a lot of animals here and all them poop."

"Okay, a buck a day an animal."

I should have talked it over with Joseph but he was at the store, picking up prescription drugs, doggie kibble, Kitty litter and rabbit pellets. Sometimes decisions can't be made in a communal fashion. Sometimes timing is all. I did the mental math and nodded.

The kid grinned and I knew I'd been had but it was *poop* so I didn't care.

"You should have dickered more." Joseph was unloading a bag of groceries. He put eggs in the refrigerator and bakery brownies in the cupboard over the refrigerator. "The kid would have done it for a dollar a day, easy."

I did not shrug or grimace or even frown. Instead, I pointed out the kitchen window to the semi-frozen brown clumps by the magnolia bush. "And you could be expected to do it for free."

"Good point."

"I would do it for free." And there he was, the proffered torch I didn't especially want but couldn't dodge, standing in the doorway holding a fifty pound bag of Purina One dog food.

"It's okay, Danny," Joseph said, "you can take a break from handling the poop. You can pet the cats and run the dogs and do whatever the hell you do with a rabbit."

"You mostly leave it alone," Danny said.

"Excellent. You can certainly do that. Besides," Joseph said, squinting at the small print on the literature that accompanied the newest batch of anti-crazy pills, "the kid probably needs the money."

Danny nodded and headed toward the back porch where the chew toys and other by-products of dedicated petmanship were kept. The fifty pound bag didn't seem to slow him down. I did not find that comforting.

"I need the car keys," I said a little too quickly. "I need to pick up the mail and water the plants and check the answering machine back home."

Joseph gave me a long look and held out the keys. When I reached to snatch them from his hand, he pulled me in for a hug and whispered, "I'll keep him plenty medicated."

"What if you make a mistake and overdose him?"

"Then he has diarrhea all night and we'll pay the kid across the alley to clean up."

The drive to my father's house took half an hour, mostly because the city was filling potholes and orange flags were everywhere. I entered through the garage and let the kitchen faucet run before filling a pitcher with cold water. The violets in the kitchen window were not flourishing, but I soaked them anyway. The barrel cactus in the den didn't need any moisture whatsoever. The orchid in Leslie's old room was dead, so I dumped it in the semi-frozen dirt by the back porch. I left the pitcher on the counter and took a deep breath. The almost empty house was not as comforting as I had hoped it would be. The rooms were cold, the silence was unnerving and there was a faint smell of barf in the bathrooms – a good-bye present from my anorectic sister.

Downstairs, there were no messages on the answering machine or faxes in my father's den. There was mail, though, piles of it spread over the dark tile of the entryway floor and some had even fluttered onto the white living room rug. The mail carriers must have hated cramming all those ads through the slot in the front door. I certainly hated sorting it out and dumping one hundred percent of it in the recycle box. Most of what I kept appeared to be bills for my father, but there were two envelopes for me. One was from the university alumni association asking for money. The other was from the school district where I used to teach. They were asking if I was interested in being on the "sub list". I tossed the former and slipped the latter in the pocket of my coat. I stuffed my father's mail into one of the self-addressed postage paid envelopes on his desk and dropped it in the corner mailbox. Then I drove back to the house that Sharon and Ralph shared with Danny.

When I walked through the front door, the smell of spaghetti sauce and garlic bread floated on warm, steamy air. Joseph's favorite opera, *Carmen*, was playing softly and Danny was on the couch, wearing headphones and watching old reruns of 'The X-Files' while petting the three cats piled on his lap. Joseph sauntered from the kitchen and said, "The pasta is almost done and it's your turn to set the table."

"I've never seen you in a frilly apron before," I said.

"What do you think?"

I found myself smiling. "I like it."

"So, this two weeks could work out for us?"

"Depends on how often you do the apron thing."

"With or without my jeans?"

"Either way," I said. "I'm flexible."

"Indeed you are."

Later, while Danny did the dishes and Joseph worked on his research paper, I took the clothes out of the dryer and began folding towels and tee shirts. I found it troubling that living with Joseph in a strange house (while babysitting a certifiable lunatic) felt far more comfortable than living in the home of my childhood. Or, truth be told, even simply co-existing anywhere with any of the members of my biological family.

December 13th

Through the magic of modern communication, Danny was in the kitchen Skyping with his mother, while Joseph was in the living room Skyping with his advisor. I was in the backyard dividing my time between Googling cookie recipes on my phone and watching icicles lengthen along the eaves of the porch. I was also hypothesizing the total number of strings of holiday lights we would need along said eaves. Notice I said "holiday" and not "Christmas". That's because I am a non-practising Jew, Joseph is a non-practising Buddhist and the owners of the house were non-religious scientists. But Danny loved lights and so there you have it. Lunacy wins every time.

Not that we – each and all – didn't benefit from the deeply rooted heritage of Christmas sales, multiple presents from Santa and all that yummy food. We did benefit and were anticipating the upcoming festivities probably as much as all of the practising Christians in the neighborhood were.

When I came inside, Danny had made cocoa with softening marshmallows. He handed me a mug of the ambrosia of my childhood. I took a sip and nodded and the worried frown on his face morphed into something almost normal.

"Tasty," I said. "Do you have any holiday decorations?"

He shook his head.

"Maybe in the attic? Or in somebody's closet?"

"No."

"So we need to go buy lights?"

He nodded.

"I – I'll check with Joseph," I said. "Maybe he can go this weekend."

"Joseph is busy," Danny said. "He has finals."

"Right."

"I can't go by myself."

I sipped more cocoa while Danny continued to stand and stare at me. For a long time. When my cup was empty he put it in the sink. His hands shook. "Okay," I said, "let me think about it. I'll get back to you."

"When?"

"Tomorrow. I'll get back to you tomorrow."

That night, while Danny was watching a NetFlix extravaganza involving every 'Star Wars' ever made, including the cartoon versions, I brushed my hair and broached the subject of holiday lights with Joseph.

"I have finals next week," Joseph said.

"Maybe he can go alone," I countered.

Joseph said nothing, in that no words came out of his mouth, but his look spoke volumes.

"You are going to be a therapist," I said. "You counsel perverts and you run a weekly group for crazy caretakers."

"*Exhausted* caretakers," he countered.

"But, my point is, you're used to hanging around with lunatics."

"So are you," he said. "Observe your own family."

I went into the bathroom and sulked. Then I took a long shower which involved shaving my legs, under my arms and washing my hair. Then I gave myself a talking to while using the hair dryer. Then I opened the door to the bedroom but Joseph was already asleep.

December 14th

Danny drove his mother's van to the nearest mall and parked in the handicap zone. "Are you sure this is legal?" I asked.

"The van has a handicap license plate."

"But you and I aren't physically disabled," I said. "We could get a ticket, not to mention how very wrong this is. What if there is someone who really needs to park this close?"

"I don't walk."

"Of course you walk. You run, too. You're signed up for a half marathon."

"I don't walk without Ralph or Sharon." His next words were muffled but I could still understand them. "And Joseph is okay, too. But I don't know about you."

A mall security car, complete with lights and a siren, turned into the lot and slowly inched our way. It eased closer and closer until it paused directly behind the van. Exhaust fumes formed dark clouds in the light rain and a woman in uniform rolled down her window. I broke out in a sweat and Danny wrenched open his door, walked to the back of the van and threw up his breakfast.

The security car window was quickly rolled up and the vehicle moved away from the steamy pile at an amazing speed. Danny motioned for me to get out, wiped his mouth on the sleeve of his jacket, locked up the van and said, "Okay. I'm ready."

I wasn't sure that having a non-obvious disability was the actual intention of a handicap license, but I kept telling myself that I would Google the matter when I got home plus there were dozens of vacant slots equally close to the main doors. That's because the mall didn't technically open for another hour.

The food court was open so we went inside. Even with the individual store gates down, the mall's holiday spirit was unrelenting. We made it as far as the pizza place before Danny started making weird robot beeps and clicks.

"Let's go back to the car," I said, but he clenched his fists and shook his head.

Santa and the elves were having some kind of pep talk in the open space by the fountain and a photographer was stuffing batteries into her digital camera. The kiosk owners were putting out leather slippers and pictorial calendars and Happy New Year banners. There were also Valentines and St. Patrick's day decorations, but we were here for Christmas lights so I didn't accidentally spit and curse at the way-too-early displays but followed Danny the Weird.

A platoon of gray-haired (or balding) mall walkers were circling the drain in their canes and running shoes. I counted four charity Christmas trees before we reached the first intersection leading to the big name stores. The trees were labeled: Infant-Preschool; Elementary School; High School; High School Homeless. There were piles of presents under every tree but the one labeled 'High School Homeless'. Apparently that group was not going to get anything from Santa, not even coal.

"Please," I said, "can we just go back? I hate this and I'm not the one who's cr..." I was going to say "the one who's crazy" but Danny ended the sentence in a voice that was distressingly metallic.

"... you're not the one who's Christian?"

"Sure," I said.

I found myself in front of the High School Homeless tree and plucked a couple of the paper bells. It had the gender, age, and the clothing need list of a teen who not only wouldn't have presents but might not even have a tree or a table. I turned to show the slips of paper to Danny but he wasn't paying attention. He was at a kiosk a few steps beyond the Information Booth. A frowning middle-aged elf stood in front of stuffed reindeer, motion-sensor Santas and boxes of lights in the various shapes of Christmas. There were angel lights and star lights and dripping-from-the-eaves lights. There were multi-colored lights and single strands of red, green and blue. There were flood lights and a cluster of lights that blinked incessantly. There were also plastic packets of inflatable manger scenes, door wreaths and three-tiered snowmen.

The mall music became even more frenetic and the lights overhead brightened. I heard the rattling clang as dozens of metal window gates slid open. I crammed the red construction paper bells into my coat pocket and felt the crinkle of the letter from the school district. I didn't know if I should let pride keep me from working, but it didn't seem fair that I was now wanted to do the same work for less pay and no health insurance. I could have immersed myself in a full blown mental rant, but Danny was gesturing wildly and beeping like a terrified alien from the planet Zircon. The elf did not look happy and two uniformed security guards were headed our way, also not looking filled with holiday cheer. I grabbed four boxes of something-on-sale, put a twenty on the cash register and pulled Danny away from the excesses of holiday cheer and back toward the excesses of another kind, also known as the Food Court.

He muttered and clicked at the condiments counter while I got us both a corn dog. I steered him through the exit doors but he wouldn't get into the van because of some no-eating-in-the-vehicle rule his also-crazy mother had received from some non-existent planet back when he was ten. So we sat on a metal bench beside the waste cans, shivering. He took a bite, chewed, swallowed and whispered, "It's just so hard. I want to be, like, normal but it's so hard."

I used my teeth to rip open the packet of mustard and squeezed a smear onto my own greasy treat. "I know," I said, "that's what my sister says, sometimes."

"Is she like me?"

"Not exactly. She can't eat without running to the toilet and puking."

Danny took another bite, chewed and swallowed. "And people get mad at her and say she's just not trying hard enough."

I sighed and nodded.

When we were both finished eating, I stood to put our napkins and corn dog sticks in the trash can and saw one of the security guards was inside. His eyes were on Danny and the bag with our holiday purchase was at his feet. I had, apparently, left it in the Food Court. The guard was tall, buff and black. He motioned me inside with the barest wave of his fingers. When I stepped through the doors, he bent to pick up the sack of lights. "He going to be okay?"

"Maybe."

"My cousin is like that." The guard's dark eyes stayed locked on Danny. "I guess every family has somebody."

"I guess." I took the bag of lights. "Are you going to ban him from coming to the mall?"

The guard looked surprised. "Why would I do that?"

"For making a disturbance."

"He's going to have to make a bigger mess than puking in the parking lot and upsetting a fat elf – especially one who comes to work half-drunk and crabby." The guard looked past me at the van in the handicap zone. "Every day I deal with snotty teenagers, toddlers who throw real tantrums and senior citizens that pee and poop in their pants then dribble in front of the drinking fountain." The suddenly sad, dark eyes returned to me. "We don't ban them."

I let go of a shaky laugh and the guard tipped his hat. "Have a nice day," he said and headed back through the Food Court.

I got in the old van and fastened my seatbelt. Danny put it in gear and backed carefully out of the slot.

"Thank you for coming with me," Danny whispered.

"You're welcome," I replied.

December 15th

It was nine days before Christmas Eve and I had stopped listening to the car radio and my jaws hurt from grinding my teeth every time I turned on my computer. That's because I was one commercial away from taking a hammer to every decibel of holiday cheer not to mention the deep desire I had to throw the flatscreen television into the street – all because of the jingling bells and Christmas choirs, not to mention the twinkling Santas and dancing reindeer ads.

"Relax," Joseph said. At least I think that's what he said. Danny had made three kinds of candy and Joseph was wrapping and periodically taste-testing the caramels. I was bagging the peanut brittle which was almost as good as the fudge which was already cut and boxed for gifts.

"We need a tree," Danny said.

Joseph swallowed and took a drink of coffee and looked at me. I folded my arms and shook my head. "We could get an artificial tree," Joseph said. "They come with lights and everything."

Danny nodded. "And we need cookies."

Joseph didn't even look at me. "I will bake the cookies," he said.

"We need the lights up outside," Danny said.

"Fine," I said. "I'll put up the... lights." I was going to say the "stupid-assed effing lights" but Crazy-Danny's face was suddenly bright with happiness. I had never seen his full-bore smile and it was a little startling to see how drop-dead handsome he was.

Joseph got up from the table and gave me a sticky kiss. "I know you hate this," he whispered, "but I will truly make it up to you."

"Yes, you will."

"It's just hard for him, being without his family over the holidays."

"It's hard for a lot of people," I said. I snagged my coat from the closet and headed for the ladder, which leaned against the front porch.

Years ago, when the house was younger and a completely different color, someone had gone to the trouble of placing little hooks along the roof line. I surmised that the purpose of said hooks was not to make the annual hanging of lights easier but to complete some OCD need to have everything line up perfectly. Some of the hooks had snapped off in the intervening years which meant this latter-day string of colored lights sank and soared and trickled and dripped and I was not inclined to change that. Instead I took a perverse satisfaction in doing a truly crappy job of putting up four strings of lights along the chipped trim of the front of the house.

Joseph, the perfectionist, looked like he might hyperventilate and pass out on the porch. Crazy-Danny didn't look sick. He smiled and nodded as if the looped and sagging lights were a bright message from his childhood. Which, perhaps, they were. Joseph put his head down, zipped up his waterproof parka and silently left in his electric car – on his way to pick out an artificial tree – while Danny moved the ladder around to the back of the house.

When Danny was back in the kitchen, boxing the caramels, I pulled on my gloves and headed out to loop three more strings of lights from the porch to the dog house and back again. Showing up once a day, the kid across the alley had done a pretty decent job with the poop, but Ralph and Sharon's smaller dog, a terrier, was what I thought of as an excitable defecator. Sometimes raccoons would set her off and sometimes, simply waiting for the food wagon to come around, her bowels would release gooey little Tootsie Rolls into the rain-sogged dirt around their dish.

I knew that and should have been aware of the potential for slippage, but I was busy grumbling about feeling unappreciated. So I stepped in one of the freshly made pellets and fell, heavily, against the doghouse. Then the ladder collapsed on top of me and my face instantly felt both wet and numb at the same time.

It wasn't my crying that called Danny from the house. It was the hysterical barking of the dogs.

I expected him to become the schizo-robot boy and huddle under a tree or crouch and rock incessantly while making clicking and beeping sounds. The whole thing might have been funny if 1) it wasn't happening to me, and 2) I wasn't bleeding all over my favorite rain jacket. I struggled to my knees only to feel a sudden stabbing pain that went from my elbow to my wrist. Plus my ankle was also doing the stabbing pain thing.

Danny took one look and raced back into the house. I lay there, trying to gain the courage to try again when I felt a package of frozen peas being held against my face. When I opened my eyes I saw that Danny was knee-deep in poopy puppy pellets.

"Your eye is really swelling," he said. "Hold this and lay still."

I tried to lift my arm but the stabbing pain stopped me.

"Use your other hand." His voice was calm and measured. Almost like he was reading instruction out of an accident response handbook. He pressed a bath towel against the gash along my arm. "Your arm is bleeding pretty bad so I'm going to have to press down really hard."

That's when my own sobs outdid the yapping of the dogs. Mostly I screamed things like, "Stop it!" "Fuck, fuck!" and "What the hell are you doing!"

"I'm really sorry," Danny said, "but we have to stop the bleeding."

And then it began to rain in earnest.

"I fucking hate Christmas lights," I sobbed.

"We need to get inside. Can you stand?"

I shook my head.

"Okay," Danny said. "Okay."

He left again, tracking poop into the kitchen which would, I knew in some distant part of my brain, make Joseph very unhappy, and brought back a magazine and some duct tape. He quickly taped the gash shut and then curled the *National Geographic* around my arm in a kind of splint.

If I hadn't been in so much pain I might have congratulated him on his first-aid response, but I was busy swearing and begging him to stop it, dammit. Stop it right now!

Then, Danny, the young man who was training for a triathlon, bent over, picked me up and carried me to his mother's van and, one-handed, opened the door and gently set me in the passenger seat.

I didn't ask the question that never surfaced, *How do you know to do this?* but he answered it anyway.

"My mom is always falling," Danny said, "and I, you know, have to know how to help her."

Danny's mother was insane, certifiably, which was how Danny came to live with Ralph and Sharon. She was also a quarter of a ton overweight and bossy, to boot. Because of her silly rules, I had eaten a corn dog while sitting on a cold bench outside the mall. But the moment I heard Danny's words, I wanted to kiss the woman.

I don't remember much about the ride to the Urgent Care facility. I do remember Danny helping relieve me of my coat and how he held my hand as I sobbed during the x-ray process. My arm was dislocated at the elbow and the doctor put in eleven stitches before she did a twisting jerk that snapped it back into place. None of this was simple or painless, but after I threw up, I did feel marginally better. The x-ray tech lost interest as soon as it was clear that my ankle wasn't broken, "merely" sprained. They wrapped it in purple because Danny insisted on an outer wrap with "healing" powers plus it wouldn't show the dirt like white or beige.

Somehow that was the sentence that brought up pain of a non-physical kind.

"I am *not* dirty!"

"No, but the animals are."

Instant deflation. "Oh. Right. Okay."

He took the proffered crutches the Urgent Care nurse insisted upon, but then carried me back to the van. Once I was settled and the seatbelt snapped into position, he handed me his cell phone.

"What's this?"

"I called Joseph but you have to call your parents."

"No."

"Joseph said you would say no but you have to call them anyway."

"They won't care," I mumbled. "They will tell me about their own owies and then hang up before I get around to telling them about mine."

"You don't know that. This time might be different."

It was annoying that Crazy-Danny was giving me life-skill advice, but I took up the challenge, if only to prove my point. He punched in the numbers I gave and when my mother answered her first words were, "I can't talk now, dear, your sister and I on our way to book club."

"But I've hurt my elbow and leg and..."

"Is anything broken?"

"No, but..."

"Well, good. Call me tomorrow. Not in the morning, I always paint in the morning, and after lunch I need my nap. Oh, and your sister and I are going shopping later on. Perhaps you could email me in a couple days."

"Mom! It really hurts and the doctor says..."

"Oh, darling, don't make a fuss, I'm sure you'll feel better after a good night's rest."

And she hung up. Danny and I locked eyes and he didn't quite shake his head in disbelief. His own mother, after all, was probably equally self-serving. He held the phone out again and this time I punched in the numbers to my father's cell phone myself.

My father didn't answer. My father never answered. His voice mail said, "Leave a message if it's important, otherwise fuck off."

"Hi, Dad. It's me. I fell down and I have eleven stitches, a variety of bandages and bruises. Bye."

"He'll call you back, right?"

"Possibly."

"Your family sucks."

"And yours doesn't?

"Sharon is my sister and she doesn't suck."

I looked at the troubled face. "No," I said, "she certainly doesn't suck. And neither does her husband, Ralph."

"Joseph is my friend and he doesn't suck," Danny said.

"Friends are important," I mumbled.

"You don't either."

My face must have reflected the confusion I felt.

"You don't suck," Danny whispered. "You're almost my friend and you don't suck hardly at all."

I laughed then. It hurt my ribs and also my mouth but I laughed long and hard and it was a few minutes before I could lean forward and whisper in Crazy-Danny's ear. "You're almost my friend, too, and you suck just enough to be interesting."

He flushed a deep crimson then gave one of those abrupt head-bobs that means "thanks" or "Oh, crap, how embarrassing please let's just ignore each other for the next hour". He stuffed the cell phone into his jacket, put the van in drive and we headed toward home.

I didn't remember my coat until after he'd carried me into the living room and settled me on the couch with the cats. Danny said it was in the back of the van and he'd bring it in later. He mumbled something about papers in the pocket, but I fell asleep before he could finish whatever it was he was trying to tell me. When I woke up the house smelled of quiche and apple crumble. The *Barber of Seville* was playing softly in the background and I could hear Joseph bustling about the kitchen, his tenor trampling over the diva's aria and joining occasionally with the chorus.

"I have to go to the bathroom," I mumbled. The crutches were within reach, but Danny lifted and carried me into that small space. He sat me on edge of the tub and leaned against the sink.

"You have to leave," I said. "I am not tinkling or tooting with you in the room."

"I'll get Joseph."

"Not with him in the room either."

"Who will pull down your pants and wipe you?"

I felt the tears welling in my eyes. "Shit," I said.

"Exactly," Danny replied.

It turned out I didn't need Joseph for the hard stuff, just the getting down to business prep work. I don't know which of us was more grateful for that.

"You know I'd do the whole enchilada," Joseph said.

"Wrong image," I replied.

"You know what I mean." The relief in his voice was palpable.

We were talking though a closed door. I wiggled back into my panties and flushed the toilet. "If you want to be a help, get me some soap and a washrag."

"For your enchilada?"

"For my hands and face."

He came in then and zipped up my pants, wiped the smeared mascara from my cheeks and kissed the tip of my nose.

Dinner was a slice of quiche (mine was cut into small pieces) and a green salad. Joseph buttered my roll and Danny's gaze followed every bite I took. I was surprisingly hungry and, when my plate was clean, Joseph put warm apple crumble in front of me and Danny got up to get the ice cream. I'm not sure how he went from Crazy-Danny to just a regular guy sitting at the dinner table but I think it had to do with our talk in the Van.

Danny put a scoop of vanilla atop my crumble and dug out another one for Joseph. "Clarice called her mother," Danny said. "She called her father, too."

My spoon, the one in my barely functioning hand, stopped halfway to my mouth. Joseph cocked his head, listening and looking moderately interested. One of the reasons I love Joseph is his studied lack of drama.

"I don't like Clarice's parents," Danny continued. "They aren't very nice to her."

"You don't have to like them," Joseph said. "But if they ever return her calls or even show up in person, you do have to be polite to them."

"I don't want to be polite to them."

"Nobody does," Joseph said, "but we will be polite anyway."

Danny dropped a large scoop into his own bowl of crumble. "Okay," he said before heading back to the freezer.

"I don't need taking care of," I whispered to Joseph.

"Of course you do," he whispered back. "And I will do my best to take complete and carnal care of your enchilada tonight."

I took another bite of my dessert and looked at the two men in my life. One was putting the ice cream away and the other wiping crumble crumbs from my chin. "Okay," I said, "I can live with that."

December 22nd

The bruise that made me look like a one-eyed raccoon had faded to a mixture of purple and yellow and the stitches in my arm itched – which a Google check had confirmed was a good thing. I had mastered the art of hopping on one foot and was capable of reaching and entering every room in the house. I had perfected the bathroom prep work and the post work, too. I had even taken a morning shower – leaning heavily against Joseph while he lathered my hair and rinsed it. "I need a lot of conditioner," I said, "but not for how you are using it right now."

"Your enchilada doesn't need conditioning?"

"Maybe we can work out something later," I said. "When I'm not worried about getting soap in my eyes."

"Danny wants to go to the mall again," Joseph said.

"And why do I care?"

"I have fifty-seven essays to correct."

"Look at me," I said. "Do you really think I can go out in public like this?"

"Yes."

"Even if I wore a bag over my head, I can't walk."

"He can push you in his mother's wheelchair."

"No."

"He's worried about the kids."

"What are you babbling about?"

"He found the paper bells in your coat pocket. From the mall Holiday tree. He wants to buy a bunch of stuff for the High School Homeless teens."

"No."

"I would go with him, Clarice, but I really don't have time."

"No, no, no."

"Do you really want me to play the guilt card?"

"What guilt card?"

"The one where I remind you who took to you the Urgent Care facility and who is more worried about you than your parents."

"You can be such a shit, sometimes."

"Better than being one all the time."

"Tomorrow," I said.

"It has to be tonight."

"Why?"

"Because the presents have to be turned in tonight."

"I am truly not up for shopping for a hundred homeless teens."

"Danny already did the shopping. Online. And he paid to have everything shipped overnight Express."

"He can afford that?"

"I guess so." Joseph was combing the tangles out of my wet hair. "FedEx, UPS and the postal service. Everything should be here by dinnertime. You just need to go with him and get the stuff to the mall."

"Are you cooking tonight?"

"No. I told you. I have fifty-seven essays to grade."

I nodded. The Mall had a Food Court. I could have an unhealthy corn dog or crappy pizza or maybe phony Chinese along with music that wasn't an opera. Besides, Danny was no longer Crazy-Danny, but almost a friend. "Okay," I said. "I'll chaperone."

As the day wore on, the street in front of the house became a rotating parade of delivery trucks and postal carriers. It turned out that one of the envelopes was for me. My father had mailed a charge card with the scribbled note, 'For your insurance deductible' No 'Love, Dad' or 'hope you are feeling better'. Just a piece of plastic.

"Better than nothing," Joseph murmured.

"Absolutely better than my mother," I replied.

By seven o'clock, my stomach was grumbling but all the boxes of backpacks, winter jackets, sleeping bags and Swiss Army Knives had been delivered and stuffed into the back of Danny's van.

"Do they have to be wrapped?"

"No," Danny said, "Santa's Elves will wrap them."

"Okay," I said. "Let's get this show on the road because I'm starving."

Danny shifted into reverse. "That's right," he said, "we need to give them food, too."

"How much food?"

"Maybe a Food Court gift card."

I did the mental math. One hundred gifts cards at $10 each was a whole bunch of credit card debt.

"You've never been poor." Danny looked at me. "You have crappy parents but you've never lived on the street."

"And you have?"

He nodded.

"I've maxed out my credit," Danny said, "but you could, maybe, buy a couple of gift cards. You had the bells in your pocket."

"You were homeless," I said, "and you've turned out okay."

"Except for being crazy."

"But you couldn't help that and you are taking your medicine." I looked at him. "You *are* taking it, right?"

"I know how it feels to be cold," Danny said. "And I know how it feels to be helpless. These kids are trying to finish school. That's a big deal."

I didn't want to think about the real meaning of presents and Christmas but the comparison between my own pathetic not-homeless family and the generosity of the young man who sat beside me could not be ignored. I pulled my father's charge card from my pocket. "I'll get the food," I said. "What the hell, we'll get Food Court cards for $20 each."

Getting the packages from the van to the Homeless Holiday tree turned out to be easy. After we got the gift cards, Danny pushed me up and down the mall corridors until I saw the buff, black security guard – the one with the crazy-cousin and the one who might have an inkling about the strength of will it took for Danny to be there. The guard listened, with crossed arms and a frown, while he stared at the wheelchair and my face and bandages on various limbs. As Danny stared at his feet, I explained about holiday lights, doggie poop, Urgent Care and Homeless High Schoolers. The guard's frown slowly morphed into a beautiful smile and he told Danny to drive the van around to the shipping dock in back. We were met by a bevy of adults and teens whom I assumed were the present-wrapping Elves of Santa. They immediately began to load the boxes into a Salvation Army truck.

"Okay," Danny kept saying. "Okay." On the way back to the house, the Christmas carols on the radio didn't bother me and I didn't mind the incessantly twinkling lights adorning every yard and roof line. When we got home, Joseph ate the cold fish and chips we'd brought and listened to us tell the story of what I later came to think of as "Christmas at the Mall". He choked a bit when we got to the part describing how we paid for the Food Court gift cards, but Joseph was training to become a family therapist so he recovered quickly.

He dipped a slab of fish into tartar sauce, took a bite, chewed, wiped his mouth and said, "Sounds like you both had fun."

"We did," I said. Danny nodded furiously.

"Ralph and Sharon emailed," Joseph said. "They wondered if it was okay for them to take a later flight back."

"They won't be here for Christmas?" Danny asked.

"No, but they will be here for New Year's." Joseph took another bite of fish and went through the same sequence. "It's fine with me but it depends on how you two feel."

I thought about the whole 'passing the torch' concept and it didn't take long for me to come up with an answer I liked. "Okay by me," I said.

"Yes," Danny agreed. "Clarice and I are good with being almost sucky friends."

Joseph did choke, then, and Danny and I laughed and laughed and for the first time in years I was looking forward to Christmas. Not only because I didn't have to deal with my crazy family but because I was privileged to deal with a crazy friend who really wasn't all that sucky when you got to know him.

DRINKING POEMS

Three of them sat in the tavern, waiting for Mac's ex-brother-in-law, a man who was perpetually late, which explained why Uncle Joe was staring at the clock, Mandy was jiggling her foot and Mac was playing pretend drums on the bar's scarred surface.

Uncle Joe took a sip of his beer and started a counterpoint to Mac's drumming. He was pretty good for an old fart and Mac smiled at their reflection in the mirror behind the stacked steins and pitchers. Joe was Mac's uncle-in-law. Mac wasn't sure if that was the right moniker for a man he wished was his own dad but, as Mandy said, labels didn't amount to nearly as much as a good hug. Mandy was Mac's best friend in the world and she was getting ready to walk down the aisle. Not the bridal aisle but the one for graduates. The robe that she rented for her doctoral speech was full enough to cover the fact that she was one week from the due-for-delivery-date of their first child.

Mandy took a long drink of her iced tea and frowned at the drummers in the mirror. Uncle Joe winked at her but she didn't smile back. "If I go into labor early," she said, "you have to promise to go up front and read my speech."

"I don't think that's allowed," Uncle Joe said.

"I spent six years doing research and taking bullshit classes," Mandy said through gritted teeth, "not to mention the two months it took to write that speech. Somebody has to read it and Mac can't."

"Because he can't pronounce the words?" Garret said as he sauntered into the tavern, shrugging out of his leather jacket and hanging it on a hook behind the door.

"Don't be such an asshole," Mac said. "I can pronounce anything you can."

"Because Mac is going to be with me," Mandy snapped. "He has to let me break his hand while I scream." Mandy didn't usually grump and snarl but she was beyond ready for the baby to arrive and lack of sleep was taking a toll.

Garret sat at the stool nearest the door and Mac handed him a cold glass of lager.

"Okay," Mandy said, "here's the deal. I have started to have contractions..."

"They're probably just Braxton Hicks; better known as false labor," Uncle Joe said and Garret nodded. Mac didn't nod. This was his first child and a new father only feels terror and bewilderment.

"Maybe false labor," Mandy continued, "but maybe real contractions and I need a backup plan if I can't walk down the aisle."

Uncle Joe put his hand on Garret's shoulder. "I'll read the speech for her and you are going to be opening the tavern," he said.

"Why do you get to be the one to read the speech?" Garret asked. "I'm a poet and I read all manner of intellectual shit. I write some, too, and get published."

"You're going to be wiping down the bar and pissing off the customers." Uncle Joe took another swig of beer and winked at Mandy. This time she smiled back.

"Am I working for real wages or just free beer?" Garret asked.

"You can drink for free, but you can't steal anything from the till," Mac muttered.

"Give it a rest," Garret said. "It was just a short term loan."

"And when do you plan to pay it back?"

"As soon as I get my bonus."

"The state doesn't give out bonuses," Mac said.

"You pay me shit – or don't pay at all – when I help out," Garret said, "and your sister needed new eyeglasses."

"My sister, your ex-wife, has medical insurance that covers glasses. Since when have you ever paid child support much less bought her –"

Mandy put her hand on Mac's knee and her face went white with pain. Mac also grunted with pain but not from false labor.

"Maybe it's not Braxton Hicks," Uncle Joe said. "Maybe we should start timing them."

"Fuck timing," Mac said. "We're going to the hospital."

The tavern was scheduled to open at noon, but that was a couple hours away and Garret couldn't see the point of going back to his apartment just to kill time. He lifted first one bottle of handcrafted ale and then another, tilting each to better see their labels. He preferred ales, when given a chance, but would drink whatever was put in front of him. Mac usually gave him a glass of house lager because it was cheaper, but tonight was different. Today Garret was drinking for pure pleasure because his mother had just been diagnosed with stage four lung cancer and in a few months he was finally going to be a free man.

The Sun was above the strip mall across the street and bright, unbroken rays skittered through the tavern's windows. One of the patrons rattled the locked door, then skulked away muttering. Garret fumbled through the old pencils, receipts and pads of paper in the drawer under the till. He tore off two sheets of lined paper, found a pencil with newly-sharpened lead and settled into his favorite booth by the hall in back. It led to the office, the restrooms and the stairwell that rose to the apartment above. That was where Mac and Mandy lived.

Garret glanced at the clock, took a deep drink of his ale and began to write...

Drinking Ale by the window

Noon's photographic plate waits.
beaded drops slip away
sunlight sifts the fog.
A shaft of white sears the far wall.
Will mother's shadow never fall?

Her dragging leg stencils the dew.
Light can't trap for others
the one who used to be.
The image this morning was snapped
just for me.

He crossed out words and considered the rhythms inherent in the lines. *Lager* not *Ale*. *Morning* not *noon*. It had too much rhyming for contemporary taste but he liked it. Finally, he sat back, reread it one more time and put his pencil down.

It was okay for now. He'd fiddle with it later. Tomorrow or the next day.

Garret's mother was 63 years old and had been diagnosed with early onset Alzheimer's ten years earlier. He had just married Mac's sister when the diagnosis came and Garret was pretty sure that was what got the marriage off to a bad start. Of course his drinking was another reason. That, plus the fact that their first daughter was born before the year was out and Jeremy was born less than a year later. When the third pregnancy showed up, Garret went to his doctor's office, got fixed and moved back in with his mother.

The rest of the family couldn't seem to forgive him for that but Garret's mother had saved his life, all those years ago, and he felt obligated to take care of her. Besides, the crying and whining of his children made him want to act like his own father and start hitting whoever got in his way. After a few years, Garret's mother had sent her husband packing and then he disappeared. Garret drank but he also held a state job and wrote poetry and walked away when he wanted to kick the dog or pound a face into hamburger. I'm not like my old man, he often told himself. I'm different.

Someone was banging on the tavern door and four sets of eyes were peering into the window so Garret put away his poem and flipped on the red neon *OPEN* switch. Then he systematically flipped the switches of the five other neon signs advertising beer, wine and chili fries. He unlocked the front door and stepped out of the way as the usual drunks stumbled in. There were a couple of newcomers who didn't look old enough to shave. They didn't have ID so Garret sent them back outside.

"Try the market across the street," one of the regulars called out. "That lady will sell anything to anybody."

The others settled onto favorite bar stools or into favorite booths. Garret went down the line, setting out stein or bottle, then he shuffled across the floor with a pitcher of beer and two glasses of wine; one house red and the other house white. He had filled in for Mac enough times to know the opening routine. He also knew things would get boring after the second round and frisky after the fourth. With any luck, he could throw the frisky ones out on their respective asses before the after-work crowd showed up.

Mandy's uncle came in just before closing. "Probably Braxton Hicks," he said, "but they want to keep her overnight. She's pretty upset and Mac is staying at the hospital with her so I'll help if you need a break."

Garret popped the cap of the craft beer, *Angry Devil*, in front of the man everyone called Uncle Joe. "That's okay," he said. "It's been a quiet night."

Joe took a long swallow and leaned on the bar, both elbows straddling the peanut dish he'd pulled his way. "I hate seeing a woman in labor," he said. "We have three kids and I don't know how my wife did it."

He wiped the bar dry with his shirt sleeve, carefully laid Mandy's typed speech down and began to read. He was silent but his lips moved and occasionally he nodded. When he was done, he drained the bottle of ale and folded the pages, lengthwise, and tucked them in his back pocket.

Garret was dumping glasses and pitchers into the sink and held the front door open as the remaining patrons slowly filed out.

"She's one smart woman," Uncle Joe said after everyone left.

"Think she'll give the speech herself?"

"You know Mandy. Tough as nails."

Garret nodded. Once upon a time he'd had a crush on her but he figured everyone who'd ever seen her had felt the flush of lust.

Uncle Joe handed Garret the empty peanut dish. "How's your sister doing?"

Garret's sister was three years older than he was and looked like a street person, begging for loose change. Her teeth were gone and one eye wandered crazily while the other eye could nail you to the wall when she was angry. Which, as far as Garret knew, was most of the time. She dropped out of high school in her junior year and ran away from home for half a decade. When she came back the first thing she asked for was money. She felt she was owed it because her parents had ruined her life.

Or maybe it was her first boyfriend, the one who destroyed her left eye, who ruined it. Or the woman at the convenience store who never asked for ID or the kid across the street who cut lawns up and down the neighborhood and showed her how to roll a joint. Maybe it was the girl in second grade who teased her about her shoes or maybe it was the man in the moon.

She was always able to blame someone, anyone, for being a drunk. Except Garret. She never blamed Garret. Not even when he quit lending her money and not even that one time he turned her into the cops and she ended up in rehab. He asked her, once, why she never blamed him and she said, "You're stuck with Mom," as if that excused anything else he might do.

Maybe it did.

Garret didn't look up from the suds in the sink until Uncle Joe asked it again. "Your sister, how's she doing?"

"Same old, same old," Garret said.

Uncle Joe grunted and pushed away from the bar. "You really don't need me to help close the place down?"

Garret shook his head and the older man drained his bottle and walked to the door. He flipped off the string of neon signs before walking out, leaving Garret with just the back bar lights and memories.

After locking the doors, sweeping the place and emptying the trash, Garret pulled five twenties from the till and put the rest in the office safe. Then he settled into his favorite booth in the back and took out his pad of paper. The hall light was all the illumination he needed.

DREAMING OF MY SISTER

It was a windless fall into despair
A quiet glide.
No splintered iridescent spin to scream her soul awake.
Blowflies gather to discover the smallest rotted speck and infest
Her best places – passion, beauty, laughter – with eggs of fear.
Creeping to the attic of this nightmare
I offer jewels: trust, hope, sorrow
but she turns away.
Reason is the key I turn to escape
It fits the latch and slides the bolt awake.

The title needed work and there wasn't enough alliteration but the nouns were good. The shape of the poem was awkward but he needed to capture the emotion. He could work on everything later. He opened another bottle of craft ale and put his head in his hands. Give it time, he thought, and scratched out another line.

He woke to the sound of the tavern phone. He wiped the drool from his face and staggered across the small dance floor to answer. "H'lo."

"It's a boy!"

"Okay."

"He's wonderful! Awesome! She's so brave! I could never stand labor! Shit, he's just the most beautiful baby! It's a boy!"

Mac babbled on for another ten minutes while Garret watched the clock's blink from 3:10 to 3:20. *Fuck, I passed out again,* he thought.

"Hey," Mac said, "thanks for helping out. I mean it. Just nice to know I can count on you. Mandy will call Uncle Joe about the speech. I'm pretty sure she can give it. Thanks, man."

The dial tone meant that Mac had hung up in order to dial half a dozen other people, but he had called Garret first. Or pretty close to first. Garret wasn't sure what that meant but he thought it meant there was a small but persistent group of people who, in spite of everything, seemed to give a shit about him. He wandered to the back booth to collect his empty bottles and wipe down the mixture of beer and snot. He grabbed the two sheets of lined paper with the poetry scribbles and shoved them in his pocket. He could perfect them later. He paused at the till, put three of the twenties back, pushing the drawer shut and quickly turning away before he changed his mind.

He left the hallway light on and headed to the front door. His leather jacket was there, on its hook, lonely and stained. Not unlike his life, he thought. There was a poem in that image, waiting to be put down with words that mattered.

Next time, Garret thought. With luck, there would always be a next time.

OBITUARY FOR AN ASSHOLE

The summer I turned fifteen, my mother's live-in boyfriend drove us all down to the Toad Suck Fair in Conway, Arkansas. It was eight states in two weeks and it seemed like we ate every meal in the backseat of mother's battered Volvo. Plus, we never stopped to pee. It averaged out to one hundred sixty-seven miles a day which wasn't bad given the flat tire we had about ten miles out of Bakersfield. Of course there was also the dropped (and dragging) muffler out of Flagstaff and the empty gas tank on the far side of Oklahoma City which resulted in Earl getting thrown into jail. It turned out that borrowing gas was illegal, even when you left an I.O.U., and throwing a punch at the service station owner wasn't allowed, either.

We camped in various parks and at night my brothers and I would climb into our sleeping bags and fantasize all the different ways we could kill Earl. Bruce (who was a junior in high school) came up with the idea of having him drawn and quartered – using the dairy herd of Old Man Sweeney whose farm was half a mile from where we lived.

"We could wait until Earl was asleep and hit him over the head," Bruce said. "Then you'd gut him and –"

"I'm not gutting him," I said. "I'm not touching him."

"Me, neither," Danny whispered. Being eleven, Danny was afraid of everything, Earl especially.

"Okay," Bruce continued, "I'll gut him."

"And I'll get the cows," I said. "I can do that."

"Me, too," Danny agreed. "We won't hurt the cows," he continued. "I like the cows."

We spent the whole trip perfecting our plan. We didn't have to worry about Earl overhearing us because *he* spent the whole time talking non-stop to our divorcee mother. That's because Earl was on uppers and was fleeing to Arkansas until things calmed down in

Humptulips, which was a fifty-cent sized hamlet nestled against the crags of Washington State's Olympic Mountains.

When we met Earl's mother and father we could see why he was so awful.

"God Almighty, you sure are a fatty," Gramma Lambini said to my mother, before turning to my brothers and me. She looked us up and down and spit tobacco juice over the porch rail. Apparently, we weren't worth an insult which was, in some bizarre and twisted way, even worse than being called a 'fatty'.

Mother immediately telephoned our father. I never knew what she told him, but he sent enough money via Western Union to buy three bus tickets back to Seattle. Only Danny grieved the loss of attending the Toad Suck Fair. He wanted cotton candy, corn dogs, deep fried Snickers bars and a white tee shirt with 'Welcome to the Ozarks' on the front and a green, goggle-eyed, bouncing frog on the back.

"We could ride the zipper and watch the pig races," Danny whined. He was good at whining and he put his heart into it but Gramma Lambini told him to shut the fuck up and he did, shocked that an old lady would actually use the F Word.

"It isn't fair that Mom gets to stay," Danny whispered as we rolled up our sleeping bags and waiting for Earl to take us to the bus depot in Conway.

"Don't be a dork," my older brother muttered and, for the first time in weeks, I agreed with him.

"Yeah," I said, "don't be a dork."

"Shut the fuck up," Gramma Lambini shouted from inside the house. So we did.

OBITUARY – DRAFT ONE

I learned about Earl's death from my mother. Her email was to the point. "His mother doesn't want a church service but he always wanted to go home to Arkansas. I know you'll do the right thing, Sharon."

Notice that I was the right-thing girl while she was in France with her new daughter-in-law and newer grandbaby. I called my brother, Bruce. "Are you and Clarice coming to the funeral?"

"Don't be an idiot."

"So, I'm supposed to handle this on my own?"

"Danny can help."

"Shit," I said, "you are going to owe me big time."

"Add it to your Big Brother's Big Time List." There was a pause. "Clare's father has hired me to supervise the Chardonnay vineyard this year. It's the smallest one, but seriously, send me the bills. All of them."

"Guilt can be expensive," I said. "Any ideas for the obituary?"

"*'Earl was an Asshole'.* Isn't that enough?"

OBITUARY – SECOND DRAFT

I spent three hours driving from Seattle to the home of my childhood – a place without electricity. After Danny and I unpacked, I sat at Mother's battered kitchen table, fingers twitching with anticipation. The doublewide trailer was steamy with the heat from a woodstove. There was a kerosene-powered refrigerator with one tattered school photo on the door. It showed a towhead with brown eyes and a smile that could break your heart. It had hung there the whole time mother lived with Earl and he'd never explained. To be fair, we'd never asked but we weren't a family that used conversation to communicate.

I picked up a pencil and after drawing a tombstone, a cross, and a hangman's tree, I warmed up with my own obituary, using a blank sheet of paper torn from my daily planner.

Known best for her groundbreaking work in butterfly migration patterns, Sharon died surrounded by her children, grandchildren, great-grandchildren, and one tiny namesake great-great-granddaughter. Sharon was predeceased by her mother and older brother, Bruce. Her younger brother, Danny, gave the eulogy.

Danny leaned over me to read. "Where's Ralph?"

Apparently I had forgotten my husband, but perhaps he had gone ahead of me because of the male-female thing, but still it gave me a chill. "This is practice," I said. "It's to get me in the mood."

"You don't want to be in the mood for Ralph?"

There were so many responses to make I was overwhelmed with opportunity and sat a moment, trying to sort things out. I tore three more blank pages from the back of my day planner.

It wasn't until I was deep into Earl's obituary that I realized the first three letters in funeral spelled "fun" and I tried to keep that in mind as the paper soaked up the ink. *Earl was an asshole, who abused our mother, assaulted her children, and lied at every opportunity. No doubt the town of Humptulips will have a memorial pot luck at the Grange Hall where the men will remember what good a poker player Earl was and the women will bring elk meat casseroles. Everybody can shoot off some guns and drink themselves blind in his honor.*

The words flowed easily, as if I'd thought about them my whole life which, truth be told, I pretty much had. I put on my coat and took the obituary down to the little white church to be copied. Ole Knutson, the choir director, proofread it and said, "There's no need to make fun of us, Sharon. Just because you went off to college doesn't mean the rest of us are damn fools."

I wadded up the smudged piece of paper and dropped it in the wastebasket by the door. Writing is about revision. I'd try again tonight, when I wasn't up to my armpits in sorting and packing Earl's crap.

"I'll do better."

"See you do."

"He was an asshole," I said. "That part is true."

"Yes, but he was *our* asshole and, once upon a time, your mother loved him."

OBITUARY DRAFT THREE

Danny was growing a mustache. He looked fearless but looks were deceiving and he thought he was going to die whenever he stepped into an airplane.

"Then stay home."

"You're mean."

"No, I'm not. I'm taking Earl, a complete piece of crap, to be buried with his kin. Some people would call me a saint."

"You don't want Mom to cry."

Hard to argue with that. I tore more blank sheets from my journal. "You lived with Earl longer than I did, help me out."

Danny scuffed his feet and flexed his muscles. He almost looked his age, twenty-four years and four months. His medication was working and he almost sounded sane, too. "Well, he liked to hunt and fish."

Okay, maybe the key to writing an obituary was to not do it yourself. Maybe a person had to have a little help. At the top of the sheet of paper I wrote, *Earl was an outdoorsman.*

"What else?"

"Earl didn't want to be cremated."

"Give it a rest, Danny."

Earl's dog whined at the door and Danny went to let it in. It was a Blue Tick Hound and slobbered unmercifully but Danny rubbed the animal's ears and boogie-woogied under its chin and I thought, not for the first time, that Danny had a lot of love to give and nobody to give it to.

Danny's voice was muffled. "He liked fishing."

"Anything else?"

"And he had a girlfriend."

"No, he didn't."

"Everybody knew it, Sharon. Even Mom."

"That was just a rumor."

"They had a little girl. Sometimes Mom would baby-sit when Olivia was working nights."

I wadded up the paper from my journal and threw it into the flames of the kitchen stove. I was stuck writing an obituary for a man who was slime. Not to mention the idiocy of my mother for putting up with it all those years.

I went outside to stand on the porch. The snow had turned blue under a sky the color of apricots. Stars blinked here and there and soon the eyes of predators and of prey would wait for the truth only night could bring. If I had to choose, I would be a predator, sharp of fang and fierce of claw, but my mother's face was always there as a reminder that sometimes things didn't turn out the way you wanted. Sometimes you started out as predator and ended up as prey.

The whine of a logging truck cut through the twilight like a chainsaw against second growth. The air on the porch was cold enough to make my eyes sting and my nose run. An owl drifted silently past the henhouse, hoping for poultry's innate stupidity to provide the feast. Hoping for a bird to act like a human.

Danny came out and wrapped me in a blanket. "You have to come in now," he said.

"No, I don't."

"I made toasted cheese sandwiches and tomato soup."

"I'm not hungry."

"I'll tell Ralph you aren't eating."

Ralph was my husband, the man I could not include in any obituary, no matter how imaginary. He was a good man, sweet, who was going to come with me this weekend, but had orals for his doctorate. "Fuck orals," he'd said. "You're more important than them."

"We're having a child," I'd replied. "Quit thinking like a husband and start thinking like a father who has to get a job."

DRAFT FOUR

Danny talked to Ralph over the battery-powered telephone because cell towers hadn't made their way past the foothills. It was like talking to someone on the Moon, or in the Alaska bush, because of the relay delay. "Let me talk to Sharon," Ralph said.

I was at the table, still wrapped in the blanket, a mug of soup in my hand. I shook my head and pulled the blanket tighter around me. Danny shifted the receiver from one hand to the other. "She won't come to the phone." We had to wait a slow count to three before Ralph answered.

"Why not?"

"This obituary is hard to write."

The static was like electric popcorn on a red hot skillet, and then came Ralph's calm voice, "*Earl Lambini, Born August 12, 1950. Died from a gunshot wound sometime in January, 2008. Found three weeks later. Memorial Service Sunday after church.* That's all she needs."

"You know Sharon," Danny said.

Ralph sighed and hung up.

DRAFT FIVE

It was morning and I was in the Grange Hall parking lot, unloading black garbage bags stuffed with Earl's plaid shirts, steel-toed leather boots, and blood-stained hunting jackets from the back of the Jeep. I piled them inside the shed that held donations for the Food and

Clothing Bank, adding the remains of Earl's life to the remnants of other lives grown useless or out of fashion. Danny was back at the double-wide, stuffing years worth of empty beer cans into even more plastic bags. The neighbors didn't want the old hound and I didn't know what to do with the chickens. Thinking about it made me tired.

A green and white Blazer turned off Highway 101. Locals liked to say Sheriff Posey was a good man but a little soft in the heart when it came to kids. "Kids don't got a choice," the Sheriff had once said. That terse sentence, in country shorthand, covered it.

He cracked the window and cigarette smoke rolled out like fog over a forest fire. "I expected to see your Mother. She always cleaned up after Earl. How's she doing?"

"Mom's in France, visiting Bruce and her new grandbaby." The Sheriff would remember my older brother, having busted him for pot on more than one occasion.

"And Danny?"

"Danny's living with me and taking his medication. He's fine and dandy. Fit as a fiddle. Happy as a pig in shit." It was funny how the homilies, the country descriptions of behavior, all came back.

Sheriff Posey got a cigarette from the pack on the dashboard, scratched the match alive with his thumbnail and cupped his hands around the flame. He inhaled and let the smoke dribble from his mouth. "How are you, Sharon?"

"I'm fine."

"Looks like you got a bun in the oven." Sheriff Posey was a no-bullshit guy and, once upon a time, I had dated his youngest son. He rolled the window down further. "Need a hand?"

"No, I'm done for now. I heard about Mrs. Posey. I'm sorry. She was a good person."

"That she was."

We stared at each other for a beat. Nobody can outstare a cop so I asked, "What do you want?"

His hair and beard were almost all white. He was probably close to retirement. "You know the story of how Earl died?"

"He committed suicide."

"The state cops aren't so sure about that."

"Why not?"

"It was a gut shot, Sharon. Suicides don't generally go out with that much pain. Coroner figures it took him twenty-four hours to die."

"I didn't do it."

"Glad to hear it."

"None of my family did." I stuffed another box of Earl's clothes into the church's shed.

"Nobody hated him worse," the Sheriff said. "You can see how I had to ask."

"I understand."

"Then I'll be getting back to the office."

On impulse I blurted out, "I'm trying to write Earl's obituary. You wouldn't have any ideas would you?"

"He was one of a kind," the Sheriff said. "Thank God for that."

After he left, I scribbled the Sheriff's words onto the back of a bank deposit slip, *Earl was one of a kind and thank God for that,* then I headed for the mercantile to pick up a cheap tablet. No sense wasting any more daily planner pages or deposit slips on rough drafts.

DRAFT SIX

It was a country store, with groceries in the front and a restaurant in the back. Sam stocked shelves with an economy of motion that could only be learned from doing the job forty years in a row. Gertie, the cook, scraped the grill in preparation for another day of burgers and home fries.

"What'll it be?" A cigarette dangled from Gertie's mouth, its ashes sprinkling over the hash browns like an exotic kind of pepper. "Three burgers with onions, one for here and two to go."

"You want cheese fries?"

"You know I do."

I ate my burger at a table surrounded by mismatched chairs. A group of snow mobilers stumbled in, faces red with cold and excitement. They headed for a back booth and Olivia took them a pot of coffee and a handful of menus.

Sam and Gertie owned the Mercantile and Olivia was their daughter, an ex-cheerleader who, fourteen years before, had gotten sidetracked by the high school basketball star. Now she had two kids by two different fathers and a desperate look about the eyes that meant she was sick-to-death of living with her parents.

The bag of take-out was greasy with flavor and I collected extra napkins. Olivia rang up the bill and followed me out the door. A pair of eagles spiraled in a lazy double helix above the river.

Olivia sucked on her cigarette. "Earl had cancer."

"I didn't know that."

"I loved him even if he was a sonofabitch and I didn't shoot him, no matter what that damn Sheriff Posey says."

"He asked half the people in the county," Sam's voice was muffled from inside the store. "Don't go getting all riled up about it."

"Earl tol' me he didn't want to die in a hospital. I went up to feed the dog and chickens and I found him. He was froze stiff." Olivia shoved an envelope into my shirt pocket. "This was on the 'frig door. There was a note saying you'd know what to do. I woulda mailed it but I didn't have your address."

I drove almost a full mile before I swerved the Jeep to the shoulder and opened the envelope. The printing inside was labored and every word was a single syllable.

"*Take me to Toad Suck Park and put me with my real son. Drop my hand tied flies in with me, too.*"

I pulled a U-turn and parked in front of the store. Olivia was still on the porch, but she'd moved further down and away from the door.

I climbed awkwardly from the Jeep, caught between anger and confusion. "*What* real son?"

"The only person he ever loved. The one he gut-shot by mistake when they went hunting up in the Ozarks twenty years ago."

It was clear that the fun had drained right out of the word 'funeral'. We stood together, watching the eagles, until Olivia's cigarette was down to the filter. "My life is shit," she whispered. "Every morning I wake up and Sam's stompin' around and Gertie's mad and I feel like I'm drownin'."

We stood together for a long time. Sam stuck his head out but ducked it back in when he saw Olivia's look. Living in back of the store was taking its toll on all of them, even a fool like me could see that.

"If you handle the service and write Earl's obituary," I said, "you can have the trailer and everything that's in it. You can have the dog and the chickens, too. I don't know who the hell the property belongs to but, as far as I'm concerned, it's yours. Every damn thing."

"What about takin' him down to Arkansas?"

"Danny and I will handle that."

Tears in her eyes, Olivia nodded. If we were men, we would have shook on it or pounded shoulders but we were women not close enough to hug so I handed her two napkins, one with my Seattle phone number and the other to blow her nose on. I climbed back into the Jeep and put it in gear. I picked up Danny and headed for Seattle. He wolfed down his burgers and shared his fries while I told him the plan. "Okay," he kept saying. "Okay."

OBITUARY – FINAL DRAFT

Conway, Arkansas was caught in the crosshairs of Interstate 40 and Interstate 65. The best I-HOP in the south nestled like a tick on an old hound that was wrapped around that busy intersection, kicking out a leg and growling now and then but mostly dozing away the hours. I had Earl's ashes under the passenger seat of the rented Subaru and Danny had the hand tied flies on his lap in a metal Altoids box.

"We'll have blueberry crepes when we're done," I said.

"Okay," Danny answered. I was liking this new medication and living with him wasn't so bad, lately, since most of what he said was "Sure" and "Okay" and sometimes "Good idea".

We stood below the dam where the banks were overhung with cottonwoods and raggedy pines. Danny pointed out some mosquitoes skating on the surface of the water and a Grampa Catfish barely made a ripple getting a morning snack. I dumped the plastic bag of ashes and said "Good-bye" without adding "Good Riddance" which was as close to making peace with Earl that I would ever get. Danny tossed in the handtied flies and we watched the current carry them downstream.

It was peaceful there. I didn't want to but I found myself smiling. It was over, I thought. I could close the door on the last awful chapter of my life. I could start a new chapter with a husband and a child that would never, if I had anything to say about it, visit Toad Suck, Arkansas.

The Lambini homestead was at the end of a single track lane. I've wondered why an Italian had homesteaded at the south end of the Ozarks but immigrants have spread all over this broad land so why not amid piney woods and croaking toads?

Earl's mother had a face like an apple left on the tree all winter, wizened, limp and scabby but still all of one piece. His father sat sullenly in the porch rocker, with a steady creak-creak to mark his days. He wore stained overalls, a yellow puddle of pee trembled on the porch between his slippers. Old-timer's Disease was what Gramma Lambini called it.

"Did 'e leave me anythin'?" she asked.

Danny and I played eyeball ping-pong but neither of us mentioned the trailer in Humptulips. I told her where we scattered Earl's ashes and I waited for her to say something soft and sad so I was surprised when she said, "He alas was a bum."

Probably Earl hadn't been a six year old bum or even a twelve year old one but bumhood might have caught up with him by the age of thirty. Shooting his own son could fill a man with enough hate that a self-inflicted gut shot might not seem like such a bad idea. The cancer was just an excuse. I handed Earl's mother his obituary and headed for the car.

"You spelt my name wrong," she said. "And who the hell is Olivia?"

I didn't turn around. From birth to death our lives are only half told and half-understood, too. I-Hop waited with bacon, blueberry crepes, black chicory coffee, and a friendly face or two.

In a few hours, I'd fly home to a husband I loved and to people who gave a shit.

Earl Lambini was the seventh son of Sharlene and Jefferson Lambini, originally of Toad Suck, Arkansas. He was predeceased by his nine year old son, Earlie, Jr. Earl died by his own hand sometime in January of this year. He leaves his fiancée, Olivia, and their daughter, Ashley.

Acknowledgements

Ralph's World – '*Stringtown*', Issue 7, 2004.

Wrestling with Demon's – '*Other Voices*', 41. Fall/Winter 2004.

My Life as a Sane Person – '*The Raven Chronicles*', Vol. 13, No. 1 (Whimsies) - 2007.

Candymaking – '*Skive*', Issue 6. December, 2007.

Garret's Lament – '*Skive*', June, 2011.

Driving Sharon Crazy – '*Prole, Poetry and Prose*', Issue 6, 2011.

Sibling Rivalry – '*Prole, Poetry and Prose*', Issue 18, 2015.

Sex and Maple Bars – '*Skive*', Issue 12, September, 2009.

The Yard Sale – '*GlimmerTrain*', *Family Matters Competition* – *Unpublished but a Finalist, Spring 2014 under the title of "The Garage Sale".*

Seven Stages of Sin – '*Prole, Poetry and Prose*', Issue 10. Spring, 2013.

Chant of Survival – *"More Raw Material" – an anthology inspired by Alan Sillitoe. Lucifer Press, Fall, 2015.*

This Is What She Knew – '*Prole, Poetry and Prose*', Issue 12. Fall/Winter, 2013.

Passing the Torch – '*Prole, Poetry and Prose*', Issue 13, Spring, 2014.

Drinking Poems – *December, 2016, in "Lucifer Press".*

Obituary for an Asshole – *'Nimrod', Awards Issue 32. "Spinning Legends...telling truths". Fall/Winter, 2010. (Honorable Mention in the Katherine Anne Porter Competition and the first place winner in the Pacific Northwest Writers Association short story competition).*

I would like to thank the many editors of the many small journals who keep this literary world alive. On a more personal level, many thanks to: Matthew Ward of "Skive" who helped direct and clarify this project. I must also give hearty thanks to Phil Robertson and Brett Evans of "Prole", Neil Fulwood and David Sillitoe of "More Raw" and "Lucifer Press", Gina Frangello of "Other Voices", Francine Ringold of "Nimrod", Elizabeth Myhr and Athena Stevens of "Raven's Chronicles", Polly Buckingham of "Stringtown" and Susan Burmeister-Brown and Linda Swanson-Davies of "Glimmertrain."

Office Use : 2002171013aFNLCrct